Second Chance

An American History Military Time Travel Novel

Book 1

By
Michael Roberts

Second Chance

Love this book? Please leave a review!

Want updates and more from Michael Roberts?

Find him here:
https://linktr.ee/sifi_author_michael_roberts

MICHAEL ROBERTS
AUTHOR

Second Chance

Second Chance

ONE: The Beginning
September 04, 2021

"We have already done it once, so don't say it's impossible," the man at the head of a cheap plastic table was saying.

We were inside the massive second-floor conference room in the recently built warehouse. The industrial lights buzzed out bright artificial illumination through the entire length of the room.

Aluminum walls had been built around a steel frame and concrete floors. Yet, for its size, and capability of holding a great deal of furniture, the conference room was virtually empty. Four white plastic tables in the middle of the room were pushed together to give the appearance of one large table.

A dark red tablecloth draped over the top to hide the fact that the men and one woman sat at four plastic tables and not some grand oak tables that they may have been more accustomed to.

Two more tables sat in the far corner. One of the tables had a coffee maker on it. The coffee maker, cups, creamer, and sugar were my contributions to this project so far. The other table had sandwiches, snacks, and sodas on it.

I stood off to the side, drinking my fourth cup of coffee today.

The man who spoke was Aden Steel, the CEO and majority shareholder of Steel Foods, Longhorn Beef, and Neptune, which was the largest fishing fleet in Canada and the whole American States of England, or what some people had called the Royal States. Aden Steel was my boss, best friend, and the smartest person I knew.

We grew up together in Los Angeles, played street cricket, and opened a few fire hydrants in the summer. Like yin and yang, he had the brains, and I had the brawn.

Aden had helped me with my homework, and I stopped anyone in school from picking on him. I hadn't been the biggest kid in school, but I also never fought fair. It was a trait I still used more frequently than I cared to admit.

My father started teaching me boxing at the age of ten. Not the Queen's boxing but the fight-to-win boxing, back alley brawling with a bit of ground fighting mixed in.

After boxing came knife throwing. Guns were illegal for civilians to own, so my father always carried two knives on him. I never learned to throw as well as my father, but I was rather decent at it. He taught me how to fight in a knife fight and made sure that I was efficient with a blade.

Post high school, I earned money bare-knuckle boxing at the Manchester Gentlemen's Club. Every Saturday night, the real men of wealth would pay to see the common man fight and bleed for them.

After a year of fighting in the ring, I managed to get a letter of recommendation from one of the members of the club. A Major in the Royal Guard had taken a liking to me after he won a large sum of money betting on several of my fights.

I was accepted into the Los Angeles Royal Police Force. By that time, Aden had already finished his first year of Harvard Business School.

Ten years later, he was worth several hundred million dollars, and I was a Sergeant in the Royal Police. Since I'd been born in the States, I had no chance of promoting past Sergeant.

I was a member of the Police Force Antiterrorism squad and taught hand to hand combat and firearms training at the Royal Police academy. Yet, I wasn't a gentleman, born in the Empire's jewel country of England, or even in the United Kingdom. That put a cap on my career aspirations, but I was content in my position.

Until the day my wife was raped and killed by a British military officer. Lieutenant Reginald Hargrave had flown over to California from London and needed a place to stay. Jenny was a flight attendant and worked the Los Angeles to London circuit.

They'd met on Jenny's return flight back to L.A. Having formed a sick attraction for her, he demanded the use of our house. While the practice of housing officials was frowned upon by most in the government these days, under the British Quartering Act of 1775, a two hundred and fifty-five-year-old British law, as an officer, he did have the legal if not moral right to be housed and fed by civilians.

As unhappy as we were with this, the law only gave him the right to stay until he found suitable lodgings. No set number of days exists in the law, but most British courts had already ruled years ago that if available hotels or military quarters were nearby, then seven days was the acceptable amount of time that an officer could sleep in our house and eat our food.

Jenny never told me, but I later learned from her best friend that he'd been making advancements on her from the first day he was in our home. She'd been afraid of what I would do if she told me. He wasn't the kind of guy to accept rejection lightly.

On the fourth morning, twenty minutes after I left for work, he raped and killed her. That is what it meant to be an officer in the Royal British military.

The British ruled seventy percent of the world, with only Russia and China holding out against them. King Charles had proclaimed that even Russia would call him King sometime in the next ten years. Capitalism was alive and well as long as the states collected eighteen percent of all earnings and the Royal family collected thirty-two percent more in the name of the great Empire. So being a military soldier for the Queen had its perks.

The call went out on my radio as I got to work. By the time I returned home, the Detective Sergeant and a few high-ranking Royal Officers were already covering things up.

The first police officer on scene said that Jenny had been stabbed but was still alive when he arrived. He found her naked in the hallway, trying to stop the bleeding from her side with a bath towel. The bastard thought that he had done a proper job at sticking her between the ribs, but he botched it. She'd lived long enough to tell the police officer what had happened before dying.

The Royal British Officer, Lieutenant Reginald Hargrave, who was supposed to be a real proper gentleman, left her there to die and drove himself to his military base where he told his commanding officer that she had attacked him. No one had believed that a young, naked, married woman, just stepped out of the shower, and attacked him, but his commanding officer didn't want a scandal. A few words and promises to the Governor-appointed Mayor, and it was declared self-defense.

Three days later, that proper gentleman and British soldier disappeared without a trace. I *may* have had something to do with it, but I was fired and arrested without any proof. Trust me, they were *never* going to find his body.

I was questioned about his disappearance, but when no leads popped up, they transferred me to military custody. I was beaten with rubber hoses, rolled-up newspapers, and even water boarded. In the end, after they realized that I wasn't going to break and admit to any involvement in the disappearance of their officer, they stopped asking questions.

They kept beating me for the fun of it, just didn't bother asking any more questions. When the word finally got out that I was in their custody and still no official charges had been filed, the base general put an end to it and had me released. I was told that this whole incident had never happened.

I had my traveling papers taken from me to prevent me from crossing state lines. It took only six months for me to lose my house, friends, and my will to live.

Like the saying goes, "You don't beat the Empire, the Empire beats you."

When I was at the end of my rope, I called Aden for advice. Aden had no love for the Empire after his two younger brothers, Edgar, and Barkley, were killed in foreign lands, expanding the Royal family's holdings.

The next day, I was on Neptune's private jet, flying to the east coast. So much for not crossing state lines. With all my government and Police training, Aden made me his bodyguard and personal head of security.

I had only been with Aden a few weeks before an attempt was made on his life. He had actually been kidnapped by Secret British Agents who wanted to make it look like a kidnapping for money, when in fact they were just going to kill him for speaking out against the crown. I had saved Aden but was forced to kill several of those agents doing so.

I shook my head, bringing myself back to reality. In this cavernous room, the other men and one woman around the table were known to me by name only. I had never met them before today, but I did each and every one of their background checks. They each had three important things in common. They were among the best and brightest in their fields, all hated the British Empire for one reason or another, and they were born here in the states. Aden had flown everyone here to King George under a pretext of different consulting jobs. Questions were asked and answered. Only after Aden felt he could trust them, and more importantly that they held the same political views about the empire, did Aden explain the real reason for their presence.

Walking up to the table, I clapped Jake on the left shoulder. Jake worked for Neptune and was Aden's private jet pilot. He had even more reason to hate the Empire than I did. Next to him was Tim. Tim also worked for Neptune and had a master's degree in electrical engineering. Tim and Jake had worked for Aden for years. It was the other three that we were not sure of.

At the far end was the famous Dr. Ronald Mallett, a seventy-five-year-old theoretical physicist who was a believer in time travel and the world's foremost expert on it, if such a position could exist. I had my doubts. He was the last to arrive and was only now being told of the real reason he was here. Dr. Mallett was also the one telling Aden that what Aden had suggested was impossible – which was a lot coming from this "expert."

Next to him sat Dr. Kyle Smith, another theoretical physicist. Next to Dr. Smith was Dr. Kimberly Rock, who had a doctoral degree in world history. The real history of the world, not that bull shit bubblegum history written by the Empire and taught in every school around the world.

A few other people were involved in all this, but they were in the main warehouse or in the other building. With the seven of us in this room and five welders and mechanics in the main work area, that made a grand total of twelve people who knew what we had and were planning. Another eight, *very* well-paid people were in the second but smaller warehouse next door, getting ready to work on their parts of the plan as soon as we knew what that was going to be.

Aden had called for a tailor, two seamstresses, a machinist, a wood worker, a leather worker, a blacksmith, and one of the best custom gunsmiths on this side of the pond. Each had their own workspace with partitions between them, special tools, and equipment. Aden instructed each of them not to discuss their work with the others. They were paid well for their work and overpaid not to ask questions.

No one here, other than Aden and me, had a cell phone, for security reasons. We confiscated the phones as they entered the property. No phones were permitted on the grounds except mine, Aden's, and the one phone at the guard shack. The guards had radios so they could talk to each other and to me. I had brought in fifteen guards to work the perimeter and they worked three shifts, each shift consisting of five men – one guard at the guard shack and four walking our new fence line. The fence and even the two warehouses had been built two miles north of King George, seven days ago.

We didn't even have time to build any type of living quarters. Aden had instructed the workers to erect large tents for every person here and a mess hall consisting of a large, open-wall military tent. Aden hired a local restaurant to bring in breakfast, lunch, and dinner, everyday. This whole project was thrown together so fast and at the last minute that, in truth we didn't know what we were doing. Aden had an idea of what he wanted done but we still didn't know if it could be done. And if we got caught . . .

Oh, Jesus, if we got caught . . .

Someone asked a question that I wasn't paying attention to. Jake raised a hand and pointed at me. "Me and Thomas did it."

"Explain," Dr. Smith demanded.

Aden strode over to the wall with the giant window that opened into the warehouse. He pulled a string and the blinds covering the window went up with a zipping sound. Everyone at the table, except Jake and Tim, jumped up and rushed over to Aden. They peered down into the main warehouse, and I smiled as their mouths hung open. Jake and Tim knew what was down there and took their time walking over. Tim grabbed a folder off the table and brought it with him.

I knew why they were in shock. The window showed the front portion of a real-life, honest-to-goodness space craft. Made of some sort of metal, like blue rock, seamless, the craft appeared to be made of one piece of whatever it was made of. The front had a pointy nose, then it widened to about eight feet before thinning to about six feet. The wide-open back of the ship had been broken off from the rest. The entire craft was a total of twenty feet long. Two seats were set in what had to be the cockpit, but that space had no windows. Streaks of dried slime, barnacles and red coral covered the entire ship. Who knew how long it had sat at the bottom of the ocean?

"What on this earth?" Dr. Rock asked.

"Not of this earth," Aden finished for her.

Everyone turned their heads slowly to him.

"One of my deep-sea fishing boats pulled it up in their nets, around twenty miles southeast of Florida," Aden explained. "They called it in to the main office who called it in to me. I had it secretly brought here under a tarp and under the cover of darkness. This whole warehouse was built days ago, just for this. We think the Empire got word of it because they showed up and confiscated my fishing ship. They're looking for me now."

"Why?" Dr. Rock asked.

"Because they'll be wanting to know what we found. The whole harbor noticed my boat pull in with it. I wanted to know what it was before the Empire rolls in and takes it from us," Aden stated flatly.

"And the crew?" Dr. Smith inquired.

"The crew of the fishing boat who found it are currently in a hotel under fake names and getting a huge bonus for their time and silence," I answered.

"What is it made of?" Dr. Mallett asked, pulling off his glasses. His voice held a sense of awe, of disbelief.

"The materials not on the periodic table of elements," Aden answered.

"Not on our periodic table," I interjected, putting emphasis on the word *our.*

"It's real?" Dr. Rock asked with a crack in her voice.

"It's real," Aden said, nodding his head.

"What did you mean by you'd already done it?" Dr. Mallett asked.

"Time travel," Aden responded matter-of-factly. "We already did it."

"Wait a minute," Dr. Mallett interrupted, shaking his head in confusion. "What about the butterfly effect? How do you know you didn't change history?"

"I don't think we did anything that could have affected history," Jake answered.

"If we did, how would we know?" I asked.

"That's why you are here, Doctor," Aden said. "You see, we *want* to change history, but we may only get one shot at it."

"Change history how?" Dr. Rock asked with alarm in her voice. I didn't blame her. The idea was a frightening one.

"That will be for you to tell us, Doctor," Aden said turning to her. "Let's start at the beginning."

Aden turned to Tim, our engineer, who coughed in his hand to clear his throat then turned to face the group.

"The craft is definitely alien. What we have here is certainly the broken off cockpit portion of the ship or craft."

"Although we are searching for the rest of it, the ocean is a big, deep place, so we have little hope of finding more," Aden said. "It was dumb luck that we found this piece."

"We have no idea what the rest of the ship might have looked like," Tim continued. "We do not know how long it was or what kind of engines it used. It's utterly destroyed and impossible to reverse engineer."

"Wait a minute," Dr. Mallett said. "You said that you traveled through time. I assumed you used the spaceship to do that."

"We did," I answered.

"But you just said the ship was destroyed," Dr. Rock spoke up.

"It is," I said.

Aden raised a hand to quiet everyone and focused on Tim to continue.

"There are two seats in the cockpit," Tim said. "The pilot's seat up front and a second or copilot's seat behind the pilot's seat. The craft has four distinct and different sets of controls on board. The first one is in the front of the pilot seat. I believe they are or were for whatever was used to physically power the ship. To fly in space and maybe in the atmosphere. The power source and engines or whatever kind of propulsion they used are missing. The second set of controls are to the left of the first. They would have to be controlled by the pilot's left hand, assuming the pilot had hands. We're guessing, but from the lay out, and design of the controls, but I believe they were used to control the ship underwater. Keep in mind that is just a guess."

"That actually would make sense," Dr. Smith said. "If another race were to come here, the number one reason would be water. Hell, seventy one percent of the planet is covered with water. Coming from space that would be the first thing they'd notice. If you consider that, why would any aliens come here if not for the water?"

"Thank you, Doctor, I hadn't thought of that," Aden said with all sincerity.

"How old is it?" Dr. Rock asked.

"We don't have any idea," Aden answered. "Virtually every facility that has the ability to carbon date is under the Empire's control."

"Or at least has an Empire control officer implanted," I added.

"At first we couldn't even guess at what the other two sets of controls were for," Tim added. "They're set more towards the copilot's seat. Until we found this in the nose of the ship."

Tim pulled out three copies of the same photograph and handed one to each of the doctors. They were photographs of a black cube with blue flecks in it.

"It's 10.35 inches by 10.35 inches by 10.35 inches," Tim said. "We have no idea if those measurements are significant, but it's a perfect square. It weighs twenty-two pounds, and like the ship, we have no idea what it's made of. We do know that it's made of a different material than the ship itself."

"So that's two elements that we don't have on our Periodic table," Dr. Rock said with a tight face, emphasizing the word *our*, just as I had.

"Yes," Aden told her.

"You'll notice," Tim said pointing to the photograph, "that there are different markings on each side."

"What do they mean?" Dr. Rock asked wide eyed.

"How would they know?" Dr. Mallett asked her in a short tone.

"Yes," Tim confirmed. "We have no idea what the markings mean. We do know that the cube is putting out enough energy to power a small city, but we can't detect any heat, and no radioactivity."

"Cold fusion?" Dr. Smith asked.

"Or some form of it," Tim answered. "X-rays won't penetrate the cube, so we have no idea what's inside. I connected a generator to some exposed . . . " Tim had to think of his next words, "not wires but similar, leading to the control panels, and the third set of controls lit up like a Christmas tree." He handed each of them more photographs showing the controls. "The third set of controls has two rows of what could be called dials, for lack of a better word. Each row has four of these dials."

"And what I'm calling an enter button above them," Jake chirped in.

"We began small, on our first and only test. We only turned the last dial on top row one click down," Jake continued.

Aden pulled out his cell phone and pulled up a video he took.

"This was two days ago," Aden said, showing them the video.

The three doctors pushed their heads together, trying to get a better look. The video showed the cockpit in the middle of the screen. Then the air around the cockpit distorted, like a shimmer over a hot desert. A light flashed and then the craft was gone.

"What happened?" Dr. Mallett asked.

"From our point of view," Jake answered, "almost the same thing. The air around us felt heavy and shimmered, there was a flash of light and a backdraft-type vacuum. If Thomas hadn't grabbed my arm, I would've been pulled out of the ship. Then, suddenly, the building was gone."

"We and the ship were suddenly in a forest," I added. "The warehouse was no longer there."

"We walked to the city," Jake continued.

"King George," I clarified.

"It was different. It was smaller, and not as much pollution."

Jake took out his cell phone that he used to take pictures and showed them. It was the city of King George, just not today's King George.

"We took this from a garbage can and went straight back to the ship," he said as he handed them a newspaper.

It was the England Post, and at the top it was dated September 02, 1960.

"It's real," Aden said.

"How did you find your way back to this time frame?" Dr. Rock asked.

"They turned the dial back up one click," Dr. Mallett guessed.

"Yes," I said. "But that did nothing."

"What?" he asked.

"We figured that must be like a zero point," Jake said. "So, we moved it one more click, for a total of two and that brought us back here."

"What about the other set of controls?" Dr. Smith asked.

"We would like you and Dr. Mallett to check out the ship before we do any more tests," Aden said. "But if we're right, then it might move the ship through space itself. I didn't want anyone touching anything else. One click of that control could put you miles into the sky or miles down into the earth. And unless you can guarantee me that I'm wrong, and maybe not even then, we'll not be touching that control panel."

"That make sense," Dr. Smith said. "Space travel would take too long for even any advance type of propulsion. This cube must somehow be able to warp through space and time. It would also explain why they would need four separate sets of controls."

"I'm sorry," Dr. Rock said raising her hand. "You mentioned changing history. How and why exactly do you want to change history?"

Aden turned to her. "I want you to take what you know about the Empire and its history, add to the fact that we have a time machine and figure out how to do the most damage."

"Damage?" Dr. Rock asked, her eyes wide again. Her face paled and she placed a hand near her neck, as if she didn't believe anything she was hearing.

"To the Empire, Doctor," Aden told her. "I want to stop them from being the sole world power. They hold almost the entire world under their royal thumbs."

"Oh," was all Dr. Rock said.

"Keep in mind, Doc," Jake added, "that our time machine seems to work in increments of sixty-one year jumps."

"And it needs to start here or close enough to this location that we can drive the ship by trailer," I threw in.

"And we are on a deadline," Aden added. "The Empire is looking for us."

"So, no pressure, Doc," I said smiling.

"No," Dr. Rock said. "There's not. I can go down the list right now for you, but I already know the answer. Four clicks down."

"Good," Aden said, smiling. "That's what I was thinking. I wanted your independent opinion. Our gunsmith will be happy to know he didn't waste his time."

Everyone's eyebrows went up at that. I'm sure they were wondering why we even had a gunsmith.

"You'll be breaking up into teams. Dr. Smith, and Jake will get the ship ready. Keep in mind we may not be launching from here. Tim, you'll find the best place to launch from, or I guess I should say the best place for the ship to launch." Aden had to think for a second and then asked, "What's the best word to say appear out of thin air?"

"Reconstruct?" Tim offered.

Aden nodded his head with approval. "Tim will find the best place for the ship to reconstruct 244 years in the past. We were lucky the ship didn't reconstruct in a tree or something last time. Dr. Rock and Thomas will come up with goals, objectives and then a plan of action."

"What about me?" Dr. Mallett asked.

"Doctor, I need you to come up with an answer to one question."

We stood there waiting to hear the one question that Aden had for the world's leading expert on theoretical time travel.

"How do we do this?" Aden asked. "We are going to send Jake and Thomas to the year 1777 to accomplish a mission to change history, and the whole timeline from then to now will be different. Do they stay there and work together? Do they try to come back afterwards? Will there be anything for them to come back to? Or do we have Jake do a turn around and bring back the ship for a second try in case Thomas fails by himself? What will happen to Jake if Thomas is successful?"

Dr. Mallett nodded, deep in thought.

"Ok," Aden said. "You all have your assignments. We'll meet tomorrow morning and go over each step of the plan, that is after we come up with one. I have to go talk to our manufacturing team in the next warehouse."

"Can we go down and look at the ship now?" Dr. Mallett asked.

Aden stepped to the door and opened it, waving them through.

TWO: Man Purse

THE NEXT MORNING, we sat around the table, getting ready to talk about what we had come up with so far. I should say we were waiting for Dr. Mallett to show up for the meeting. Aden had sent Jake down to the salty-smelling ship that we'd dubbed *Second Chance*, and Jake was literally dragging the doctor. out of it. He complained loudly as they walked up the stairs to the office door. We waited patiently until he sat down and was ready.

"He was up all night studying the *Second Chance*, then he slept in it, last night," Jake said as he sat in his chair.

"I was trying to find answers to Mr. Steel's question," Dr. Mallett explained.

"Good," Aden said, jumping in and taking control of the conversation. "And, may I ask sir, what answers you have for us?"

"Well, first off," Dr. Mallett said, "there are two predominant theories with regards to the construct of time.

The first is that time is linear and the second, that it is circular."

"Which do you believe is correct, Doctor?" Aden asked.

"Well," Dr. Mallett said, taking off his glasses and rubbing them with the edge of his shirt, "I've debated, contemplated and argued for both at one time or another through the years, and last night I finally figured out the truth of it."

"And?" Aden asked.

"Who cares?" the doctor told him.

"What?" Aden's face was a mask of shock, an expression he didn't often wear.

"Who cares?" the doctor said again. "We have a working time machine down there. When we are done, the result will be that we'll have changed the timeline and will never have this conversation, so who cares how it works?"

"Ok, but what about the whole paradox problem?" I asked.

"There is no paradox problem," the doctor answered.

"But wait," Jake jumped in. "If I go back in time and kill my grandfather then I will never be born. If I'm never born, how did I go back in time to kill my grandfather?"

"If you kill your grandfather, then you'll never be born in the new timeline," the doctor said. "That doesn't change the fact that you were there and that you did kill your grandfather. Like they say, it is what it is. You were part of the timeline, then you became part of the new timeline taking yourself out of the old timeline that no longer exist anyways and if you go back to the point you left, well then you'll be part of that timeline again, just have never been born."

"That makes no sense," Dr. Rock said, shaking her head.

"Just trust me on this," Dr. Mallett said.

"OK, so what about the rest of us?" Tim asked.

He shrugged his shoulders. "Can't say. If Mr. Cain kills your great-grandfather, then you'll never be born. Otherwise, you should be ok."

"The laws of chaos say . . ." Dr. Smith began.

"The laws of chaos cannot be predicted or controlled," Dr. Mallett finished. "So why worry about them?"

"And what about me?" Jake asked. "Do I stay, or do I come back with the ship?"

"You have to come back," the doctor answered. "You'll be our compass, our judge as it were. If Mr. Cain fails, nothing here will have changed, and we can try again. Since you'll be the only person here who remembers how history was, you'll have to tell us if anything *has* changed. Keep in mind, whatever changes are made will, from our point of view, be the way it has always been, and we may think you're crazy."

"And if he's successful?" Jake asked.

"In the case of Mr. Cain's success, it'll be up to you to destroy the ship," he answered Jake, but his eyes were on Aden. "Time travel is great in theory, but in reality, it will cause chaos. You'll be the only person alive to remember the old timeline."

"How will he remember how things were, if history has been changed?" Dr. Rock asked.

"The rest of us will be part of the new timeline. He was part of the timeline that will no longer exist, but that non-existing timeline is still the one he lived," Dr. Mallett answered.

"Well, there it is," Aden said. "Jake, you get to be Dr. Who for the day, but without the sonic screwdriver. Are you up to it? It's a lot to ask, being the only person alive who knows the truth."

"The truth is the truth," Dr. Mallett said. "For us, we'll be living the truth. Just a different truth than Jake will remember. Let's not use the word truth and instead say that Jake will be the only person alive who remembers an alternate timeline."

Jake bobbed his head. "I feel like I need to make a Tardis joke."

I laughed at that. "Well, the ship is blue."

"Will there be two of me here when I return?" Jake asked. "I mean in the new timeline?"

"Yes," Dr. Mallett said.

"I've already made arrangements for that," Aden said. "Jake will be taking three million in gold with him. No matter what Thomas does to the timeline, gold will always have value. With three million, Jake will be able to disappear and live a comfortable life. I'm also giving him my cell phone. I left a video message for myself on it. If you run into any problems, find me and play that video."

Jake nodded his head. "Thank you, Mr. Steel."

"Any other questions?" Dr. Mallett asked.

No one said anything, and most were focused on Jake, thinking about what kind of life he would have if he returned to a different timeline.

"Good," Aden said. "Tim?" Aden prompted him to cover his part.

"The biggest problem is the terrain. Not knowing exactly how things looked in 1777 is the problem. We run the risk of reconstructing in a small hill that we never knew about because it eroded away, a boulder that was moved, a tree that was later cut down or even a person that happens to be walking by. I started off with a twelve-mile diameter from here, searching at any spot that might work. I was only able to find one perfect spot, within the area. An open field. The ground soil is mostly made up of clay and rock, so no crops or trees grow there. I even found a painting on the internet of the area from 1810. Looks the same now as it did then. Should be perfect, and it's only ten miles from here so we can be there minutes after loading the ship onto a truck."

"What's wrong with right where it is?" I asked. "Maybe we did get lucky, but it worked right there, and we were fine."

"You went back sixty-one years," Tim said. "That's a drop in the bucket when it comes to time. It's clear here and now, and you were ok sixty-one years ago, but who knows what was there two hundred and forty-four years ago. That was my first plan. I wasn't able to find anything in the history books about this place."

"We'll call the open field, plan A, and the warehouse plan B, for now." Aden raised his voice to get our attention.

Aden then turned to me and Dr. Rock. "Were you able to come up with a plan?"

Dr. Rock stepped forward and repeated some of what she had gone over with me last night. "First, most of what you were taught in school about the Colonists' rebellion is wrong. We were taught that the colonists were a greedy bunch of traitors. In truth, many were loyal to the crown. They only wanted freedom and the right to rule themselves. Plus, the king was taxing the shit out of them."

She seemed to take herself by surprise with her language. "The colonists lost for many reasons. The war was lost officially in 1779, but let's focus on 1777, since that is where, or I should say, when Mr. Cain will be going."

She counted them on her fingers. "The death of General Washington in the city of King George in 1777 was the single biggest blow to the colonists' efforts. Back then, King George was called Philadelphia. Washington was captured in Philadelphia and hung in the streets."

She held up another finger. "The Battle of Saratoga was a complete loss for the colonists. Many believe that if the colonists had won that battle, the French may had joined in the war." She held up a third finger. "The loss of twelve thousand men, most to starvation at Valley Forge, crippled the colonists' whole regular army. Then, after the British took, and held Yorktown, it was all but over. By 1779, the British had fifty thousand soldiers throughout the states. King-appointed Governors, enforcing the King's rule."

"So, what's the plan?" Aden asked.

"We send Mr. Cain back. He saves George Washington, helps turn the battle of Saratoga, saves the men at Valley Forge, and prevents the British from getting a bigger foothold on the States. If he can prevent the British from keeping Yorktown, and he can get the French to join the war, then he will have forever changed history."

"Ok, that's great for the States, but what about the rest of the world?" Dr. Mallett asked.

"The British were able to take over most of the world because of the States. The manpower and the resources that they took from the States between eighteen fifty and nineteen hundred is what made them the world power they are today, just with the gold, oil, and steel alone." She smiled. "If you take the States from them, you take the whole world."

"But there's one problem," I said.

"What?" Aden asked in alarm.

"George Washington was captured on September ninth and killed on September tenth," Dr. Rock said. "He was killed two hundred and forty-four years ago, five days from now."

"We have only five days to get ready, launch, and travel to King George," I said.

"Philadelphia," Dr. Rock interrupted.

"Sorry, Philadelphia," I repeated, "and save George Washington."

"Then travel on foot ninety miles in a week to New York to help out at Saratoga," Dr. Rock added.

"Saratoga," I repeated, "then back south ninety miles to Valley Forge to make sure twelve thousand men don't die."

"Of starvation," Dr. Rock added.

"Of starvation," I repeated.

"Ok," Aden said, handing Dr. Rock a new cell phone. "This is the newest smart phone. Download all the maps, battle timelines, British moments, drawings or paintings of important historic people, and bios of General Washington and anyone else that you think is important." After a second, he added, "Include as many how-to books that you can think of."

"How-to books?" Dr. Rock asked.

"Yeah, you know," Aden answered. "Everything that Thomas might need. How to ride a horse, how to build a fire, and so on."

Aden turned to Tim. "How far is this field of yours from King George?"

"Philadelphia," Dr. Rock and I said at the same time.

"Philadelphia," Aden repeated.

"Not far," Tim told him. "Like I said, ten miles from here and two more miles to the city."

"Twelve miles on foot, through the wood and hills," Aden said.

"Yeah, Ok. It's far when you put it that way."

"Ok, and our last team," Aden said turning back to Jake and Dr. Smith. "What about the ship?"

"I could study it for a lifetime and still not fully understand it," Dr. Smith admitted. "The control panel seems to be working, and the cube is hooked up correctly, I think, or as far as I can tell. I studied the layout and configuration of the control panels all day yesterday and all last night. I am now convinced that your preliminary conclusions about their purposes and functions were correct."

Dr. Smith took a deep breath before continuing.

"I do need to point out that, although your assumption that each turn of the dial is sixty-one years is a logical one, it's not a scientific one. We know nothing about the race that made that cube or their concept and degree of mathematics. One click is sixty-one years, but two clicks could be six hundred, or six thousand years. Not only do we not know anything about their mathematics, but we also don't know anything about how they think or what would be logical to them. Remember, our concept of time, started with the day. We call it a day, because that is how long it takes the planet to spin one time on its axis. We call a year *a year* because that's how long it takes the earth to travel around the sun. As far as seconds, minutes, hours, and months, we invented those to help us explain a concept of time. From our point of view, it could take a week or month for an alien's planet to spin around or five years for their planet travel around the sun. What we think of a day, a segment of time, cannot be the same as their segment. It would also explain why one click is a weird number like sixty-one years, instead of say ten, or twenty or twenty-five years."

"Noted," Aden said. "What else?"

"Well, the last dial on the first row is the only dial that you'd tried," the doctor continued. "The bottom row may be single years, months, days, and hours. We can't know without experimenting. I'm sure that the second row would narrow down when in time you would end up, but without more testing, we can never know."

"We're done experimenting," Aden said. "No more tests. We can't afford for anything to go wrong. The next experiment might blow up the ship or who knows what. We know the function of that one dial, and our plans will be based around that. Anything else I should know?"

"I also disconnected that cheap, noisy gas-powered generator you'd been using. I'm going to attach an independent industrial noncombustible Honda generator to the inside rear of the ship. It will last longer, run cleaner, and has less chance of any unexpected problems, like power lag, surges, or interruptions. Thomas sent one of the guards to King George to pick one up for me. I'll install it today with some help from one of the welders. That set you back another seven thousand dollars."

"Why?" Aden asked. "This is a one-way trip, and we'll most likely will not get another chance."

"Well," Dr. Smith said, "none of this will matter if there's a problem and they never make it to their target location in time. We may have to try again if Mr. Cain fails. And finally, what about Jake? It may not be a one-way trip for him."

Aden's eyes went wide as he realized how insensitive what he'd said sounded.

"Yes," Aden said quickly. "I'm sorry Jake. Anything you can do to improve Jake's chances is fine with me, Doctor. Thank you for thinking of that."

Jake nodded his understanding.

The doctor continued. "Jake, and two of the warehouse guys, are welding a door and makeshift wall, to the rear of the ship, so that should take care of that backdraft problem."

"Well," Jake said, jumping in, "we couldn't weld to the ship itself. The ship's material will not heat up or accept a weld. We had to bend several steel bars and wrap them around the entire back end. Today we'll be welding the wall to the bent bar. By the time we are done it will be airtight and waterproof."

"Perfect," Aden said. "So, we have a plan, and we'll have a ship by tomorrow. As soon as Thomas's equipment and gear are ready, you'll have a go."

The next day Aden ushered me over to the smaller warehouse.

"Everything is ready except your weapons," Aden told me. "The gunsmith says that they'll be ready by tomorrow morning. He says you'll be happy with what he's made for you."

"What exactly did you tell him to do?" I asked.

"I told him the truth about what we are doing and what you needed," Aden said. "Except I told him we were filming a Sci-fi movie. I also told him that you insisted all the weapons be real for demos and movie promotions. He's extremely excited to be a part of this movie."

An oblong table was situated in the middle of the large workspace. We approached the table, and I was amazed at how Aden had thought of everything – four pairs of thick black wool socks, four pairs of underwear, and two sets of long johns for cold weather. Next to that was a white loose long-sleeved shirt, the kind of shirt a pirate might wear, and a short green coat that would serve better in the woods. The coat was more of a jacket by today's standards. It was also waterproof, filled with goose down, and had a fur lined hood.

Also on the table was thick black leather vest that Aden had crafted specifically for me. It was made from the same materials as a level three bullet proof vest. He slapped it.

"The bad news is that muskets fire rounds the size of a fifty-caliber rifle. The good news is they travel at about one-fourth the speed and are round balls, not pointy bullets. This will stop one easy enough."

"But?" I asked.

"But," he said slowly, "it might break a rib. It will definitely hurt, so don't get shot."

"Good advice," I told him. "Don't get shot. Can you write that down for me, so I don't forget?"

He laughed. "I already did."

He opened the vest and on the inside the words "Don't get shot," were written in white magic marker.

I had to laugh.

The vest had four brass buttons in the front and two larger brass buttons where chest pockets would be, except these buttons were not brass. They were painted to look like brass, to blend in. They were really hardened C4 explosive shape charges. *You never know when you might need some C4,* I thought. The backside of the charges consisted of double-sided tape, so I could stick them to almost anything. They could be set to explode on a thirty second timer, or thanks to a tiny mercury switch, they could be set to explode if they were moved.

A pair of military boots in my size were covered in brown suede and appeared homemade. The right boot had a four-inch knife sheath attached to it, containing a sharp, double-bladed throwing knife. The pants were tan with some brown flecks in them, made from an anachronistic polyester and cotton blend of rip-stop fabric with buck skin sewn on the knees. The pants were cut in military BDU style – warm, comfortable, and had cargo pockets. The belt was like a cargo strap but with a more historically accurate belt buckle.

Aden even had a backpack made for me. Sewn in a modern backpack style, like a backpack that you might buy at a sports store, this one was made of deer leather to blend in better. On the bottom of the backpack, a thick rolled up wool blanket was tied with two straps.

"It's a thermal blanket," Aden said, pointing to it. "I had wool blankets stitched to the outsides."

"Three blankets in one," I observed. "That will help keep me warm." After living in California for so long a time, the extra warmth in cold weather would be welcome. I had read the history books – I knew how cold the winters had been in colonial times.

I picked up one of four twelve-inch-long matching knives. The blades were constructed of titanium, with deer antler handle grips. Aden didn't think I could pass as a land-owning gentleman, so he wanted me to go with the mountain man or army scout costume – a militia man. George Washington had fought in the Indian wars, so Aden thought he would be Ok with the wilderness get up. That suited me fine. I didn't know the first thing about being a wealthy landowner.

I changed into the clothes to start getting used to them. I had to admit the clothes were much more comfortable than they initially appeared. The tailor came out and double checked his work, making sure I was happy and that everything fit as it should. I tucked the rest of the clothes into the backpack.

Then I attached one of the knives to my belt in the small of my back and the other to my front left side for an easy cross draw. The other two I placed in my backpack. Aden picked two first aid kits off the table and handed them to me.

"Combat kits," he said. "I also put in four bottles of extra strong pain killers. Hydrocodone. Extraordinarily strong stuff. Plus, bandages and extra blood clotting powder, just in case. The syringes are morphine, for emergencies only." He narrowed his eyes at me.

Aden then grabbed a cardboard box and pulled it to himself. He pulled out plastic bags of beef jerky, smoked salmon, a bottle of vitamin C, two canteens of water, two dozen granola bars and other food stocks.

"The canteens are plastic," he said. "They are covered with rabbit fur, so no one will know. I'll have someone take the food out of the plastic wrappers and rewrap them in wax paper."

Aden handed me a leather, drawstring purse. It was heavy and clinked. I opened it and poured out a handful of gold and silver coins into my palm – large silver coins, smaller gold coins and some the size of nickels, with King George's picture stamped on most of them. They were incredibly clean and in fact appeared brand new.

"Are these real?" I asked.

"They are real gold and real silver, if that's what you are asking," he answered. "But they are fakes. We made them ourselves. No one will know the difference."

Hopefully, I added to myself. I dropped the leather purse back on the table with a heavy thud. Also, on the table sat a brown powder horn with a gold cap at the large end and a gold pouring spout at the small end. A brown leather strap, long enough to go around a man's body, was attached to each end. It appeared normal enough. I picked up and investigated it. It was really a GPS transmitter with its own power source.

"Why so big?" I asked. "They make these the size of quarters now a days."

"Yes, but there are no satellites in 1777," he said. "It has to have a strong enough power source to put the signal out two miles or so. Plus, it has a battery that will last at least three months. I downloaded the app on your phone and mine. Just in case we must come back to find you, I can use this."

"You mean, if I fail," I said. "If this plan works, you'll not remember me. You may know a version of me, but it won't be the version of me that is stuck in 1777."

"Yeah," he said sadly, averting his eyes. "In case you fail."

Aden shook his head as if forcing negative thoughts out of it. He then handed me a worn, brown leather bag with a strap with the name *Nelson* stamped on the top. Nelson used to be an immensely popular name brand in leather bags and purses.

"You're giving me a man purse?" I asked, lifting one eyebrow.

"No," he said, missing my attempt at humor. "It's a satchel. Quite common back in the day, mostly used by messengers. You carry it across your body."

Two brass buckles held the flap shut. I put the satchel over my head so that the bag part itself sat on my left hip.

"Call it a satchel if you want," I said. "But it's still a man purse."

I lifted the flap to peer inside and found two different gun cleaning kits and a zippo lighter. He'd even put in a high-power monocular with a brass housing, which made it look old-fashioned. On closer inspection, it was anything but old-fashioned. It was a five to fifty-five power magnifier with a build in range finder. The biggest surprise was the military grade night vision goggles.

"Night vision?" I asked.

"Yeah, don't lose them," he said.

I made a mental note to put some writing materials, duct tape, gloves, earplugs, and few other items I thought I might need into the satchel. Aden reached under the table, slid out a wooden British military crate, and flipped the top open. He pulled out six high explosive grenades and handed them to me.

"Really?" I asked. Now I was incredulous. This was too much.

"Just in case," he said.

I didn't argue. Instead, I double checked the pins and made sure the pins were bent to a point that they wouldn't slip out. I placed four grenades in my satchel, and two at the bottom of my backpack. Aden was staring down at the satchel, and he chuckled.

"What so funny?" I asked.

"You just put four grenades in your man purse!" he said.

We stood there for several minutes, laughing at how absurd the situation was. It felt good to laugh again. I couldn't remember when I had laughed like this. But the moment was bittersweet –there was a chance it would also be the last time.

The next morning, Aden and I sat at the table in the mess tent and talked over coffee and donuts. Aden kept glancing at his phone and when he finally got the text message he was waiting for, we trekked back to the small warehouse and met with the gunsmith. He had a table with numerous guns laying on it along with two large stacks of ammo. His smile went from ear to ear. He was terribly excited to show us what he had come up with.

The gunsmith first handed me a leather shoulder holster with a large pistol in it. I slid my arms into the holster, and the leather strap went around my back. The pistol sat under my left arm facing down and toward the back. A strip of leather laid under my right arm with loops designed to hold eight more rifle rounds. I managed to pull the pistol out fast but smoothly.

"It's a Thompson Center Contender," the gun smith explained. "A single shot pistol used for hunting and competition shooting. It uses a 30-30 Winchester round. You can take down a deer with that, easy. The barrel is black steel, and the frame and grip are made from a single piece of smooth redwood. The front sight is fixed, so while it can't move, the rear sights adjust left or right for windage and up or down for elevation. It breaks open like a shotgun to load it."

I found the locking bolt and released it. The gun snapped open like a single shot shotgun might.

"It's a single shot modern pistol. I think it will blend in nicely, even in 1777," he said. "Keep in mind that the average musket is only accurate up to one hundred yards. This pistol is accurate for a man size target, over three hundred yards. More if you're a fair shot."

It was a graceful piece of art designed to kill from long range. The pistol grip was smooth and had finger grips carved on the inside.

The smith shifted to the other end of the table where three flintlock pistols lay. He picked up one that was different from the others.

"First, I took an eighteenth-century German flintlock pistol just like those two," he said pointing at the two he left on the table. "I stripped it down to the wooden frame. Then I took a 9mm Tec-9 pistol machine gun and tore it apart."

The smith tilted his head to Aden and explained.

"Most modern pistols load through the pistol grip," he said to Aden. "That can't work with the shape of the flintlock pistol. The Tec-9 loads its rounds in front of the trigger, like a military rifle. So, copying the Tec-9 design, I fabricated the barrel, trigger, springs, chamber, firing pin and magazine well. I had to reshape and resize some parts to rebuild it inside the flint lock's wooden frame. I had to cut a square opening underneath the wooden frame, in front of the trigger, for the magazine to fit in. The flintlock pistol was large enough to allow the cut. I also reattached the original hammer on the outside and cut down the ramrod, so it still fits in the gun, under the barrel, just for looks. The hammer and ramrod serve no purpose, other than aesthetic. I also attached a larger, fake copper barrel over the real Tec-9 barrel, so it will fool anyone who sees it. As long as you don't let them look too closely," he added.

Four-dozen two-inch magazines lay on the table next to several piles of ammunition of both calibers. He handed me one of the small, loaded magazines.

"They each hold six 9mm rounds," he told me. "When inserted, the bottom will only stick out a half inch. That's seven rounds if you chamber one in the chamber first."

Then he picked a four-inch brass tube with threads on the end.

"What's that?" Aden asked.

"A suppressor," I answered.

"Yes," the smith said with a slight smile.

The threads went inside the pistols fake barrel and threaded on the outside of the Tec-9 real barrel.

"It's really a Tec-9 with a wooden frame now," the smith said. "I test fired about two hundred rounds, and it's accurate up to twenty-five yards or so."

Next, he handed me a brown leather gun belt designed to go around my waist like a cowboy's gun belt. The gun sat low on my hip.

"Wrong time frame, isn't it?" Aden asked.

"In real life, this gun belt would make people look twice," he said. "You see, most people didn't walk around with their flint locks loaded unless they were planning on using them. The gun powder and ball would just fall out. But it will look cool for a movie. It will make for a stellar script too, since the bad guys in your story would assume your pistol is empty."

"You mean because he would carry the pistol facing down, everyone will assume it has to be empty?" Aden asked.

"Well, in your movie?" he asked. "Yeah, it would be a natural assumption."

Aden and I glanced at each other. He had to be thinking how useful and lifesaving that information would be.

"My only words of advice," he added. "I know you have shot guns before, but these are more unusual. You should practice before you try shooting at a demo or movie promotion."

"That's a good idea," I said. "I'll take all the ammo you have."

We shook hands and I thanked him. Aden laid it on thick with promises of movie credits and future work for other movies.

"If you're going to practice shooting," Aden told me as we left, "do it now, because you leave tomorrow night."

THREE: Short Goodbyes

IN THE OPEN FIELD, the darkness covered us like a heavy blanket. We stood around the broken ship, waiting for Aden to say something inspiring or comforting. The ship had been off-loaded from the truck and the workers had set up some lights and generators. I wore my costume, satchel, and both guns. My backpack with extra food and water sat safely on the ship already. Jake was videotaping us with the cell phone Aden had given him. Aden inspected me up and down for a final once-over.

"Well," Aden said finally, addressing those of us in the field, "I want to thank the six of you for your hard work. My only regret is that if Thomas is successful, then in whatever timeline Jake comes back to, none of us will ever know what risks we took. The Empire rules most of the world and has gone crazy with power. It must end. As someone once said, if not us then who? If not now then when? Well, I say it must end. That it's up to us. And now is the time."

Dr. Rock raised her hand, killing Aden's train of thought. Aden didn't even bother calling on her.

"I mean two hundred and forty-four years ago is the time."

Everyone laughed at that. Then he lowered his head and closed his eyes as if in prayer. I realized that he really was praying. Or perhaps thinking of those he lost and the reason behind this entire crazy enterprise.

He opened his eyes. "Thank you all."

Aden walked over to me and wrapped his arms around me in a hug. It was the strong hug you gave your brother. I realized then that not only would I never see my best friend again, but that my best friend would not remember me if we were successful. Hell, if there was a new timeline, there might be a Thomas Cain, in it, but I would not be *that* Thomas Cain. I could see the same thoughts in his eyes.

"Not too late to back out," Aden said, shaking his head slightly.

I shook my head in an adamant *no*. "If I do this right, I'll never get to meet Jenny, but Jenny will be alive."

If nothing else, this gigantic risk was worth the sacrifice if Jenny were to live the fullness of her life that had been robbed from her. I swallowed the lump in my throat that formed as I thought on that potentiality.

"I never told you why I am letting you do this and not doing it myself," he said, breaking me from my thoughts.

"I always assumed you knew I wanted to go," I responded.

"Yes, Thomas," he said. "But we all want to go. Look around. Is there a single person here who wouldn't jump at the chance to do what you're doing?"

42

From the intensity of the serious faces around me, I realized that he was right. I could tell that every one of them wanted to get on that ship.

"Why me then?"

"You are a haunted soul, Thomas," he said. "You have lost something that you have not been able to replace or move on from. It's my hope and wish that you'll find the peace you so desperately need. If you can't find it here, maybe you'll find it there."

He was right, and as my mind drifted to Jenny again, I pushed slowly away from Aden and walked to the ship without another word. Jake made a point of shaking hands with everyone, then came over to me. We loaded up in the ship, shutting the newly crafted door behind us. Dr. Smith had set up lights inside the ship so we could see what we were doing. Since we weren't using the main controls the set near the co-pilot's seat, Jake sat there, and I took the pilot's seat.

Jake turned to me. "Ready?"

I was afraid my voice might crack, so I gave a thumbs up sign. He then keyed his radio mic and narrated what he was doing. Aden had a radio and would be listening.

"Turning last dial, of the top set, of the third control panel, one click down, to what we think is the zero point," Jake said. "Now turning last dial, on the top set, of the third control panel, four more clicks down, to what we hope is our target. You guys want a count down or should I just push the button?"

Aden's voice came over the radio. "Give us a count down from five. And God speed, Second Chance."

Jake keyed the mic again. "Five, four, three, two –"

I closed my eyes and held my breath.

"One. Launch."

The air felt thick and tasted of ozone. My fillings vibrated in my teeth. Even with my eyes closed, a flash of light permeated my lids. No vacuum this time, so I guess the door held. I opened my eyes. Nothing in the ship looked different. Jake turned his head to me with raised eyebrows as if to ask, *Did it work?*

I went to the back of the ship and turned the latch holding the door shut. Jake moved to the lights. I nodded my head and he flicked them off. The ship was pitch black except for the two control panels. Once my eyes adjusted to the dark, I gave a thirty count. Opening the door about six inches revealed that it was still dark out. Cold air rushed into the ship, colder than it had been when we entered the ship. Aden, the lights, and the trucks were gone. The field appeared the same, but the grass was taller. Pushing the door, the rest of the way open, I stepped out of the ship.

"What do you see?" Jake whispered.

"Nothing," I said. "They are all gone."

Jake stepped out behind me, his eyes wide.

"Did it work?" he asked.

"Well, it worked, but the real question is, is this 1777?" I asked.

Thunder rumbled low in the distance, and the air was colder. A cool breeze was blowing from what I believed to be the north.

"A storm's coming," Jake said. "It's colder than it was, and I can hear thunder."

The thunder had a rhythm to it. Eight or nine thunderclaps then four more from farther away. Eight or nine and then four further away. No lighting preceded the thunder. No bolt of electricity sticking the ground, just the rhythm of the thunder.

"That's not thunder Jake," I commented.

"What is it?" Jake asked.

"Cannon fire," I said, tipping my head. "From the north."

"How far?"

"No idea," I answered. "I've never heard cannon fire in real life before. Depends on how big the cannons are."

"Guess," he insisted.

"Well," I said. "How far you can hear a cannon depends on how big they are, and the presence of any noise blockers, like trees. Dr. Rock said that the average cannons were six pounders. Most of the times armies would put cannons on top of hills. They must be five to ten miles away from here but no way to say for sure without knowing more."

"What now?" Jake asked.

"You go back to Aden, and I find a safe place to sleep until morning," I answered.

I turned to face him, and he had his hand out to shake mine, barely visible in the dark. I grabbed his hand, and we each held a strong grasp. We had no idea what laid before Jake on his return trip, but we knew this would be the last time I spoke to someone from my own century.

"Good luck," he told me in a wavering voice.

"You too, Jake," I answered back.

"Do this right, Thomas," he said, as a tear coursed down his cheek. "You do this right and give them hell. For both of us and those we love."

He was thinking of his family and everything that Empire had taken from him. I nodded my head. We slowly let go of each other's hand – each of us knowing we had to, reluctant. Once he pushed that button, there was no going back. I stepped back a few feet away and he stepped back into the ship.

"Should I give you a count down?" he asked.

"No," I answered. "Just be safe."

"Oh. One last thing."

"What's that?" I asked.

"If anyone asks, don't tell them that your last name is Cain," he said.

"Why not?" I asked.

"1777 was a puritanical time," he said. "The whole Cain and Able thing may make people distrust you. Try a more common name, like Smith."

Ducking into the ship, he reached out and handed me my backpack. Then he closed the door, and I turned my back on the ship, walking for the tree line. A bright flash lit up the night from behind me. I shifted around to look, but the ship was just gone. An imprint of crushed grass laid on the ground where the ship had been, but no ship.

I was alone.

I made it to the tree line and went down on my right knee, trying to get my bearings. I didn't need to use the small compass attached to my watchband. The field really hadn't changed much in the last two hundred and forty-four years. The cannon fire was to the north, and Philadelphia was southeast. The quickest way to Philadelphia was as the crow flies, eleven miles southeast of me. The downside was I couldn't count on road signs or a GPS anymore. If, I was a little off, I might miss Philadelphia by miles.

My second choice was to walk the ten miles back to where the warehouse was, or will be one day, then the two miles from there to Philadelphia. I thought I could do that, but we took a lot of back roads to get to this field so as to avoid any check points. I knew basically where the warehouse would be, but not exactly in this time period.

The third and safest option was also my longest. I could walk east until I ran into the Delaware River, then follow it south until I reached Philadelphia. That trek would be about twenty miles, taking a lot more of my limited time. On the other hand, if I got lost, I might not make it to Philadelphia until after George Washington was hung. After an internal debate, I elected to play it safe and go the long way.

First, though, I decided to stay where I was tonight and start out at the crack of dawn. My father had taken me camping a few times, but navigation by the stars at night in the woods wasn't something we ever went over. The cannon fire was still firing with rhythm, but it sounded like fewer cannons were going off. I untied my thermal blanket and wrapped it around my body. I laid down between a large brown bush and some trees, then checked my guns one last time to make sure they were loaded, chambered and ready to go.

A giant emptiness surrounded me. With nothing but the wispy sound of the wind through the maples and cedars and the distant echoes of cannons, the world suddenly seemed strange. Sleep was elusive and I needed to distract myself, so I had the energy for tomorrow. On a whim, I pulled out my cell phone, turned it on, and scrolled through my and Jenny's wedding pictures until I was tired. I needed to save the battery's life, so I forced myself to turn the phone off, and fell asleep.

As the sun's pale rays broke through the trees, I blinked awake. It had dropped to about forty degrees over the night, and even though my breath came out in smoky puffs, the thermal blanket had kept me warm enough. Something was different with the morning light. It took me a minute to realize that the cannon fire had stopped. With a flush of panic, I whirled around, but I was still alone.

My first thought was to make a pot of coffee, but then I realized where I was. I wasn't just camping, and I had not brought any coffee with me. Old habits died hard. I'd have to rely on the cold air to do the work of my missing caffeine.

Stretching and yawning to wake up, I rolled up my blanket and laced up my boots. I pulled out some powdered eggs and beef jerky and ate quickly. I desperately craved a cup of coffee, but I was out of luck. Then I placed four granola bars in my cargo pocket to snack on later as I walked. I didn't want to stop to eat lunch, and the bars would help with my energy. I took my morning piss on a pine tree and swung my backpack on. Again, I didn't bother to use my compass. The sun had risen, breaking the gray eastern horizon, so heading due east was easy.

Glancing at my Swiss Army watch, I noted it was almost seven o'clock. With some quick computations, I figured between the woods, hills, and creeks, and with no roads or trails, I would most likely walk about two miles an hour. If I was right, I had about twenty miles to reach Philadelphia. Including rest breaks, I rounded it up to a twelve-hour trip. I wasn't sure if I wanted to walk into Philadelphia at night or sleep right outside the city limits and walk in first thing in the morning. Then I risked having only one day to stop Washington's execution.

The first three hours of moving cautiously though the woods passed virtually incident free. Other than some squirrels and a fat gray rabbit, I didn't see another living soul. Then, as I broke from some bushes, I thought I heard voices. I froze in place.

The voices sounded straight ahead of me. The gurgling of running water in the distance told me that a stream was up ahead. A horse whinnied and snorted from the same direction – maybe someone was watering their horses? I dropped to my stomach and crawled through the leaves to the next set of trees. I picked out a multichromatic tree that was large and had exposed roots for better cover. Peeking my head over one of the roots, I watched as two British soldiers sat down on a log that laid partway in a stream. The stream bubbled from the north and just south of where the soldiers sat, it turned east. The water was shallow, maybe a foot deep. The horses stood in the water, drinking, while the soldiers washed their feet.

How cold is that water? Their feet must have been disgustingly dirty to make them want to stick their feet in it. They had their muskets across their laps and were laughing as if one had just told a joke. They faced opposite directions, so that one had his back to me, and the other was facing me. About forty feet extended between them and my hiding space, and no cover existed past the tree I hid behind. I could back away and work my way around them, hoping they didn't come across me on horseback. My other option was that I could shoot the men right now, take their horses, and get to Philadelphia even faster.

The second choice seemed to be the most logical one, but I didn't know if I could kill two men in cold blood. My thoughts flashed to Jenny and how I wanted to kill these British soldiers to avenge her, but I also knew that Jenny would not approve of such senseless violence. I laid in the dirt, telling myself that this was war. Yesterday it wasn't my war, but when I stepped into that spaceship, I made myself part of it. Nothing else mattered but getting to Philadelphia and saving George Washington. Still killing two men while they sat there washing their feet felt wrong. One of the two raised a hand to silence the other and they scanned their surroundings. Something had them spooked.

Shit, I thought. Had I made a noise?

"Who's there?" the taller one yelled. I held my breath.

49

They grabbed their boots and waddled out of the water. Without knowing I'd done it, I realized that I had my Thompson Center Contender in my right hand. I hadn't even realized that I had pulled it out. If I hadn't pulled it sooner, I would be going for it now. What worried me was I wasn't sure if I had pulled it *after* they'd heard me talking to myself, or had I already made up my mind to kill both of them but didn't care to admit it.

They didn't bother to put on their boots. Dropping their boots to the ground, they aimed their muskets into the tree line, fanning them from left to right, trying to find me. If they saw me in my costume, they'd take me for American militia and probably shoot me.

"Drop your muskets," I yelled. "Drop them or die."

The taller must have seen me, or guessed where I was from my voice, because he fired his rifle and the round hit the tree root about two feet from my right, spraying dirt and wood splinters across my back. One of the two horses pulled at his bridle, trying to be anywhere other than where they were right now. The other horse stood calm as could be, obviously used to gunfire.

Shooting the taller one first if it came to that had seemed a sound plan, but now his musket was discharged, and his buddy was bringing his rifle around to my direction. I fired precisely without thought and the man flew back like he'd been hit with a sledgehammer to the chest. The taller one dropped to a knee and scrambled to reload his musket.

I thumbed the release bolt, and my Thompson Contender broke open. Pulling out the spent round, I replaced it with a new one. I closed the action and brought my pistol back up, aiming down the barrel. The taller one was pulling his ram rod out of the barrel when his head exploded. The soldier's body stilled for a second, then it fell back into the stream with a soft *plumsh*. Reloading my Contender again, I laid in wait to see if anyone else would come running. After two minutes, I stood, brushed off the woodchips, and strolled over to the two men, nudging them with my boot to make sure they were dead. The horses seemed to be calming down, and I patted the first one on the neck.

"Easy boy," I said. "Easy." Not sure why I patted his neck, he was the calm one and didn't seem to need reassurance.

He was a tall, radiant chestnut with a white face and white lower legs. He had a lot of spirit but also seemed calmer than the other. He turned his head and tried to bite at me. The other was a lighter brown with a white stripe down his nose. He seemed younger and a little more skittish and reminded me of the horse little Joe had on the T.V. show *Bonanza*. He pushed me with his nose as if to say, "I have a neck too, dummy."

I liked this spry one better, plus he was smart enough to want to run away from the shooting. I took off my backpack, tying it to the back of the saddle. Saddle bags were fastened to the horses, and both sets of saddle bags contained some food and a few personal items. The taller horse's bag had some coins that I added to my own. The other horse let me climb onto his back with no problems.

"Ok, Little Joe," I said, naming the horse as I tied the bridle of the chestnut to the horn of Little Joe's saddle. "Let's mosey on."

Leaving the British bodies where they lay, I rode at a walking pace down river for about a half mile to hide my tracks. Taking out my compass, I evaluated my location and turned Little Joe due east. I'm not going to lie; I didn't realize how tired my feet were until I sat on that horse. The last four miles went easy. A couple of times, musket fire in one direction or another caught my attention, and I turned away from it and nickered the horses into a canter for a little distance.

I made it to the Delaware River in decent time. At the grassy riverbank, I gave the horses a rest and refilled my canteens. I also dropped in a couple of water purification tabs into each with a measure of uncertainty. This water appeared cleaner than anything I was used to already – probably cleaner than anything unbottled in my time. It sparkled as it ran over the rocks, but then I thought of the dead Brit I'd left in the stream and decided purification was a sound practice.

One of the Red Coats that I had killed was kind enough to have had a bag of grain tucked into his sack, so I took the time to feed the horses, cupping the grain in my hand as their soft lips sucked at the food. After the short rest, I turned Little Joe south and we were off down the path along the river frontage.

An old man rode up the path in a cart built for two horses but was only being pulled by one old nag. Not that I knew what a nag was, but that was the word that came to mind at the sight of the poor horse. The man's cart was filled with mostly corn and apples – he must have been a farmer. His apples were edible but barely. They were smaller than I was used to and didn't have that waxy sheen that the apples in the grocery store had back home. He was dressed like a farmer and wore a blanket across his shoulders, and he stopped to chat when I waved him down.

He introduced himself as Old Ben. His strong and distinct accent claimed him to be Irish. According to Ben, I was heading in the right direction and was only a few miles outside of Philadelphia. I asked if he knew where the British were. He spat on the ground and told me that they were getting ready to attack Philadelphia.

When I asked about George Washington, he said, "Damn fool is preparing his new continental army. He wants to meet the British on the battlefield."

"You don't think he can win?" I asked.

"Ha," he barked out a laugh. "Lad, the British may be the biggest bunch of fecking aristocratic, dictators, tyrants, and sons of bitches, the world has ever known. But how do you think they got that way?"

Then he answered his own question. "By deploying the most disciplined, well trained, and well-equipped army the world has ever seen. And right now, lad, there are about eighteen thousand of them, well-trained, well-equipped, hardened soldiers camped outside of Philadelphia. They are waiting for that damn fool Washington to step his high-born, highly educated ass out onto the field and meet them."

Then, while nodding his head to his own words, he spit to the side of his cart and stuffed what must have been a tobacco leaf in his mouth.

He chewed the leaf for a few seconds before continuing. "And you think a bunch of half-trained, well-intended, farmers, clerks, furriers, and black smiths, are going to stand up and trade shot for shot with the greatest army alive, guided by the greatest generals ever produced? Washington's a fool."

I nodded agreement, since I knew he was right. I filled the saddle bags with apples he offered and handed him a gold coin. He squinted one eye at it.

"Lad, that's too much and I do not have any silver to give back," he said.

"No need, Ben," I said taking a bite of an apple. It was sour.

I nodded my thanks and kicked Little Joe in the flanks to get him moving. I made it to Philadelphia two hours ahead of schedule. It was still day light, so I didn't have to sleep outside the city, but the sun was racing into the western horizon.

1777

FOUR: Drinks at the Tavern

THE CITY WAS SITUATED on the banks of the Delaware River, and the breeze whipped up more cold air from the east. The city was laid out with a mix of dirt and cobblestone streets going north and south and east to west in straight lines, a functional grid, throughout the whole city. The roads started off as deep mud and then turned to hard cobblestone. I tried not to appear like a green foreigner, but my eyes had a mind of their own, trying to take in all the sights at once.

Two-story buildings made of red or brown brick lined the streets. Some men were dressed in tattered cotton or wool and covered in dirt and filth. A few wore blue coats with white pants. Others, who were not in the regular army, wore brown pants, or if they were gentlemen, then they seemed to compete with the ladies in colorful outfits, reminding me of strutting peacocks.

I came into the city from the north and tied the horses to a hitching post in front of the large Continental Congress building. I cut one of the apples in half and stuck each half in front of the horses. They each took the half apple and chewed greedily. The tall one almost took off one of my fingers. I hung my backpack and coat over Little Joe's saddle horn but kept my satchel. Turning around, I gazed up at the Continental Congress building. That's when it really hit me. I was here, walking through history. I shook my head in amazement as I headed up the steps and into the building.

I entered into pure chaos. Men scrambled around in every direction. Bloodied, wounded men lay in the hall and were trying to sit up with their backs against the walls. Doctors performed primitive surgeries on rickety tables right there in the Congress building. A low moaning consumed every corner. It turned out that British soldiers had attacked the Congress building in hopes of arresting General Washington, but the attack had failed because Washington wasn't there at that time. The soldiers had fled after losing half of their men. Some of the soldiers were seen running off, to the north and south while able-bodied Continental soldiers had rushed out to search for the British soldiers.

I inquired about General Washington, and one of the Doctors informed me that he wasn't in the building. He was planning tomorrow's attack with his top advisors at a more private location. That made sense – the Continental Congress was too crowded with nonmilitary workers, and the General, being a careful man, didn't want anyone overhearing his plans. He moved with his advisors and commandeered a tavern on the north-west side of town. No one knew if the General had been notified about the attack yet.

I ran out of the building, leaving the horses at the Congress building and searching the taverns. The cobblestone streets I ran on were so neat and unusual – I could hear footsteps of men and horses along the road. I thought I'd found him at the third tavern I checked the Lady Love. Two Continental soldiers held up their hands at me, stopping me in the doorway. A red curtain hung behind them, blocking the interior of the tavern, yet men's voices carried to the door.

"I have a message for the General," I said with an air of urgency, and neither seem to care.

Their blue coats were ripped, faded, and wore through. Their dusky white shirts and pants were in newer conditions and slightly cleaner. The man to my right pressed a hand on my chest to stop me from going any farther. His rifle hung on his back, but the one to my left maneuvered his rifle with his left hand and grabbed my left arm. The one with his hand on my chest pushed me back a foot out of the doorway.

"No entry until you hand over your weapons." His voice was tight in a way I assumed the believed to be authoritative. I narrowed my gaze at the men.

As they moved, their boots caught my attention. They were newer, and the tops were shiny black but fresh mud had splattered their ankles. If these men were assigned to Washington, why were there mud on their boots? He surely would have stayed in the center of town and not the outskirts, and the streets weren't that muddy. Their gun powder tins or holders, or whatever they were called, weren't horns but brass containers. They were the same style of powder holders, with the same markings, I'd found on the two British soldiers I'd killed.

"Ok," I said, playing along. "Let's kick this dog in the ass and see which way he runs."

It was a saying my father liked to use when I was a boy, and it seemed more than appropriate here.

Both men's eyebrows curled in confusion at me. My right hand snaked behind my back and grabbed the twelve-inch knife that laid in the small of my back. I shifted up my left hand in the air and wiggled my fingers as it went above my head. Their eyes followed my left hand, watching the fingers move. It was a simple distraction I sometimes used before I sucker punch someone. People fell for it all the time, which continued to surprise me. I hoped it worked here.

My right hand shot out, and I struck hard. My arm exploded with power as I twisted my upper body, slamming the tip of my knife up into the soft pallet under his jaw. The razor-sharp blade went through the bottom of his mouth and through the roof of his mouth. The knife didn't stop until it penetrated his brain.

My left hand came back down and forward, grabbing the other soldier's throat as he overcame his shock and pushed toward me. I squeezed as hard as I could against his windpipe to stop him from yelling. The man to my right fell straight down as his knees buckled when his brain was turned off, and he struck the floor. I released the knife, and with my hand balled into a fist, struck the other soldier square in the nose. His hands were occupied, trying to pull my hand away from his throat and his rifle clattered to the floor. I yanked him close, and my knee came up into his nuts. I felt more than heard the air in him exhaled from his lungs in a rush, bathing my face in hot, fishy-smelling breath.

I then pulled my other knife in the cross draw and jammed it up into his ribs and penetrated his lung. When I extracted the knife, a wet sucking sound whooshed out as his lung collapsed and filled with his own blood. He was alive, but out of the fight and not alive for long. He dropped to the floor in a writing heap. The men laid there on the wooden floor. I wiped my knife off on the dead soldier's pant leg and put it back into its sheath, then did the same with the knife in the dead man's chin. I pulled out my Tec-9 pistol and peeked past the curtain.

General George Washington himself sat in a chair with his arms secured behind him, a rag tied around his eyes, and another shoved into his mouth. I pushed the shock of seeing the mighty man in the flesh and assessed the situation.

One British officer, a pistol in hand, stood behind him, eyeing at the curtain that I was peeking through. Two more men stood to his right and three men to his left. They were staring at the curtains and at me. That is when everyone in the room except Washington and the officer behind him aimed their pistols in my direction.

"Shit," I cursed under my breath as I dived to the side.

Five loud gunshots rang out and ripped through the curtain. A hammer strike landed on the left side of my chest. Crashing down on my face hurt, but I kept my head in the game and rolled to my side.

The first man burst through the curtain with his empty pistol in one hand and a two-foot-long bayonet in the other. I raised my pistol and shot him in the face. He snapped back without a word, but his hand grabbed and ripped the curtain down as he crumpled to the wood floor. The other four soldiers' heads popped up, two of the men held knifes and two were reloading their pistols. The two with knifes stepped forward towards me. I fired two shots into each of their chests and they thrust back, blood spraying one of the tables. One man landed on the same table, sprawled out like a starfish, and the other fell to the floor. The men reloading their pistols snapped their head up, expecting to see four men holding pistols after hearing four-gun shots. Instead, they only saw me with a single pistol. Their brows furrowed in confusion and they stood there with their mouths hanging open. That was their mistake.

I raised my Tec-9 as they shook themselves and tried to finish reloading. By my count, I only had two rounds left and fired one shot into each of their faces. They tumbled backwards. I dropped my Tec-9 and pulled out the Thompson Contender, then came up in a roll, stopping on one knee. The British officer held his pistol to the General's head, and the man's eyes were as wide as teacups. He watched me shoot seven rounds from what he thought was a flintlock pistol without reloading, and his brain couldn't process what he was seeing. He stood behind the General, and my lips pulled into a side grin at his ignorance.

I'm an excellent shot. I used to teach firearms at the police academy. The pistol I was holding was used for competition shooting, and I could hit a six-inch circle from about twenty-five yards, easy. Hell, it was one of the reasons Aden tapped me for this gig. This soldier was no more than fifteen feet from me. He believed the General shielded him, having half his body exposed, when all he was doing was making it easier for me by holding still and letting me take aim. I wanted to marvel at how far firearms and our behavior about them had come in the past two centuries, but I had a job to do.

"How?" was all he said before I put a bullet between his eyes and blew out the back of his head. He fell backwards on top of his own brain matter.

I stood up and then stumbled back down. My vest had worked as advertised and stopped the bullet that should have killed me. I wasn't sure if I had any broken ribs or not but damn, it hurt. I struggled to breathe, but I was catching my breath, so I didn't think I punctured a lung. My left leg began to burn. My pants were ripped, and my leg was bleeding. When I had dived to the side, one of the rounds hit the back of my thigh. It didn't seem to be bleeding too badly, so it could wait.

I reloaded the Contender and picked up my Tec-9, ejecting the magazine and replacing it with a loaded one from my man purse. I had to remember that I only had six shots this time, not seven. I then limped over to where General Washington sat tied up. Men yelled outside – whether Brits or militia, I couldn't guess. I slipped the blind fold off his eyes, and he blinked several times as his left eye adapted to the lamp light in the room. His right eye was swollen shut and a mess of red and purple. He also had a knot on the back of his head, with dried blood caked around it. I pulled the rag out of his mouth, and he worked his jaw as he viewed the carnage.

"Are you Ok, General?" I asked.

"Fine, I think," he said, then asked more than stated, "thanks to you?"

"Yes, sir," I answered. "I got lucky with the element of surprise."

Men rushed into the tavern as I cut Washington's hands free. He held up his right hand before someone misread the situation and shot me.

He glanced over to the other side of the room, where two dead men laid.

"Your advisors?" I asked.

"Yes," he said. "The bastards came in and charged us. How did you know that I'd been captured?"

"In truth sir, I didn't," I answered honestly. "Not until I noticed their boots."

"Their boots you say?" he asked.

He stood up shakily and staggered over to the first two soldiers, observing their boots.

"Newer, finely made, English boots," he said. "Well polished but muddy."

He nodded his head in some silent agreement with himself. With the toe of his boot, he rolled the head of one soldier, exposing the wound under his chin. He shifted his gaze to the other soldier who had since died.

He altered his gaze over at me, his eyes hooded and powerful. Commanding. "Very observant of you, young man. Who are you, sir?"

"Thomas, sir, at your service," I answered. Jake said not to tell anyone that my last name was Cain, but I never came up with a new last name.

"Very well, *Thomas*," he said, picking up on the fact that I had not given my last name.

One of the men in the room had retrieved a sword belt that was on the floor and handed it to Washington. He nodded his thanks as he buckled it on.

He studied me with those same hooded eyes. "Are you one of my scouts, son?"

"No sir," I said, figuring that staying as close to the truth as possible was the best policy.

"Then why were you looking for me?" he asked with a measure of suspicion in his voice. I didn't blame him. Time to put on the show.

"The British, sir," I said. "I have news of them."

"News. What news?" he asked.

"May I speak to you in private, sir?" I asked as I glanced around at the men coming in the door.

He lifted his eyes and knew what worried me.

"Very well, Thomas. Come with me," he ordered.

He stopped and asked one of the officers to take care of the advisors' bodies, then I followed him upstairs to his room. One of his men was studying the empty magazine that

I had dropped. Without pausing, I plucked it out of his hand as I walked by him, dropping it in my satchel.

"Hey!" he yelled at me.

"Mine," I announced, not turning around. Better not to engage with questions I couldn't answer. And I'd have to be more cautious about things like that in the future.

I limped up the stairs, still bleeding. The pain burrowed deep into my leg, but I couldn't help myself and took a minute to look the revered General over.

He was a tall man for the time, standing six foot two inches, with wide shoulders and thick chest, well suited for the military. He carried a little excess fat on his frame, but it only made him appear bigger. Understandably, he was upset and insulted after being captured in his own city. He talked and held himself like a true gentleman, but history told how he fought in the hills and woods of this country and had seen his share of death. As a result, he had a stern, lined face but sad eyes. This was a man who had fought in so many battles, witnessed so many young men die; a man who knew he was going to see many more die before he was done, but understood his fight was just. I liked him from the start and had to admit just being in the same room with him was electrifying.

"You're bleeding Thomas," he said as he entered his room.

"Yes sir," I answered. "A bit."

I pointed towards a chair in a silent request to sit. He nodded his head in assent. I pulled off my satchel and sat it on the floor next to the chair. Digging into the satchel, I took out a packet of blood clot powder and a bandage. Then I removed my gun belt and sat it on the floor next to my satchel.

"Forgive me, sir," I said, as I pulled my pants down below where the bullet had grazed me.

I was lucky. The bullet ripped through my skin, but not deep, and had already started to slow. I poured the powder on the wound and wrapped the bandage around my leg tight. The bleeding stopped and I gave myself an antibiotic shot that I had also taken out of my first aid kit. Washington watched every move I made with forceful intensity. He was taking mental notes that I knew he was committing to memory. The man didn't miss anything.

"Are you a doctor, Thomas?" he asked in an even tone.

"No sir," I answered. "Just a man who has seen his share of fighting."

He sauntered over to a wash basin and poured in water from a pitcher that sat next to it. He lifted a small towel and soaked it in the water. After ringing out the water, he rubbed the back of his head, washing off the dried blood. He then pulled out a small but sharp knife and cut his own face, right under his swollen eye.

Like me, this wasn't the first time he had done field medics in his life. He knew to hold the towel under the eye to catch the blood that poured out, releasing the pressure, and opening up his eye.

"How did you kill eight men with only two pistols?" he asked while wiping the blood off his own face. I had been expecting the question.

"Luck and surprise," I told him. "Lots of luck and surprise, sir."

"I may have been blind-folded Mr. Nelson, but I do have ears, you know," he said.

I raised an eyebrow at him quizzically. *Why did he think my name was Nelson?*

He turned and pointed to my satchel on the floor. "You're not the only person in the room who's observant."

The brand name "Nelson" stamped into the leather satchel. His assumption made sense. People didn't exactly have brand name tags in 1777, so it might have been common to stamp the family name on one's own satchel.

"Eight men in that room," he said. "All trained British soldiers, and they are now dead. Two of them you killed with knives, unless I miss my guess. They were not even able to give warning to their associates. Five of them emptied their pistols at you from about ten feet away. Somehow, they all missed, other than that one, which is nothing more than a scratch," he said waving a hand towards my leg.

"It's more than a scratch, General," I said. "And one of the soldiers dropped his musket, giving some warning to the others."

My breathing was still labored. I needed to check my ribs, but not in front of him. *That* would be hard to explain.

"Sir, may I make my report on the enemy activity that I've observed?" I asked, hoping to change the subject.

He nodded his head slowly, still holding the towel to his face as he listened.

"About eighteen thousand British troops are camped outside your city and more arrive every day. They are here for two reasons only." I paused for dramatic effect before continuing. "To kill you and take this city."

"I know that young man," he said flatly. "I will meet them on the battlefield in the morning."

"No," I countered. "You can't."

"Can't?" he stated, obviously not accustomed to being told what he could and couldn't do.

"Sir," I said in a calm voice. I wasn't sure what to say next, so I repeated Old Ben's words. "Right now, you have eighteen thousand, well-trained, highly disciplined, hardened soldiers camped outside your city. They are waiting for you, sir, to step out and meet them on the field. No one else. A field and time of *their* choice, may I add. No disrespect intended, sir, but you have a bunch of half-trained and well-intended, farmers, clerks, furriers, and black smiths. No matter how noble your intentions, you can't stand up and trade shot for shot with the greatest army alive, directed by some of the greatest generals ever produced. They are setting a trap."

"What would you suggest then, Mr. Nelson?" he asked as he perched on the edge of the table in the room. "Should I run like some coward?"

"No sir," I answered. "Not run."

"Good. Because if they see us leaving the city, they will attack and run us down. I'll die on my feet before I live on my knees, young man."

"Luck and surprise," I said, getting his attention again. "That's how you win the war. But first you have to break out of the city and survive."

He opened his mouth to argue, so I held up a hand.

I tried to back up and start again. "If you fight and die, the whole country loses. If you fight and are forced to run, those who live to run will die of starvation, and again, the whole country loses."

I could see him calculating, his eyes shifting to the right. He was pondering losing and having to run or die. I needed to push him harder.

"A bad war is fought with a good mind," I continued. "If you order your men to strip the city of all the horses, wagons, and food, you can hole up somewhere and finish training your men. Then, when *you* are ready, you pick the battle, you pick the time, and you pick the location. With a little luck and surprise, you can turn this war around."

He stood there and rubbed his hand over his chin. I waited for him to ask how I came to know all this, but he didn't. He realized what he was doing and forced his broad hands down to his sides.

"Valley Forge is only twelve miles from here," he said to himself as he turned his back on me. "It would buy us time to train and grow."

He turned and strode quickly out of the room, like a man who just made an important decision.

"Come along, Thomas!" he yelled over his shoulder.

I scrambled after him, cringing in pain with every step. I'd have to take some pain killers first chance I got.

When I strode outside, night had come, and the city was lit up with torches. I caught up with the General halfway to the Continental Congress building as he was yelling for his command staff. Officers came running from every corner, and Washington gave orders to form up the men.

"We are leaving in four hours," he yelled. "Tell the men to grab everything they can carry. If they can ride it, shoot it, or eat it, then it's coming with us. Leave nothing behind for the British."

He yelled for someone to get him a horse.

"Sir," I said, getting his attention. I pointed at the hitching post. "I have two horses. Please take the chestnut. He's calm under fire. You'll need a calm horse like him."

He stepped over to the chestnut and patted his neck.

"He's a fine mount, Thomas. Thank you. What's his name?"

"I haven't named him, sir," I said. "In fact, I only recently acquired him from a British soldier who no longer needs him."

The General laughed, catching the joke.

"Calm under fire, you say," he thought out loud. "I'll call him Nelson, after someone else who stayed calm under fire."

He then mounted Nelson and spun the horse in two tight circles. I wasn't much of a horse rider, but it was evident that the General was.

"I hope you'll be coming with us to Valley Forge, Thomas?" the General asked. "I do believe I like you."

"No sir," I said. "I'm heading up to New York, to help out at Saratoga. I think the British will be heading there next. They'll be needing a resourceful scout. I'll find you at Valley Forge," I said.

Washington pulled the horse up and stared down at me with that intense gaze of his. It was enough to make any man tremble, including myself.

"Who are you, Thomas Nelson?" the General asked. I swallowed and took a shallow breath before answering.

"Just a man who hates the British and wants to help you win this war sir."

"Not good enough, sir," he said, that fierce gaze narrowing.

"Fine, General," I answered in a sturdy voice. "A man whose wife was raped and murdered by a British officer."

With a sad expression overtaking the hard, chiseled lines of his face, he nodded his head as if that explained everything.

"May I ask a favor of you, Thomas?" he asked, holding my gaze.

"I did say I was at your service, General," I answered.

"I know you have already saved my life and given me a fine mount," he said. "I do not want to sound ungrateful, but General Howe wants my head. He will never let us pull out of Philadelphia. He has kept his distance so far, but only because he wants to give me room to come out and fight. One of the reasons I hadn't pulled out days ago is, as I said already, as soon as we try, he will attack and run us down. You seem to me to be very," he paused a moment to choose the right word, "as you say, resourceful. Would you be willing to do a small but hazardous task for me?"

"You want me to cause a distraction?" I asked, raising an eyebrow.

"Aye. A distraction. Is that something you would be agreeable to?" he asked.

"The harder the conflict, the greater the triumph," I said glibly.

"I like that. You're correct Thomas. The harder the conflict, the greater the triumph!"

"General, strip the city bare and form up your men," I said. "Keep them quiet and in the city until you see my signal."

"I assume I'll know this signal, when I see it?" he asked.

I flicked my eyes to the large tower clock that we stood in front of, then glanced at my watch. The clock said it was nine o'clock, and my watch read ten till nine. I'd would have to remember that I was ten minutes behind the clock.

"Shall we plan for one in the morning by this clock's time?" I asked, pointing at the clock tower.

"Very well, Thomas," he said. "But will you be able to keep track of the time? Have you a pocket watch?"

"Oh, don't worry about me, General. Just be ready to pull out of the city," I told him with a smile.

I reached into my backpack and pulled out one of my two pairs of long johns and handed them up to the General. "It's going to be a cold winter sir. Take these."

He ran his hands over them, feeling how soft and warm they were. He smiled for the first time since I'd met him.

"Thank you, Thomas," he said. "I hope to meet you again."

He heeled his horse and galloped down the road, waving to his men as he went.

I pulled out one of my canteens and drank deeply from it. If you have never been in a gun fight you might not know it, but cotton mouth is a common after effect. After the whole adrenal dump in your body wears off, you feel tired and thirsty, and I had to wait until after my interactions with Washington before I could drink. I was parched. I downed the whole canteen with two pain killers for my leg and chest. The other thing about adrenalin is that it really helps hide pain. When the adrenalin's gone, the pain is even more noticeable.

Now that the General was gone, I stepped to the side of the Continental building under a flickering torch and took off my vest and shirt. A softball-sized, purple bruise blossomed across my ribcage. I fingered it gingerly, but the ribs didn't feel broken, so I had that going for me. General Washington was safe for now and not going to be hung in the streets, and that was also a point in my favor. A great start thus far and I might have already changed history. But if I didn't come up with a sound plan to distract the British, they'd attack, and instead of Washington dying before his men, The General would starve with them, and nothing would change. I gazed up at the quarter moon, and that did give me some ideas.

I sat down on the steps of the Congress building and ate some smoked salmon and drank some of the other canteen of water, while I got dressed again. Filling the canteens back up from a well pump, I dropped in a few more water purification tablets and drank deeply before heading out.

FIVE: The Distraction

ME AND LITTLE JOE rode out of the city the same way I came in. I knew about where the British camp was, but once I was out of sight of anyone around, I pulled out my cell phone and powered it back on. Scrolling through the maps that Dr. Rock had downloaded for me, I found the map that showed where and the layout of General Howe's army. I took a minute to plan out the best course to come up behind them without being seen. I spent the next two hours riding wide around the camp, planning to come up from behind them in the dark.

I found a safe hilltop and stayed low as I climbed it on foot, leaving Little Joe tied to a tree. Moss along the tree trunks had started graying in the chillier weather, and I was fortunate enough that it was early fall, so most of the foliage helped cover my approach. Walking up the hill caused my leg to throb, so I took two more pain killers. With my high-power monocular which was magnified and able to bring in enough star light to see, I could observe Howe's camp. I studied it to commit it to memory.

Thousands of tents lined perfectly straight rows, interspersed with several larger mess tents. Dozens of cannons sat ominously at the far end, facing the city, ready to rain down destruction, next to numerous ammo dumps, or whatever they called them in the eighteenth century. Behind the cannons stood wagons filled with black powder, cannon balls, and other barrels and crates. On the south side of camp, where I was, several hundred horses were tied up to picket lines. I groaned deep in my chest as I wasn't able to spot General Howe's tent. My plan A was going to be to snipe him from the hilltop or throw a grenade into his tent. Well, plan A was out and now I had to come up with plan B.

The camp was mostly quiet and still. From my experience, you can always count on the British to go to sleep when they were told to. They did have a lot of two-man sentries walking the perimeter, which made my job more complicated. I took a minute to stare up at the night sky. The stars were so bright – I had never seen the sky so clearly before in my life. The world was like new here, and the people who lived on it had not yet discovered electricity, giant skyscrapers, mass pollution, or a hundred other things that would later hide this clear view of the heavens from us.

Dark clouds were moving my way, and they would block out what little moon light there was, as soon as they got here. I pulled out the brass suppressor that the gun smith had made for my Tec-9 and screwed it on, feeling the balance of the gun. The front end felt a little heavier and the barrel wanted to dip downward. I had to get used to holding it slightly different than I was accustomed to.

My watch said that we had just over an hour before General Washington would be ready to leave the city. The next thirty minutes was spent watching and timing the guards patrol around the camp. The camp was huge. I counted the patrols that went by and so far, had not seen the same two men twice yet. It must have taken each patrol over an hour to walk around the whole camp. The patrols were a consistent six minutes apart, like clockwork, walking in a clockwise direction from south to east to north to west and south again.

I slipped my night vision goggles on my head and climbed down the hill towards the closest horse picket line. I approached the horses that were growing nervous and shaking their heads and snorting. After a few soothing words and pats on the necks, they calmed down. I ducked between two of the horses and waited for the next patrol to go by. My heart thrummed in my chest, hoping they didn't notice any changed behavior in the horses. It was so dark in this area shadowed by the tents and lacking any torchlight, that the men marched by about twenty feet away and never even lifted their eyes my way. Once they were out of sight, I untied the horses, about thirty of them, until I gritted my teeth, realizing I was taking too much time. I was doing it the hard way, and I slipped out my knife and cut the picket line. None of the beasts seemed interested in going anywhere at that moment.

I then crept over to one of the ammo dumps. I could hear men snoring and some chatting as I crept among the tents. Making a brash decision, I stood up straight and strutted as if I belonged there. It was too dark for anyone to see me well, the clouds had obscured the moonlight, but just in case someone did, they would think I was one of them if I walked with determination.

The area where they kept the black powder was draped in darker shadows than the rest of the camp. They didn't allow any torches or fires anywhere near there, and for good reason. With my night vision goggles, I saw everything with green tinted clarity.

I found several wagons on the south side of the camp, west of the horses. Some of the wagons were filled with black powder, shot, wads, extra rifles, cannon balls, and other items that I didn't recognize. Piles of these items were stacked on the ground next to several empty wagons for quick distribution to the troops. The wagons had drivers sleeping under them, wrapped in their threadbare blankets against the cool night air.

I stopped at the first wagon. Moving as silently as I could manage, I went to work lifting one of the small quarter barrels of black powder off the wagon and setting it on the ground. A cork plugged the top, and I popped it out. Setting the barrel on its side, I let the gun powder pour out and made a small mound in the dirt. I picked up a dozen or so boxes of shot – steel balls the size of marbles which the muskets used as ammo. Then I gingerly stacked the boxes of shot on the side of the barrel, facing the camp. When the barrel blew up like a bomb, the shot would fly into the camp as shrapnel – like hundreds of rifles firing at the same time, not to mention blowing up the gun powder on the wagon, and would kill a lot of men.

I grabbed a second barrel and again yanked out the cork on top. I tipped this barrel over and poured the black powder on the ground while walking backwards. I still didn't have a plan for a timer, merely an idea – I was making this up as I went. I made it back to the outer perimeter of the camp when voices carried from the west. I took a knee, leaned toward the sound, and clenched my jaw. The next patrol was coming my way.

Two men were walking in step right at the horse picket line. One of the men was talking about his woman back home, and the other laughed at whatever he said. Keeping my eyes focused on them, I withdrew my Tec-9 out, and from about twenty feet away, I pulled the trigger twice. The gun emitted a *thunk thunk* sound, and both men fell backwards in front of the horses. Hunkering deep into the shadows, I glanced around, but didn't see any other movement. Exhaling heavily, I tucked my gun away and resumed my task.

I poured the powder in front and across the horse picket line, around the dead soldiers. I flicked my eyes at my watch – I had eight minutes. But the next patrol would find the two bodies in about five minutes.

The General better be ready to go.

I poured the rest of the powder into a small mound, then ran over and dragged the two bodies to the small pile of black powder. I extracted one of the four hand grenades from my satchel, sent up a silent thank you to Aden for his forethought, and then pulled the pin. I tucked the grenade under the chest of one of the two face-down soldiers where it was immobilized between the soldier's body and the ground.

My hope was that the first thing the patrol would do would be to turn the body over to check and see if he were still alive. The spoon would fly off the grenade with a loud ping and then the grenade would go *boom*. I had never done anything like this before, but if my seat-of-my-pants plan worked, then this explosion would set off the gun powder. Then the ignited gun powder, which I had poured in front of the picket line, would scare the hell out of the horses and send them running into the camp, adding to the confusion. Shortly after that, the several hundred balls of shot would kill more than a few soldiers. I wanted their attention to the rear of the camp and not on the city. The whole set up was a desperate, crazed Hail Mary.

My trap was set up, so I then took off at a run up the hill to the north, stopping at the top. I removed my goggles, laid in the cool grass, and waited. I didn't see the patrol walk up or discover their dead comrades, but I did see the grenade go off. The two men must have been killed instantly. The explosion set off a powder flash from the pile of gun powder and then, like in the movies, the trail of powder ignited and shot down in front of the picket line, a glowing snake in the night. The horses went crazy and broke the picket line and ran away from the smoke and powder flash straight into the camp. They didn't bother galloping around the tents, just crashed straight through them, trampling the men inside who were sleeping or more likely, shocked awake by the explosions.

At the same time as all that was happening, my snake of fire worked its way around the picket line, and straight to the wagon. The next explosion was the biggest I had ever seen. I squinted as the heat struck me with a painful ringing in my ears, and I was knocked flat on my back. I wiggled my finger in my ears, as if that would help. A fireball soared in the sky and lit up the night. The fire reached for the stars and lit up a crater where the wagon had been a few moments ago. Washington had to have seen this and knew it was his cue.

A row of tents for about a hundred yards went missing, obliterated by the boxes of shot. It had been even more effective than I'd imagined. The ringing in my ears was soon replaced by the sound of men and horses screaming. Thousands of men raced out of their tents – some were trying to catch the horses; some were firing their rifles into the hills around them, thinking they were under attack, but most were milling around, waiting for someone to tell them what to do. Tents caught on fire and chaos took over and ruled the night. As the harbinger of that chaos, I smiled.

The sure destruction of what laid before me was a little over-whelming. It took me a second to regain my senses and focus on what needed to be done next. With the fires lighting up the night, some of the soldiers finally noticed me and starting yelling and pointing in my direction. Time to leave.

I ran down the other side of the hill, my legs pumping for all they were worth before the soldiers decided to start shooting at me. Little Joe was still tethered to the tree waiting for me with skittish movements at the raucous noise. I jumped on his back and dug my heels into his flanks. He leaped forward as if sensing my urgency, or he knew that some rough shit was going down and he wanted to get out of dodge even faster than I did.

"What do you think, Little Joe?" I yelled to my poor horse as he ran. "Did the General see that?"

I rode hard for about a mile then turned east and slowed Little Joe to a walk. He was breathing hard so after another half mile, we stopped at a stream. I fed Little Joe two of the granola bars that I had in my pocket, and then let him drink from the stream. In a passing thought, I realized I'd have to start feeding him better. While I was patting him on the neck, I heard rumbling, like a train but far off. But it couldn't be trains – too early for that technology. It was too dark to see well, and small hills surrounded me. But the sound of a hundred horses riding straight at me grew louder. The British were storming the hill four or five hundred yards behind me, their torches lighting their way. So many torches, cresting the hill and coming my way fast. Little Joe, skittered to pull away from me, wanting to run. I tightened my grip on his bridle.

"Good idea boy," I said to my horse. "Let's get the hell out of here."

Dawn was a long way off, and the moon was had hidden behind the clouds. I reached into my satchel and pulled my night vision goggles back out before I climbed back in the saddle. Little Joe took off without any encouragement from me. I learned fast that I could count on Little Joe to want to run away from danger – a practical philosophy in my estimation.

With my night vision goggles on, I was able to ride faster than the soldiers chasing me. Not a lot faster as they were better riders than I was, but enough to stay ahead of them, which was all I needed to do. With night vision, I could weave in and out of the pine trees without running into any branches. The soldiers were going too fast to avoid the branches as dark as it was.

Little Joe and I continued east for a few miles. I didn't want to run him to death, so I focused on trying to lose the British and not out run them. We turned north and after about a mile, I shifted again, heading back east. We lost the soldiers several times, but they kept breaking up into smaller groups, splitting up and gaining. By the time the sun broke across the horizon, about twenty tenacious soldiers pursued us. I no longer had the advantage of my goggles, and they were closing the distance between us.

Little Joe was tiring and wasn't going to be able to keep up this pace. As far as I could tell, the soldiers really didn't care if they ran their horses to death. An open field emerged on my right. I yanked Little Joe's reins, and we trotted straight down the middle. The field was wide open for about three hundred yards from end to end. I was about two hundred yards in, fully exposed, a gunshot zinged in the air. The soldiers breaking through the pine trees right where I had come through. Half the soldiers rode hard to cross the field while the other half stopped as they broke through and started shooting. I was already out of range for their muskets, so I didn't worry about them. I focused on reaching the other side.

As soon as we reached the tree line, I pulled hard on Little Joe's reins and brought him to a skidding stop. Leaping off Little Joe, I then withdrew my Thompson Contender, and side-stepped behind a pine tree. The Brits were about a hundred yards into the field when I fired my first shot with the benefit of greater range than they could imagine. I missed the first shot. I was breathing hard and jerked the trigger. Grunting with rushed frustration, I took a deep breath as I reloaded and fired again at the same target – the man closest to me.

He tumbled over backwards, landing face first on the ground, a solid shot. I reloaded and fired again. The soldiers were only a hundred yards away now, so this was a far easier shot, and a second man clipped backwards off his horse. I was in a rhythm now. Fire and reload, fire and reload, fire and reload. The last two soldiers came straight at me. They had experience fighting on horseback because they were calm and deliberate, unfazed by my superior firepower. The soldiers leveled their gun barrels and fired their muskets. The first and closest soldier hit the tree I was behind, sending a rain of bark down on my head. That wasn't an easy feat, considering he was riding full speed on horseback. And he kept coming.

The second missed me and the tree. They dropped their muskets and rode past me. I figured they would have stopped and got off their horses, but they continued for about twenty feet, then pulled their horses up and swung them around. I suddenly realized this was smart – if they had pulled up in front of me, they would have been at a disadvantage while dismounting. They heeled their horses and pulled flintlock pistols.

"Screw this," I said under my breath.

I pulled my Tec-9 and fired at the first one who was threading his horse through the trees. It took me three shots to hit him and when I did the bullet caught him in the shoulder. He dropped his pistol, but he managed to stay on his horse. Impressive. The second one fired before I could swing back around, and the round clipped my left arm in a spark of pain. Pushing the pulsing sensation to the side, I focused on my target and waited until he was right on me. Then I fired two rounds into his chest.

He flew backwards and hit the ground with a solid *thump* as his horse continued right by me. I swung around as the first soldier was coming back, right at me. I'm not sure if he fell or jumped but he landed right on me. My arm exploded as we rolled on the ground. He popped up with a knife in his uninjured hand and smiled when he saw that I was still holding what he thought was my unloaded pistol. I didn't have time to smile at his ignorance as I shot him in the chest.

The ground vibrated with the sound of the other soldiers coming up on the tree line. I rolled over to peer into the field – they were only thirty yards away. I grabbed another grenade, pulled the pin, and threw it halfway between me and the soldiers. I scrambled behind the abused pine tree again. The grenade detonated, and the trees echoed with the screams of men and horses. I reloaded my Tec-9 with a fresh magazine and stepped out from behind the tree.

Four of the soldiers were on the ground while six more clung to their horses. The first two soldiers were shell shocked. They were wide-eyed, dazed, and didn't seem able to focus on anything. I skipped them for now. The next two scanned the field, not sure what had happened. Taking careful aim, I shot them each in the head. The last two shifted as if they were going to run. I moved to aim at the first one, but I decided against it. I let those two ride away in retreat. No sense wasting the ammo.

The first two soldiers that I had skipped still sat on their horses, walking them in circles. I ignored them still. Enough killing for today, and they were harmless. I dashed into the field and checked on the four soldiers on the ground. They didn't move and appeared quite dead, so I left them alone. I went back to the tree and lifted my empty magazine off the ground. I'd reload it later when I had a chance. I investigated my left arm as the burning pain of torn flesh caught up to me. He had missed the bone so I could still move my arm, but the bullet still in there, grinding against muscle. I needed to stop the bleeding and get the bullet out. I flicked my gaze to Little Joe, but the four-legged traitorous coward was gone.

"Just great," I said to no one.

I trudged over, grabbed four of the British horses, and tied them in a line. At least I wasn't in want of a ride with my loss of Little Joe. Then I peered at my arm again. I wasn't going to be able to cut out the bullet now and here, so I bandaged it, swallowed some more painkillers, and turned to lead my four horses out of the forest.

The next thing I knew, I was on the ground, face first in leaves and muck.

What happened?

Cool dirt clung to my face and from the corner of my eye, I could see the horse's leg.

Please don't step on me, I thought wildly.

My face was dripping, and I wanted to stand but couldn't. I brought my right hand up to my face and felt sticky wetness. My hand came away, covered with blood. I rolled over onto my back. One of the two soldiers that I had spared still sat on his horse. He had a pistol in his hand and was reloading it. I reached down for my pistol but struggled to pull it out of its holster. The other soldier that I had spared was still on his horse as well and came up next to the first.

"Is he dead?" the second soldier asked.

"No," the first soldier answered. "But he soon will be."

I tried to focus my eyes on them, but they rolled in my head. My fingers didn't want to obey my brain. I brushed my fingertips against the butt of my pistol, I just couldn't grab it. The first soldier finished loading his pistol and gripped the flintlock in his right hand, he carefully and slowly, pulled the hammer back into the cocked position.

Holy shit. I didn't think I'd die on my second day in.

Two gunshots rang so close together that they almost sounded like one long gun shot. I slammed my eyes shut, but when I realized I still felt the pain in my arm and head and wasn't dead, I peeked them open. So, I *wasn't* dead.

The British soldiers slipped off their horses and landed hard on the ground. I laid there, desperately trying to wrap my fingers around my pistol grip when voices came from behind me. My head wouldn't turn so I couldn't see who spoke. One of the voices was male and the other was female. Leather-covered feet under a brown dress entered my range of vision, walking up to stand in front of me. I assumed she was looking down at me. The male voice spoke in a gruff voice.

"I'll retrieve the cart."

Then the world started to fade. A circle of black closed in on my vision, and the pain lessened. I was passing out or dying.

My last thought was that I hoped I was passing out.

SIX: Butterfly

I WOKE UP some time later but had a hard time opening my eyes, like my eyelids were too heavy for my eyes. My brain didn't want to work, and my thoughts were fuzzy. My heart raced as I tried to figure out where I was. When I was finally able to force my eyes open, I found myself in a bed, under a thick, blue quilted blanket. The room was dim and small, and a narrow glow of light that might have been a candle flickered on the other side of the room. I shifted to sit up and a sharp, pounding pain stabbed through my brain. Darkness overcame me again and I fell back into sleep.

The sound of laughter tinkled in my ears. Children's voices, I thought as I came to awareness. I laid there with my eyes closed, listening. A horse whinnied, and the voices giggled again. *Girls*, I thought. Two young girls, laughing. I pried my eyes open and the sun light in the room penetrated like a hundred needles going through my eyeballs and jabbing my brain. I groaned and slammed them shut and tried to recall the last thing I could remember. My body jerked and my eyes shot open again as a cold, wet cloth wiped my forehead. My hand shot up to grab the wrist holding the cloth. My vision slowly focused, and the needles were plucked from my brain, one by one, as my eyes adjusted to the light.

"Easy sir," a woman's voice said in a strong Irish accent. "You're safe here."

My eyes focused on her. She might have been about thirty-five years old by twenty-first century standards of easy living. Here, though, I guessed she was more like twenty-eight to thirty years old in the hard life of the eighteenth century. She perched on the edge of my bed in easy reaching distance. A few wrinkles were etched her bright blue eyes. Her long, bright red hair that was pulled back in a loose ponytail showed some gray creeping in by her ears. She was slender but appeared strong, felt strong if I were judging by her hands on my head. Like many women in this time, she wore no makeup, but she had a natural beauty and didn't need it. She smiled gingerly at me, and with her other hand she grabbed my wrist lightly and pulled my hand from hers with extraordinarily little effort.

"Try not to move," she commanded in a pleasant voice.

Her brown dress covered a loose white shirt. A carved wooden cross hung around her neck on a leather thong and sat at the top of her cleavage. I had neither the time nor the inclination to really pay much attention to women since my wife had been murdered, and a wave of hot guilt washed over me for noticing her ample cleavage, which was only magnified by her thin waistline. She noticed my eyes lingering too long in that area and her face burned red. I felt mine do the same.

"Who are you?" I asked, breaking the awkward silence.

"My name is Annie," she answered. "You are in my father-in-law's house."

"I'm Thomas," I said, then added, "Thomas Nelson. What happened?"

"We heard a lot of shooting," she explained as her hands wrung out the cloth and reapplied it. "My father-in-law and me. By the time we got there, you had already killed most of the soldiers. I don't understand why you didn't kill the two on horseback, but one of them shot you in the head."

I reached up to touch my head as fear shot through my body. She grabbed my hand, preventing me from touching the wound.

"Don't," she said. "You might pull your stitches. It's a graze. I think the bullet might have bounced off your skull. You're incredibly lucky, but I would say you'll have a long scar. I was able to stop the bleeding and stitch up the wound. Your skull felt unbroken, so you'll live. If I had to hazard a guess, I'd say that the soldier who shot you didn't load his shot with enough gun powder. Since I was already stitching you up, I also removed the bullet in your left arm and stitched it up as well. Oh, I took care of your left leg too. You seem to like getting shot. My oldest daughter stitched up your shirt and pants for you."

I wondered if I had a concussion. What was I thinking? Obviously, I had a concussion. Focusing on the woman's ramblings took all my energy.

"Thank you," I said in a scratchy voice.

She grabbed a glass of water and reached her right arm under my neck, slowly raising me up. She put the glass to my lips, and I sucked in several sips. After lowering me back to the bed, she stood up. She was shorter than I'd initially thought, maybe five foot two at most.

"How long have I been here?" I asked. The water had eased the stress of my throat and it was easier to speak.

"We found you yesterday," she answered. "I'll get you some chicken broth. It will help you regain your strength. You were a bloody mess."

She exited the small bedroom, closing the door behind her. Her two girls laughing again outside the window. I scanned the room and noted my satchel and weapons stacked in the corner. At least I hadn't lost those. My mended clothes laid across a chair next to a dresser. The door opened and in walked Old Ben.

"Ben," I said with a painful, shocked smile.

"Lad," he said, smiling back. "We meet again. How are you feeling?"

"Alive," I answered. "Thanks to you."

"Not I," he disagreed. "My daughter-in-law performed surgery on you."

I slid my feet over the side of the bed and slowly sat up, waiting for the dizziness to fade.

"You shot the soldiers?" I asked, putting a hand on my face, trying to estimate the damage.

"Aye," he said. "One of them. Annie shot the other."

"Oh," I said. "I'm sorry."

"I'm not," he said. "And neither is Annie. The British killed her husband, my son Patrick, two years ago." That explained why Ben was willing to bring an odd stranger into his home. That or the hope for more coin.

"Grab my clothes for me, please," I asked.

"I think you should take it easy, lad," he answered, unmoving.

"I will," I said. "I promise. The British will be searching for me, and I have imposed enough on your family. I need to get as far away from here as I can."

"You let me worry about that," he told me.

"You brought me here on the cart?"

"Well, I certainly didn't carry you." His voice held a nuance of humor. At my state or at this entire situation?

"The British will find their dead soldiers and follow the cart's tracks," I said, not hiding the concern in my voice.

"A lot of those horses ran off," he said. "They'll think you were on one of them. If any of them come around asking, I'll tell them that we found all those dead soldiers and left the area as fast as we came. No reason for them not to believe us."

He sounded earnest, but I wasn't sure I believed him. The Brits were renowned for their harsh tenacity.

"Did you bring the four horses I had tied?" I asked.

"Aye lad," he said. "Plus, the two the soldiers who shot you were on. And one more we found. Seven in all."

Well, that was something. Though I wasn't sure what he would do with seven missing British horses. Sell them? He handed me my clothes and helped me stand while I dressed. My pants and shirt were stitched nicely – Annie's daughter had a fine sewing hand. Ben was slower about handing me my vest, feeling its weight, and trying to figure out what it was made of.

"It's from Germany," I lied with a twinge of guilt. "Latest fashion."

He nodded his head as if he understood, but it didn't quite reach his eyes. Then he handed me my weapons and satchel.

"I've never seen guns like those before," he said.

"Also, from Germany," I responded, hoping that would be the end of it.

As I finished belting both guns back on, Annie sashayed in, and we knew there'd be hell to pay for me not staying in bed. She set a steaming hot bowl of chicken broth on the dresser and then crossed her arms while standing in the doorway.

"I own this house, lad," Ben said, tipping his head toward Annie. "But I don't run it. You're on your own."

"Why are you out of bed, Mr. Nelson?" Annie asked with an edge scorn in her concerned voice. "Why didn't you stop him, Father?"

Her question to Ben had less tenderness but more volume.

"Your children are in danger if the British find me here," I told her. "And the fresh air will do me good."

She laughed at that. "As if the air is fresher outside then inside. It's all the same air, you fool. Now sit down before you fall down."

I opened my mouth to protest her science, but Ben got to her first.

"Oh, Annie," Ben said. "Let him at least sit on the porch. He can have some of your delicious broth while we figure out what to do with him."

She tapped her foot against the worn wooden floorboard and eyed me up and down like I was an errant child.

"Fine," she said. "But no tricks," she added and wagged her finger. "Don't you dare try to ride off until I say you can!"

I dropped my satchel onto the floor and shrugged in surrender. She graced me with a tight, hesitant smile at that and stepped out of the way. I plodded out of the room and down the narrow hall on unsteady feet with Ben behind me, supporting my back.

The front door stood open as I entered the main room, which resembled a museum or movie set. The ceiling was lower than I was used to, with rough wooden beams running across. Off-white plaster walls showcased drawings in glassless picture frames, of people whom I guessed were family members. A large round table sat near what would have been the kitchen area that housed a hand water pump and a large, blackened wood-burning stove. The fireplace was constructed of gray, round rocks, and concrete-like mortar. A musket hung above the fireplace in an easy-to-grab location near the door.

When I walked outside, six horses tied to the picket post grazed on the thin grass. The cart I had last seen Old Ben riding was still out front with the same nag tied to it. To my right were two girls playing with a horse. The girls were about eight and ten years old and the spitting image of their mother. The horse wasn't tethered and ran free. He trotted from them and then when they would stop chasing him, he would turn and chase after them in a skittish gallop.

"Little Joe!" I yelled.

The traitorous coward turned and regarded me with one deep brown eye. He trotted over to me as if he had never deserted me in a fight. In all honesty, his cowardness was one of the things I liked about him – it showed he was smarter than the other horses and gave him personality. He nudged against my chest with his nose. I searched for another granola bar in my pocket and finding one, unwrapped it. I held the bar out for him, and he took it with his teeth.

"Hey! That's our horse, sir," the younger of the two girls said boldly. "We named him Butterfly."

"Now girls," Ben yelled from the porch behind me. "I told you that horse was his."

The girls' faces fell in matching frowns.

"But Grandpa," the little one entreated. "We never had a horse of our own."

"Molly, Regan," Ben said, raising his voice and calling the girls by name.

"How about a trade?" I asked the two little girls.

"What kind of trade?" the older girl asked with more than a little suspicion in her tone. She narrowed her blue eyes at me, and I smiled in return.

"I'll trade you, Butterfly here, for five of those six horses," I said pointing to the six horses tied to the post.

"Five?" the little one squealed.

"Five," I confirmed. "That means each of you get your own horse, your grandpa gets two new ones for his cart, and your mother has one for herself."

"What's the trick?" the oldest one asked.

"No trick," I answered, holding up my hands. "I'll even let you two pick out your horses first, before I pick the one, I will keep."

"Deal!" they yelled at the same time.

"Wait a minute," Annie said.

I turned to her; my smile still plastered on my face. "Giving away five horses, which I don't want and can't use, in exchange for saving my life is not a terrible deal."

The girls ran to their mother. "Please, please, please!"

"Very well," Annie sighed, resigned, and ruffled her girls' hair. "Only if Mr. Nelson, agrees to sit down, and sip on some chicken broth."

Then the girls scrambled over to me, grabbed my hands. and dragged me back to the porch. The younger one pushed me into a rocking chair, while the older one ran into the house, yelling that she would get the chicken broth.

Two bowls of chicken broth and two surreptitious pain killers later, I was feeling better. The pounding in my head lessened to manageable, and my wounds didn't ache quite as much.

The two girls investigated the six horses, trying to pick out the best ones for themselves. I found it funny how they pretended that they knew what to look for in a horse. They peered into the horse's eyes, lifted their lips to check the teeth, patted their sides, and even inspected their tails. It was no surprise when, in the end, they picked out the two shortest horses.

Ben brought me a glass of what turned out to be fine whiskey in a horn cup. I sipped on it, surprised when Annie didn't object. Either she didn't think it was her place to tell a stranger not to drink, or she thought it would do me some good. It did help further numb the pain in my arm and leg. Nothing seemed to help the pain going across the right side of my head. Ben was nice enough to bring me a small mirror and help me remove the bandages.

Annie was right – I was going to have a hell of a scar. A long thin strip of hair was missing with stitches going across my head from back to front. Ben rewrapped the bandages, his eyes flicking back and forth, trying to finish before Annie found out that we had messed with them. He didn't want to get caught disobeying her medical directives. Ben had spoken the truth – Annie did run the house.

I spent the night on the floor in the main room in front of the fireplace and considered my next move. I needed to help General Washington, but I was in no shape for another fight. Had he known the explosions were the diversion? Had he made it out? I fell asleep thinking about what I should do next.

The next morning, I awoke to the heady scent of bacon and Annie busy at the black cast-iron stove. She served me that bacon with bread and strong black tea for breakfast. She said that she preferred milk tea, but that Ben liked his black and energizing in the morning. I ate breakfast and refilled my cup. My strength was returning after several real meals and a solid night's sleep, and I could walk a straight line again.

I went a little heavy on the pain killers, but that was something I couldn't avoid. My head injury really did turn out to be a graze, a deep laceration. The skin was ripped, and it looked a lot worse than it really was, the headache notwithstanding. Added to that, my arm still hummed with a dull ache.

Annie invited me to go for a ride with her around Ben's property. I wanted to check the area for English soldiers anyways, so I agreed. Annie had picked out a black horse for herself and named him Ben, after her father-in-law.

When I stepped outside, frost glittered on the ground and the weather nipped at my exposed skin, cold and invigorating. Couple more days and it might start snowing. We rode about a half mile out before Annie reined her horse around, and we made a huge circle around the property. We saw no signs of the British, and my shoulders relaxed slightly. She must have noticed the worried lines on my face and slowed her horse to a walk.

"What's wrong?" she asked me.

"The British," I told her. "Why haven't we seen any signs of them?"

"Well, maybe Ben was right," she answered. "I was there, and a lot of horses were running off in different directions."

"Maybe," was all I said, doubtful. There had to be another reason.

"Or maybe they never found the bodies," she offered. "You said they were getting ready to attack General Washington. Maybe they went back to their camp as to not miss the fight."

"Yeah, maybe," I said again. "The problem is I don't like unanswered questions, and I hate maybes."

"Where are you from, Mr. Nelson?" she asked suddenly. Oh, the cursed question for which I didn't have an easy answer. "I have been trying to place your accent but can't."

"Mr. Nelson?" I responded. "Call me Thomas, please."

"It's not proper to call a married man by his Christian name when we are out here alone," she explained.

Her eyes glanced down to my wedding ring.

"My wife was killed by the British. I'm from a place further west than even the King's empire has gone."

"Family?" she asked.

"No," I said. "My mother and father died years ago. My wife was my only family."

Annie cleared her throat. "No one?" she asked with sadness in her eyes.

"There is a man who is like a brother to me," I admitted to her. "But I will never see him again."

I patted Little Joe on the neck. "I have Little Joe," I said, trying to lighten the situation.

We dismounted down and ambled next to the horses in silence for a while. It was nice to stretch the legs, and my strength was returning faster than I could have hoped. I think I had needed the sleep more than anything else.

I flicked my eyes furtively to Annie as we walked. My time as a widower was catching up to me, and I didn't hesitate to admire Annie's figure when we were walking.

Then she broke the silence. "Ben seems to like you."

"Ben seems to be a nice guy," I answered back.

"Guy?" she asked, not familiar with that word.

"Sorry," I responded, swallowing hard. "A nice man."

"My girls like you, too, and they love Butterfly," she continued, gesturing a pale slender hand to my horse.

"His name is Little Joe," I said smiling at the beast. "And I like your girls and so does he. You have a beautiful family.

And if I may say, they are lucky to have someone as strong as you."

A thick lock of her red hair fell in front of her face as she smiled, and her chin lowered. Was she blushing at the compliment?

"You know the farm could always use a man around," she said slowly.

My breath caught in my throat. She couldn't be suggesting what I thought she was suggesting. I'd only met her the day before – was this how society functioned in the seventeen hundreds?

"The farm could?" I asked in a low voice.

"We all could," she answered, lifting her head to me. There it was, that strength, even when suggesting a mad proposition.

A slight breeze kicked up, and this close, she smelled like flowers. I had no idea what kind of flowers, but she smelled clean, fresh – something I hadn't experienced in a long time.

"What are you saying, Annie?" I asked in that same low voice.

"Well," she said, pulling her mount to a stop. "I'm just pointing out that Ben and the girls all like you. There is more work around the farm than we can handle. And you don't seem to have a home to go back to."

She pointed to a stream, and we led our horses down to it. We tethered the horses to a low branch, giving them enough lead to drink from the stream. She sat down in the dank shade of a large white pine and primly smoothed out her dress.

"And what about you?" I inquired. Was she offering a position on her farm, or something much more personal?

"What about me?" she asked.

"Are you asking me to stay?" I clarified my question.

"And if I am?" she asked coyly. "I don't have a husband, and you no longer have a wife. They were killed by the British. We need someone to be with and somewhere to be. You seem to be a strong, capable, and honorable man. You are not unpleasant to look at, even with your new scar."

This sounded like some crazy arranged marriage scenario, but I smiled at that last part. She was a strong woman who spoke her mind. I couldn't fault her for that.

"I have a job to do," I said flatly. I didn't have time for romantic interludes, no matter how lovely the woman was.

"I know that," she told me. "I see that fire in your eyes, every time you mention the British. I saw it again just now when you mentioned your wife. It burns to your soul. You'll not quit until you have done whatever you need to do. But do not let that fire burn you up. The war will not last forever, and you'll need a home to return to when it's done. Until that day is here, maybe a place to drop by and visit from time to time."

The thickness in my throat choked me as a heat throbbed under my belt. I was attracted to her – I couldn't deny that. She was strong, smart, stunning, and caring. It had been a long time since I'd been with a woman. I was going to be stuck in this timeline for the rest of my life, and there wasn't a thing I could do about it. I had never given any thought to what I would do after my mission was over – if I lived or managed to change the timeline. Die trying, most likely. Until this moment, I was ok with the idea of dying, if I died hurting the British. Aden's final words came back to me in a flood.

You have lost something that you have not been able to replace or move on from. It's my hope and wish that you'll find the peace you so desperately need. If you can't find it here, maybe you'll find it there.

Aden was still the smartest person I had ever met, and it appeared he was still watching out for me. He had a better idea of what I might have been searching for than I did.

"When the war is over," I spoke slowly, "or at least when my job is done, I will need to decide what to do next with my life. If I had a reason to return here, that would not be objectionable to me."

She leaned forward and kissed me on the lips – her kiss was dry and gentle and surprising. So much for the supposed social and religious constraints regarding coupling. And what was I doing? This woman didn't even know me! But I wanted to know more about her, so perhaps that was something.

"Maybe I can give you a reason to return and want to call this place home," she said, pressing against me. And after so long without my wife, I could only respond to her.

Several hours later, we rode back to the farm, taking our time as the horses ambled through the woods. As we broke from the tree line, Old Ben's cart sat in front of the house. His nag was no longer tied to it, and I didn't see any of the British horses tied to the picket post. The little hairs on the back of my neck stood on end, and Annie kicked her horse into a full gallop before I could utter a word. As we pulled the horses up short of the steps, Annie leapt off her horse and rushed into the house, screaming for her daughters.

"Molly! Regan! Dad!" she yelled over and over.

I moved to follow but then noticed lots of horse tracks in the clinging dirt. They came from the tree line east of the farm and stopped here before continuing west towards the corn crops. I squinted into the distance, trying to surmise where these potential riders had gone.

I slid off my horse with my hand on my Thompson, searching for any movement in the trees. I didn't see anyone.

"Thomas!" Annie shouted from inside the house.

I ran up the steps and into the house. Annie knelt in front of Ben who was lying on the floor. Blood streaked his face and hair. Annie held a towel to the back of his head, huffing as she bit back her sobs. By fortune and providence, Ben was alive, and we got him into his bed. He'd been pistol whipped to the back of the head, causing a bloody gash. Annie tried to stop the bleeding, while I search the rest of the house and barn for the girls. Nothing. They were gone. I returned to the house, and Ben now had his head bandaged and eyes squinting open.

Annie faced me, in wide-eyed panic and tears running down her cheeks. "They took them. They took my girls, Thomas."

Her tone wrenched my chest. I regarded Ben pointedly for answers.

"They rode in an hour ago," he told me between coughs. "They asked about you. I told them that we never saw you, but the British officer leading them pulled Molly to the side and she didn't know what to say. Poor lass. He got the truth out of her, and his lads took to beating on me. They took the girls and said that if we wanted them back, you needed to come to them."

A muscle clenched in my jaw. "Where?" I asked in a hard voice.

"The Johnson's farm," he answered. "Must have been about thirty of them. They seemed to be terribly upset with you. Something about their horses and a personal insult to General Howe."

"The Johnson's are decent people," Annie said. "They would never let the British use their property. If they're on their farm, then they have already killed Jacob and his wife."

"Kids?" I asked.

"No," she answered, her hand fluttering to her bosom. "The boys are grown. They are with General Washington."

"Where's this farm?" I asked, hearing the biting anger in my own voice.

"About five miles north of here," Annie said.

"Did they say when?" I asked.

"Sun-up," Ben answered. "On the Johnson Bridge."

"Bridge?" I asked, flicking my gaze to Annie.

She nodded her head. "The stream we were at today comes from the Johnson's property. It's deeper on their property, and a few years ago they had to build a bridge across it."

"Can you draw me a layout of the property?" I asked Annie.

"Layout?" she asked confused.

"A map," I corrected and cleared my throat. "But a map of only the property. Start with that bridge, then show me where the house is from the bridge, then the barn and then anything else on the property big enough to hide in or behind."

"There is some parchment with pen and ink in the library," she told me. "As soon as I take care of Father, I shall draw you a map. But I'm going with you."

I wanted to argue, but that would have been a waste of time I didn't have. From the stubborn squint in her eyes, I knew there was only one answer for her. I nodded my head in acquiescence and peered back at Ben.

"Did this officer, say what his name was?" I asked.

"Aye lad," Ben said. "He said his name was Captain James Bonifield. Quite the proper pompous ass he was. Typical Tory."

I stepped toward the door, and Ben called me.

"Lad," he said in a low voice, "I got the distinct impression that this particular red coat will not go back to General Howe without your head on a pike."

I nodded again. Then, stepping out of the house for privacy, I took my cell phone out of my satchel. Powering it on, the battery life was down to eighty-seven percent. I pulled up the library of books and text that Dr. Rock had downloaded and searched for the name James Bonifield. Two hits for the name appeared on the screen.

The first was in a book about General Howe that mentioned General Howe had promoted Captain Bonifield to Major in 1778, for all his hard work in crushing the rebel forces in the Massachusetts campaign. The other source referenced a book written by a man named Thomas Jefferson. It contained photocopies of a handwritten book and on one page Jefferson mentions a Captain Bonifield. He detailed the looting of Boston and took the time to mention Captain Bonifield specifically. Jefferson described Bonifield as a war criminal with no respect for life, other than his own. The text even included a poor, childlike drawing of Bonifield. He resembled the other British officers I'd seen – tall, thin, sharp nose, and high hair line. In a few side notes, he mentioned that Bonifield was a feared swordsman and preferred to kill with his military issued, sharpened sword.

Jefferson also mentioned that Bonifield led one of General Howe's light cavalry regiments. Bonifield was a natural horseman but was reputed as being cruel to his horses. General Howe was known for letting Bonifield do as he wished without any accountability. If Bonifield participated in the major battles and kept killing the rebels, General Howe didn't care. The recklessness of this Brit struck close to home, and the sting of bile rose in my throat.

I powered down my cell phone and tucked it back in my satchel. I needed to walk and make a plan, so I collected our horses we'd left in the yard and tied them to the post. This nutbag sounded like a real psychopath. He enjoyed killing, and now he had two little girls in his violent grip.

I pursed my lips as my mind worked. This was my fault. If I had left Annie's house as soon as I'd woken up, the girls would have told him that, and the British would still be after me. Who knew what those poor girls were going through right now? I had no doubt he'd kill them if I didn't show up. Men like that always did. I marched back into the house, ready for Annie to strike out with justified blame. Instead, she sat at the table with a quill and ink, already drawing a map.

"Annie," I said with heaviness in my voice.

"Don't!" she exclaimed and lifted her hand at me. "This is not your fault. The British think they own everything and everyone. After they killed Patrick, I knew it was only a matter of time before the war came to my front door."

"This is not the war," I said. "This is a murderous bastard who took your children to get to me. I'm sorry."

"Just promise me we'll kill him," she demanded.

I sat down next to her and placed a hand on hers that didn't hold the pen.

"I promise," I told her.

With an ink-stained fingertip, she turned the parchment towards me so I could see what she had drawn. She'd drawn a house in the middle of the parchment, with a barn and several other buildings surrounding it. A bridge and a road leading up to it were sketched near the bottom.

"What are all these buildings?" I asked.

She pointed to them, one by one. "Horse barn, outhouse, chicken coop, and tobacco drying barn."

"Is the house two story or one?" I asked.

"Two," she said. "Why?"

"They'll have lookouts," I explained. "Two story means they can see farther away. Where is the tree line?"

"Here," she said, as she sketched rough trees on the paper.

"How far is it from this tree line to the house?" I asked as I pointed to the north side tree line.

"Maybe two hundred paces," she guessed.

"What about the east and west tree lines?"

"At least three hundred paces, maybe more."

"You said they needed a bridge," I said. "How deep is the water?"

"This whole area," she said, as she scratched her pen down the paper, drawing the stream, "is about up to my waist deep, and maybe six feet wide."

She misread what I was thinking. "The bank is too steep on both sides. The horses cannot cross it. We have to use the bridge. The soldiers will have realized this as soon as they saw it." She tipped her head thoughtfully for a moment. "Or we can cross on either side a mile upstream or downstream."

"How far is the bridge to the house?" I asked.

"Only fifty feet," she said. "But the tree line is at least five hundred feet beyond the bridge."

We had three hours of daylight left. I told Annie to make sure her father-in-law was Ok while I went back to work. I had to put myself in Captain Bonifield's head. What would I do if I were in his position?

Then I realized that I *couldn't* put myself in his position. I had the advantage of almost two hundred and fifty years of history to fall back on that he didn't have. All my antiterrorism training, firearms training, and not to mention a lifetime of watching war movies added to my knowledge. He was trained in military warfare in 1777. These guys stood in a line and shot at each other. That realization meant Captain Bonifield would be in the main house like a proper British Officer. The children would be in the house with the captain, where he could keep an eye on them. Maybe a few of his men joined him to watch the kids and keep them out of his hair. The rest of his men would be in the barn with their horses. They would have guards out, somewhere between the house and the tree lines. Plus, one or two guards watching the bridge.

Had he left any men behind to watch this house? I tapped my teeth together – I didn't think he had. The arrogant fuck would think that we'd know when we were beaten and do as told.

Taking hostages for ransom or trade had always been done, throughout history. It wasn't until the nineteen seventies that antiterrorist teams were created. Until then, terrorists always had the upper hand. This was our one advantage – the natural assumption was that we would just do as we were told.

But I didn't want to take any chances. Bonifield might be smarter and more cautious than I was giving him credit for. We would keep the farm dark and when it was safe, Annie and I could sneak out. My only question was, would he have men hiding in the tree lines around the Johnson's farm? I know I would, especially after the chaos I'd unleashed on General Howe's camp.

Annie came into the room and asked about my plan.

"I'm still working on it," I told her honestly. "We'll not be leaving until nine or ten o'clock, so get some sleep while you can."

"How am I supposed to sleep?" she asked me, desperate hurt in her voice.

"We have a long night ahead of us, and we may be on the run tomorrow," I said, resting my hand on her arm. Her skin was hot from her panic and anxiety and sweat was seeping through the thin fabric of her dress sleeve. "Your girls will need you to be awake and alert."

"My girls will need you to be alert more than they need me," she said. "You get some sleep, and I'll wake you in a few hours."

I knew she was right, so I nodded my head and laid down on the floor in front of the hearth.

"No, Thomas," she said, gesturing to the scruffy wooden door next to her father's bedroom door. "Use my bed."

I stood up to walk to her bedroom when she stopped me with a hand on my chest. She kissed me and put her head against my chest crying. We held each other for several minutes with her crying into my shirt and me kissing the top of her head. She finally pushed away from me and pointed to her bedroom, with her unspoken words clear to me. She picked up a flintlock pistol that she had already loaded. She sat down in a rocking chair that she had placed in the center of the room, facing the front door. After what felt like a second later, someone shook me awake.

SEVEN: Bayonets Hurt

"THOMAS," ANNIE'S VOICE softly called to be from beyond the void.

I blinked my eyes open to find her standing over me.

"The horses are tied out back," she told me in a hushed tone. "Ben is resting comfortably. We should go soon."

Had it been a few hours? It felt like I had closed my eyes for only a second, but the room was darker. Nodding my head, I stood up, mentally readying myself. I washed my face with a wet towel to help me fully wake up. My skull was throbbing again, so I took two more pain killers. My leg and arm were also hurting but I didn't even notice them much – the throbbing of my head overwhelmed all the other pains, and I needed it gone so I could think clearly.

I picked up my two guns and strapped them on. Then I replaced the 30-30 ammo I had used, filling the slots on my shoulder holster with more rounds, and placed an extra box of twenty rounds in my cargo pocket. I removed one of the grenades and six extra magazines for my Tec-9, also placing them in the same pocket. As I did this, I mentally checked off my weapons and tactics for this extraction.

Gearing up for a fight didn't change, no matter what century I was in.

I planned on leaving my backpack and satchel behind, wanting to travel light. I slipped off my bullet proof vest and had Annie put it on. She lurched as she took it and peered at me questioningly. I explained that it was strong enough to stop a bullet, and once I said that she tried to hand it back. She argued with me until I told her she wasn't coming unless she wore the vest. I also asked her to change into a pair of her husband's pants before we left. She did as I asked without argument.

Since I wouldn't let her light a fire, she covered Ben with two extra blankets. I gave him two painkillers to help him sleep, and he took them readily enough. Then Annie and I snuck out the back door and crept with the horses into the trees.

I put on my night vision goggles when Annie was behind me so that she wouldn't see me put them on. I could see clearly, and if Annie stayed behind me and back a few feet, it was too dark for her to see them – I really wasn't ready to answer any questions about them.

We trudged along for several hundred yards and then halted. Slipping the goggles off, I asked Annie to stay with the horses while I backtracked, checking to see if anyone was following us. Overly cautious? Maybe. After about twenty minutes, I was satisfied we weren't being followed. Then we rode to the stream and walked along it until we were about a quarter mile from the Johnson's farm. I had Annie tether the horses to a tree while I made sure we were still alone. So far so good.

Soon, Annie indicated we were a few hundred yards away. She thought my plan was crazy, but after some convincing, she finally agreed to it.

"Come on," I said, as I climbed down the bank and into the freezing cold water. "Get in."

"Can't we go closer before we get into the water?" she asked. Her face was starkly pale and bright even in the dark. I might be used to dangerous tasks, but she wasn't, and it showed on her face.

"We don't know where the guards are," I explained. "And we don't know if they have any lookouts. The water is the one place they won't be watching."

"And for good reason," she said, shivering as she climbed down the bank.

The water was only three feet deep here, and I had Annie stay behind me, telling her it would make us harder to spot if we were at least ten feet apart. This was only partly true – I also wanted to slip the goggles back on my head.

By the time we neared the bridge, the water was above my waist. Annie's teeth chattered loud enough for me to hear. Only a few feet of the wooden bridge were visible, but as soon as we rounded the next bend the whole thing would appear. Pushing my goggles up onto the top of my head, I paused and waited for her.

I put my finger to my lips as she waded close and pointed to the bridge. She strained to see what I was pointing at, so I whispered in her ear. I handed her my goggles and told her to wait for my signal. Her mouth dropped open, probably in surprise and to ask about the goggles, but I interrupted her, instructed her to keep them dry, and promised I'd explain the strange goggles after.

I sunk down into the water, going as deep as I could, then kicked off towards the bridge. The trick to swimming under water is to go slow, that way you don't stir up the water as much or accidently splash the surface. Plus, with less effort exerted, the less oxygen you use – a few useful tricks learned from military amphibious training. Even with my training and knowledge, the water was so cold, it made it hard for me to not go as fast as I could.

The center of the bridge loomed over me, and I slowly came up for air. This close I didn't need my goggles to see the two soldiers standing guard with torches on the farmhouse side of the creek. The wooden bridge was strong and well-built, mostly constructed with six-inch diameter pine logs. It rose about six feet above the water line, so that in heavy rain, it would still be passable. Shaped like a lazy arch, the center was the highest point, and the entire bridge was about thirty feet long with a railing on each side at least three feet high.

As slowly and quietly as possible, I climbed out of the water and onto the bank. Cold mud clung to my knees and hands as I climbed the bank. I had to wipe my hands on my pants to get the bigger chunks of mud off them, and then again on my shirt to clean off the rest. Pulling out my Tec-9, I made sure the suppressor was still tightened. A real flintlock would have been worthless after it was dunked under water. Not so with my guns. I crouched under the bridge, getting as close as I dared to the soldiers. I picked up an egg-sized rock from the muddy bank and tossed it into the water west of the bridge.

"You hear that?" one of the two soldiers asked, spinning around.

"Yeah," the other soldier said in a bored voice. "It was just a fish, jumping."

I picked up another rock a little smaller and square, throwing it in almost the same spot.

"There," the first soldier said. "I heard it again."

The darkness receded, replaced by the light from his torch, and his shadow loomed over the water. The soldier loped down towards the water at an angle away from me to investigate. He held his torch high to see what had splashed in the water, and I aimed my pistol as he moved farther away. With a slow steady squeeze, I fired one round and my pistol coughed out a *thunk*. The soldier's hat flew off his head comically as he fell face first into the mud. The other soldier laughed at his partner.

After a few seconds, the soldier said, "Get up you fool. If the Captain finds you playing around, we'll both get flogged."

His torch came closer but more slowly than his dead friend's had.

"Hey," he said in a loud enough whisper that he might not have even bothered. "Get up, you pig."

His torch kept getting closer, and then his foot came into view.

"Did you trip, you fucking dumb bull calf?" he said in a lowered whisper.

As his body and head came into view, I aimed for the back of his head. He stopped and must have sensed me because he slowly rotated his head to face me.

We made eye contact one second before I pulled the trigger and put a round through the bridge of his nose. I gave a low bird whistle to get Annie's attention, not that I knew what birds in this area sounded like. But I figured the British didn't either. Keeping as low as I could, I dragged the second body under the bridge and went back for the first. I dragged him by the arm, then grabbed their muskets, carrying them by their slings.

Annie was under the bridge and put on the second soldier's coat and hat, wiping her own muddy hands on the dead soldier's white shirt. I handed her one of the muskets, and she held my goggles to me. I kept them out, knowing I'd need them again. I donned the other soldier's coat and hat as Annie retrieved the two fallen torches from the edge of the bridge. We scurried up the bank with the muskets in one hand and the torches in the other. Brackets had been mounted to the bridge to hold the torches, and I placed mine in one as Annie did the same.

"Stand back from the torches," I said. "I want things to appear normal, but I don't want our faces exposed."

We stood on the bridge, talking as if everything were fine for about five minutes to make sure that no one saw anything. A small puddle formed at our feet as our clothes dripped onto the ground. If anyone noticed the bridge guards gone, an alarm cry would have been given. We remained in place about ten feet away from the torches with our hats pulled low and coat collars high. Annie didn't like this part of the plan, but she had to stay at the bridge. I wasn't going to risk her rushing the British army with only a musket.

I set the musket I held against the bridge railing, then handed her the soldier's flintlock pistol that I'd taken from him. Now she had two muskets and two flint locks, just in case. I reached into her coat and removed one of the C4 explosives from my vest she was wearing. She was shivering uncontrollably from the cold air and soaking wet clothes. I gazed into her face for a short moment, wanting to kiss her for good luck, but if soldiers were watching, that might raise a concern to say the least. Instead, I gave her a curt bow of my head, then took off toward the farm.

I held my goggles up to my face as I walked to the outhouse that stood between the barn and the house and strolled inside as if to use it, but kept the door open an inch. With the magnification of light from the goggles, I noted several candles burning on the first floor of the house and one in one of the upstairs bedrooms. I didn't see anyone in the windows. This didn't surprise me because I was betting, they'd be looking out the upstairs window on the other side of the house toward the more exposed backside. That someone might stroll right up to the front door didn't concern them as much.

One lazy guard sat in a chair on the front porch. I glanced over my shoulder toward the barn where one guard leaned against the front of the closed barn door, picking at his fingers with a thin knife. The whole scene screamed boredom. I scanned the open field as I stepped into the outhouse but didn't see anyone else, which was fortunate because my eyes started watering. The outhouse was made of thin boards, a simple square shape design with nothing more in it than a wooden box with a hole cut out. I was glad it was dark and couldn't see any real details inside. The outhouse reeked of use, as though thirty soldiers had just used it. Breathing shallowly against the foul odors, I stood inside the outhouse, figuring out my next step.

The barn was about thirty feet northwest of me, and the house was about thirty feet northeast. They had placed the outhouse in a centralized spot, so I was equal distance from the soldier on the porch and the soldier standing in front of the barn. The soldiers had lanterns with them so they might be able to see each other. In the end, my decision on who to take out first was decided by the fact the guy on the porch was already sitting down.

I ducked out of the outhouse and made my way straight to the porch. Darkness covered me, preventing the soldier at the barn from seeing my face, but he must have been able to see the outline of my body. With my goggles on, I was able to watch his head move sideways. He was tracking me, but didn't appear worried or suspicious, so I assumed he was simply curious to why I left my post. Lowering my goggles from my face, I shoved them into my coat pocket.

I marched straight up the steps of the porch and into the incandescent glow of the lantern light. The soldier at the barn could fully see me now, if not clearly. My footsteps woke the lazy soldier in the chair, and as he ran his hands over his face to help wake himself, I turned my body to shield my right side from the soldier at the barn. Bending my wrist upward, I raised the barrel of my Tect-9 without lifting my arm. As the soldier's eyes focused on my face, I fired two quick rounds into his chest – *thunk, thunk*.

He jerked twice and fell forward, almost out of his chair. I grabbed his shoulder with my left hand and pushed him back into the chair with as little movement as I could manage. From a distance, he should appear to still be a lazy, sleeping soldier. I covertly holstered my pistol before I made a show of stretching my other arm out and acting like I was talking to the soldier in the chair. I wanted to appear like we were talking, without garnering the attention of anyone in the house. Or of the nosy soldier by the barn.

An empty bucket sat on the warped porch next to the chair, and I picked up the rope handle. With as much nonchalance as possible, I marched back down the steps and straight to the soldier in front of the barn. I hoped he'd assume I was bringing him something that was in the bucket – water to drink or wash his face. A slim premise, but it seemed to buy me time.

As I got closer, he stood a little straighter. He wasn't going to be caught off guard like the soldier on the porch had been. I wasn't sure what I was going to do with him yet, but I had about twenty seconds to think of something.

I didn't know if anyone inside the barn was still awake, so I couldn't just shoot the guy and hope he didn't fall back against the door, warning the soldiers inside. *That* would not go well for me. Once I stepped into the light of his lantern, he'd know I wasn't one of them.

I paused right outside the circle of light and went down to one knee like I was checking my boot. He was still about twelve feet away, and although I could see him clearly, his own lantern was killing his night vision. He probably couldn't see me as well. As I pretended to be adjusting my boots, he stepped forward about two steps, and I stood up. His arm shifted to raise his rifle when I threw my four-inch boot knife that I had grabbed when I was bent over. The knife went forward and imbedded in his right eye, piercing his brain. Clean and silent.

I jumped forward as his head fell backward and grabbed him by the shirt before he fell but not before his rifle hit the ground in a clatter. Gritting my teeth at the noise, I lowered him to the dirt softly, then spun around with my Tec-9 in my hand aimed at the barn door. Counting to five slowly, I listened for movement and tried to control my breathing.

My heart pounded like a sledgehammer in my chest as I waited. If that door opened, I wasn't going to survive the ensuing encounter. I hadn't even reloaded my pistol yet. Great time to remember that I only had two rounds left. The barn door remained shut, so I gave it another five seconds. My breathing had slowed back down, and my heart rate went back to something close to normal. The only thing I could hear from inside was a few horses snorting.

Exhaling the breath, I'd been holding, I placed my pistol in my left hand, then reached down and yanked my boot knife out of the dead soldier's eye socket. With a sickening wet sucking sound, his eye pulled out with the blade. I grimaced, my lips pulling tight as I wiped the blade on his shirt, freeing it of blood and the round orb. As I slid the blade back into my boot sheath, I thought to myself that this was a sight that I'd never forget.

Working quickly, I withdrew the C4 from my front pocket and removed the back of the two-sided tape. The smell of horse dung made me wonder how anyone could be asleep in there, distracting my train of thought as I stuck the explosives to the old, dry, plank-wood door and activated the mercury switch. If that door moved more than an inch, the C4 would go off. I didn't think it'd kill more than the person opening the door, plus anyone next to him, but it'd give me plenty of warning and really freak out the rest of the soldiers and horses inside the barn. Chaos often worked well as cover.

I blew out the lantern on the ground and strode back to the house. I took the hat off my head and dropped it on the ground as I walked. Reloading my pistol, I put the mostly empty magazine in my other cargo pocket so that I didn't grab it on accident. With the round I still had in the chamber, I was reloaded with seven rounds. Solid.

I shrugged out of the coat and after removing my goggles, let the coat drop to the ground behind me. I again climbed the steps to the house, but this time I took slow, carful steps, trying not to make a sound. I blew out the lantern next to the dead soldier and slipped my goggles back on, then moved to the thick brown front door.

The brass lock on the door turned with an audible *click*, and I slowly pushed the door open. Stairs rose up straight in front of me. A formal dining room was to my right, and a door stood at the far end of the room to what I guessed was the kitchen. On my left was what I could only assume was a parlor, with curved, padded chairs and a finely hewn coffee table centered amongst them. Beyond the parlor was a hallway. I wanted to run up the stairs, certain the girls would be held in an upper bedroom, but I didn't want someone to walk up behind me either.

I flicked my eyes up the stairs longingly. If the kids were up there, then that was where I needed to be. But they weren't getting out if I dropped my guard and was killed for it. I had to slow down, control my emotions, and secure the scene. I had to think like a cop again. Clear the downstairs first, then clear the upstairs.

The hallway first it was. I slinked down it to find two doors to my left and one straight ahead that I thought to be a backdoor. Too many lit candles burned my eyes and ruined the efficiency of my night vision goggles. I blew out each candle as I walked past them. By the time I came to the first door, I had blown out every candle on the first floor. The hallway fell into complete darkness. I turned the knob and pushed open the door. The door swung with a long, loud squeaking from hinges in desperate need of oil. My breath caught in my chest, and I cringed before my eyes focused on the two girls sleeping on the floor with their hands tied in front of them. They weren't upstairs. Glad I listened to my previous life's training.

"Who's there?" a voice to my immediate right called out.

I peered around the door to discover a soldier sitting on the floor in the corner. He must have been asleep a moment ago, but the room and hallway were so dark he couldn't see anything.

"Captain," he asked, "is that you?"

"No," I answered, then I fired two rounds into his forehead.

Blood, bone, and brain matter splattered the wall behind him, as his head went back against the wall, only to flop forward again, resting against his chest. The girls opened their eyes but fortunately didn't squeak a word out of fear.

"Shhh," I told them, holding a finger to my lips out of habit – not that they could see the movement. "Be quiet."

"Mr. Nelson? Is that you?" the little one, Regan, asked.

"Yes," I whispered. "Butterfly sent me to come get you."

"No, he didn't," the older one, Molly, said with a shocking pragmatism attitude given our situation. "Our mother sent you. Didn't she?"

"Yes," I answered in a whisper. "I'm going to cut you girls loose. Don't make any noise and don't move."

I kneeled next to them and cut their ropes with my knife.

"Do you know how many men are in this house?" I asked.

"Three," Molly said. Ahh, there, her pragmatism paid off. "There was one in this room with us."

"Don't worry about him," I told her.

"Then the one in charge," she said.

"He's mean," Regan added in a petulant whisper.

"And a big soldier with a lot of stripes on his arm," Molly continued. "I think the mean one in charge is upstairs, but I don't know about the big soldier."

"Ok," I said. "Stand up and hold hands. I'll lead you out of here."

They held each other's hands, and I took Molly's other hand in my left. First, I scanned up and down the hallway to make sure it was still clear. Muddy footprints led from the front door to where I stood. I led the girls out of the room, to the front door and opened it. I went down on one knee and pointed to the bridge.

"See that bridge with the two torches?" I asked.

"Yes, sir," Molly answered.

"See that soldier standing at the bridge?"

"Yes, sir," Molly answered again.

"Ok," I said. "That's not a soldier, that's your mother."

They gasped in unison. "Shhh," I said. "You have to be quiet."

Molly put a hand over Regan's mouth to quiet her.

"Ok," I said, still kneeling next to them. "This is especially important. You need to walk, not run, to your mom. Don't say a word the whole way. Do you understand?"

"Walk, don't run, and don't talk," Regan repeated.

"Good girl," I said. "When you get to your mom, tell her that I said to run for the horses. Don't wait for me, just run."

"What will you be doing, Mr. Nelson?" Molly asked.

"Tell your mom that I'll be keeping my promise to her," I said, rising and pushing them out the door.

They didn't walk like I had told them– they raced wildly toward their mother as I had expected. When they were about fifteen feet from Annie, she lost control of herself and dropped the musket she was holding and ran to her girls. The three embraced in a hug. They were chattering excitedly, and as Annie hugged them, she kept glancing my way. Then she turned and the three of them ran across the bridge, down river to the horses, leaving the two muskets and one of the two flintlocks behind. For the second time that night, I let out a heavy breath.

I could have snuck out with them, but Bonifield and his army would come after us as soon as someone found the dead soldiers. No, I was going to have to kill that son of a bitch. Maybe not all his men. If I killed him, they might return to General Howe and quit searching for me.

My hopes of that went up in flames as I turned around to find an exceptionally large British soldier standing behind me, and an immense fist flying at my face.

The lousy thing about having night vision goggles on is the tunnel vision. You can only see what is right in front of you, so you must turn your head to look around. Fortunately for me, I no longer had to worry about my night vision goggles getting in the way, because his fist knocked me across the room, and the goggles flew off my head. My Tec-9 dropped out of my hands and bounced on the floor.

Fuck. A fist fight with a giant, angry British soldier. A definite turn for the worse.

I tumbled over the dining room table and ended up on the other side. He'd seen me before, because I had been standing in front of the open door and what little moonlight there was had silhouetted me. I'd been an easy-to-see target.

He slammed the door, and we were plunged back into darkness. The only light was the few rays of moonlight coming through the slit in the window curtains, as I had blown out all the candles. I crouched low behind the table and waited.

His heavy footsteps treaded closer, followed by the unmistakable sound of a knife being drawn from its sheath. The wrappings around my head came loose and unwrapped a little. The end of the cloth brushed against my face, and I tugged at the whole wrapping, ripping it from my head, and dropping it to the floor. I drew both my knives and offered up a silent thank you to my dad for taking the time to teach me how to knife fight. I held the one in my right-hand, blade up and the one in my left-hand, blade down.

"Come 'ere, lad," he said to me in the dark. "Sergeant Major Brown won't hurt you... much."

He sounded close. Maybe six feet and to my right a little, but still on the other side of the table. I bent lower and crept my way around the table towards the kitchen door.

"What in the holy hell is going on down there, Sergeant Major?" a voice yelled from upstairs.

A lamp lit the upstairs landing, but it only shone on the stairs, and we were in the dining room, so it didn't do us any good.

"He's here, sir," Brown yelled.

Instead of going for the door, I continued to creep around the table.

"Who's here?" the voice upstairs yelled back down.

"The fucking bastard we've been chasing," Brown yelled even louder, irritation in his voice. "If you'll forgive my language."

Then as an afterthought he added, "Sir." He then muttered under his breath. "You fucking twit."

A fool thing, to keep talking. With that last part, I knew right where he was – about three feet straight in front of me. In a quick lunge forward, I thrusted my right hand. The knife sunk deep into his flesh, then a hand grabbed my wrist and yanked me up. I knew instinctively that I was heading for his blade, so I ducked and twisted my arm towards his thumb, breaking his grip on my wrist.

His knife breezed against my hair as he swiped it over my head. I dove and rolled, popping up several feet away, in a fighting stance. He'd heard me roll behind him, so I knew he'd would have turned to face me. He didn't know where behind him, but then I wasn't certain if he had moved either.

"Can you handle this, Sergeant Major, or do I need to do it for you?" the voice yelled out with a note of derision.

Thank you for the distraction, I thought as I switched the knife from my left hand to my right. My other knife was still stuck in the Sergeant Major. I could hear what sounded like heavy boots stepping on the wooden floor and then, the swoosh of a swinging knife. Step and swoosh, step and swoosh.

His stupid, heavy tread. *The better to hear you with my dear*, I thought wildly.

With his next step, he put himself within three feet of me. Breathing shallowly, I waited for the sound of the swing and then I stepped forward, slashing out with my own knife hard and fast. The blade bit deep into his flesh again. Resistance slowed it, but the knife went through easily, telling me I didn't hit bone. A gurgling broke the darkness – I had cut through his jugular.

His knife fell to the ground with a heavy *thud*. Most likely, he'd dropped his knife to grab his throat with both hands. He was an easy kill now, and I step forward to slash out again, but felt his whole weight plow into and down on me. Maybe not so easy a kill.

A knife went straight through my left shoulder in a bolt of searing pain as I landed on my back, his dead weight on me. And I did mean *dead* weight – the soldier wasn't moving. The tip of the knife stuck into the wood floor beneath me. I was completely stuck, pinned literally to the floor. The rushing drip of his blood pouring from his neck and onto the wooden floor was right next to my left ear. I could feel the hot blood running against the back of my head and neck.

I groaned deep in my chest, disbelieving. He didn't grab his throat, hoping to hold onto a few more seconds of life, like any normal human would have. No, the Sergeant Major released his throat, knowing he was letting his life's blood pour out, so he could stick me. He must have had two knives on him. I wasn't sure if he was the sickest, most twisted mother fucker, I had ever come across, or the bravest, hard corps soldier I ever had to fight against. I suddenly realized that I was glad I didn't have to fight him in the daylight, or I might be the dead weight right now.

Either way he was dead, and I was still alive – on my back, pinned to the floor, under two hundred pounds of dead British muscle with a knife sticking out of my shoulder, but alive. The knocking of the captain's boot steps announced he was coming down the stairs. Light from his lantern reached the front door now, but he still couldn't see me because I was right off the stairs and out of his line of sight.

"Sergeant Major," he yelled. "Report Sergeant Major."

"He can't, you fuck!" I bellowed hoarsely. "He's dead, and you're next."

The footsteps stopped. I could almost hear him thinking – come down or go back up? My Thompson was out of reach, what with the Sergeant Major laying on that half of my body. I turned my head, searching for anything I could use as a weapon. My Tec-9 was now in view, thanks to Bonifield's lamp light, about four feet to my left, almost directly in front of the stairs.

I was trying to reach for it when the floorboards shook under me, from an explosion outside in the direction of the barn. I groaned at the movement.

"Damn," I cursed under my breath.

"What in God's name was that?" the captain asked to no one in particular.

Screaming and yelling erupted from the barn. One of the soldiers must have heard the Sergeant Major's yelling and opened the barn door to investigate. Men were shouting and the horses were going crazy. Despite my agonizing shoulder, my lips curled into a half smile.

I guess he didn't want to face down the unknown by himself, because the captain's footsteps pounded back upstairs. I pushed the Sergeant Major over and off me with my good arm, then rolled to my right to pull the knife out of the floorboard, hissing through my teeth as I moved. The knife tip came out easier than I thought it would, but also pulled the blade deeper into my flesh. My other knife was still sticking out of the Sergeant Major's belly. I tried to pull it free, but it was deep in the muscle, and I didn't have the strength. I let go of the knife, hating to leave it, but I didn't have time for this.

I moved forward on my hands and knees, glancing up the stairs. Captain Bonifield stood at the top and seeing my face pop into view, he threw his lantern at me. I pulled back out of sight, but the lantern crashed to the wooden floor between the stairs and the front door. Glass shattered and liquid fire exploded across the floor. Almost half of the front room was instantly engulfed in flames. The window coverings caught and only helped the fire spread out of control.

I returned the knife in my right hand to its sheath and crawled to my pistol at the foot of the steps. Ignoring my throbbing shoulder, I grabbed my Tec-9 and got up, running for the stairs. I swooped up my goggles that laid a couple feet away as I went. Men burst through the front door now, but the fire slowed them down.

The first two who came in bravely leaped over the flames. I turned on the stairs and shot them each in the chest. The men behind them fired their muskets. Sharp air caressed my face as bullets flew passed me, and I suddenly wished I had listened to Annie and kept my vest.

I ran up the stairs but didn't see Bonifield. A door at the end of the hall was shut, and I knew he had to be behind it. I investigated my shoulder with my eyes and fingers before moving to the door, and I had to pause in a moment of surprise. The Sergeant Major had stabbed me with an awfully long bayonet, not a knife. That explained how it went in so easy and why another six inches still stuck out the front. I should have realized that earlier. Most soldiers carried both a knife and bayonet.

Two more men scrambled through the fire while I was investigating my injury. They both had knives in their hands and started for the stairs. I shot each of them twice and watched them fall backwards. Then I changed magazines as I moved to the door. My left arm wasn't working like it should have, so I had to rely on my right arm.

Glass breaking crashed inside the room. *Bastard's going out the window.* Well, in all fairness, the house *was* on fire. I stepped forward, then leaning back I kicked the door open with my right foot just in time to see him drop out the window and onto the ground. I ran to the window ledge and glanced out. Shots zipped through the window frame, and I ducked back in and out of sight of those below, as the shots smacked into the ceiling above my head, showering me with dust and wood chips.

The soldiers down below were covering their Captain in an attempt to protect him from whoever had chased him out a second-floor window. I raced back out of the room to the stairs as two more men ran up the stairs straight at me. I emptied my pistol into them and watched them fall backwards, tumbling over to the floor. As I ran down the stairs, I reloaded yet again. Gritting my teeth, I took a couple of tries to get the magazine into the pistol. My stabbed arm was aching and hindered me. And it was only getting worse.

A gruesome pile of bodies rested at the bottom of the stairs, and I had to jump over several dead soldiers. Then I turned to go down the hall and out the back door, but on the other side of the now open backdoor, two soldiers stood right outside, waiting for me. I dropped to the floor as they fired their already raised muskets. The rounds went through the hallway, over my head. I jumped up and ran outside past them as they were reloading their muskets. Taking advantage of their slow reload, I put one round into each of their faces from only a few feet away.

Once outside, I pulled out the grenade from my cargo pocket and replaced it with my goggles. I pulled the pin of the grenade and held it as best I could with my left hand, still holding my pistol with my right. When I peeked around the corner of the house, six or seven soldiers still aimed their rifles at the upstairs windows.

The barn was on fire, and panicked horses ran in every direction; some with saddles most without. A few soldiers were trying to catch as many of the horses as they could. I had to adjust my grip on the grenade, when it started slipping out of my grasp. To be honest, I didn't think I could throw with my left hand with the bayonet still sticking out of that shoulder.

Acting decisively, I holstered my Tec-9 and reach down to grab the grenade with my right hand. My left arm was practically numb, and I was afraid I would drop the grenade if I tried to raise my left hand up to my right. I was lucky that hadn't dropped the grenade at my own feet. With a side arm throw, I tossed the grenade to the ground right in front of the group of seven and watched it bounce once and roll to the middle of the group. Two of the men looked down at it, as if it were a pinecone that had fallen from a tree. I turned and ran around the house in the opposite direction.

I made it to the corner when the grenade went off. More screaming followed and with the house and barn on fire, the entire property was bathed in orange and yellow flickering lights.

One soldier had tied two horses to a tree and was calming down a third horse trying to pull away from him. I took three deliberate steps forward while drawing my Tec-9 and shot him in the back of the head. The horse pulled away and ran off through the open field. I was willing to let the soldiers run away when I first got here, but now I wanted to make sure none of them lived to report what had happened. Both for my sake, and for Annie's.

In sure panic, Captain Bonifield yanked one of his own men off a horse that didn't have a saddle. He grabbed the horse's mane, and like a skilled rider, he swung onto the animal's back. He paused to inspect the farm, burning house, and the tree line in the distance. I knew his eyes were searching for the dozens of enemy soldiers who were attacking him and his men. His gaze landed in my direction. His eyes took in the pistol in my hand and the blood that covered my face and shoulders. I stood there, my eyes locked on him, chest heaving as I sucked in oxygen to fuel my muscles. Seeing just me and his own dead or fleeing men on the property gave him the realization of the truth, that one lone, crazed, and vengeful man had just wiped out the whole of his command, and that struck him like a steel fist to the gut.

He spun the mount under him and galloped off with three of his men also mounted on horses. The soldier he'd pulled from the horse ran after them on foot. None of the horses had saddles, so they weren't running as fast as they could. Taking aim, I shot one more soldier who was trying to mount another horse.

Holstering my Tec-9, I pulled my Thompson out and aimed for Bonifield's back. My arms were exhausted, and my pistol felt heavy. I forced my hand to stay in the air as I sighted for the center of his back. I moved the front sight forward, slightly in front of the captain, adjusting for the running horse. As I started to squeeze the trigger, two more soldiers ran around the corner of the house, and ran straight into me. I stumbled back a few feet, barely managing not to fall onto my back. Out of instinct, I shot the first one in the chest with the bullet I had intended for Bonifield.

The soldier I shot fell to the ground unmoving, blood soaking through his shirt. The other soldier quickly recovered from his surprise and raised his musket at me. I knew I was as good as dead. His loaded musket was too far for me to dive on, and he was too close for me to run away. Frankly, I was too exhausted to do either, even if I could have.

He smiled and then as he aimed, his throat erupted with blood. With the barn and house on fire, and the horses running in a panic, screaming, I hadn't heard the gun shot.

He first opened his hands, dropping the musket to the ground. His hand rose to his throat as he dropped to his knees with a flabbergasted look on his face. He slowly fell forward onto his face, and a small cloud of dirt kicked up around him. A stark-faced Annie stood behind him, holding a flintlock pistol. I stared at her in shock for half a heartbeat, then smiled. It took me three tries, but I holstered my Thompson, not just because it was empty but because I didn't think I could hold it any longer. My overworked right arm was giving out. I felt like a wet, tired, stabbed, beat down dog. I slumped to my knees, and Annie dropped her pistol to the dirt as she scrambled over to me. She grabbed my shoulders before I fell on my face.

"Oh my God, Thomas," Annie cried, bringing her right hand up to my head.

I felt her finger probe my head and when she pulled her hand away, it was covered in blood, and some of my hair clung to her blood-covered fingers.

"It's not my blood," I told her. "Belongs to one of the soldiers."

"Thank God for that," Annie said. Her fingers moved down to the bayonet sticking out of my shoulder, "This, however, is your blood."

"He got away," I gasped between breaths.

"He rode off with three of his men, plus one on foot," she told me.

"I need to go after him."

"No, Thomas," she said calmly.

"What? Why not?"

"He has no food, no guns, no ammo, only four men, and three horses, none of which even have a saddle," she explained. "He must go back to General Howe now. Plus, you can't even stand."

"Girls?" I gasped, unable to speak in full sentences. Even breathing now hurt.

"They're fine," she reassured me. "We ran to the horses. I figured they'd be safe there. So, I came back to check on you."

"Just in time," I said in a ragged hoarse voice. "You saved my life, again."

The house was ablaze now, and steam wafted into the air from my wet shirt as the fire's heat reached my skin through my clothes.

"We need to move away from the house," Annie said. "Can you walk?"

She wrapped her arm around my waist to help me stand and walked me over to the tobacco barn. I sat down heavily on the ground, leaning my back against the wooden wall. I started to pass out when the bayonet poking out the back of my shoulder hit the wooden barn wall. My eyes shot back open with the flood of pain. Inhaling deeply through my nose, I could smell the tobacco leaves that hung in the barn, drying. The Johnson's wagon was still in the barn. Annie raced outside and was able to catch two horses. This far from the fire, they had calmed a little bit. She tied them to the wagon and then loaded me up on the back of it.

I had managed to pour some blood clotting powder on my wound around the bayonet that was sticking out the front of my shoulder. I was no longer in danger of bleeding to death unless I had already lost too much blood. But every time I moved, the bayonet shifted, and agonizing pain careened down my arm and across my chest.

Annie was an exceptionally practical woman, and she spared a few minutes to gather up the rifles, flintlock pistols, shot and gunpowder that she could find from the dead soldiers near the barn and laid them in the back of the wagon next to me. She must have also checked their pockets because she dropped in a handful of coins. Then she managed to gather up about ten more horses. The rest of the animals had wisely run off away from the fires. I may have been bleary and losing my ability to function, yet I still marveled at her skill under pressure.

Somewhere on the slow bumpy ride back to Annie's farm, I lost consciousness.

EIGHT: Snakes In Trees

I WASN'T SURE if I passed out from blood loss, exhaustion, or from my head wound catching up to me. I woke up sometime later, to find that I was tucked into a bed. The bayonet was no longer in my shoulder, and I had on yet another bandage. I slipped back into darkness again. I woke several more times, and each time, the pain wracked my entire body, causing me to pass out again.

I had no idea how much time passed in this semi-conscious state, but the next time I woke, I forced myself to stay awake. Thin shafts of sunlight pressed through gaps in the wood-paneled wall and the curtain in the window. I gazed around, noticing that this wasn't Annie's room. *Where am I?*

My throat was dry and raw. I was starving, and my stomach groaned. I moved my left hand and arm against my bare chest. The numbness was gone. Then I realized so were my clothes.

"He's awake," Molly yelled from the foot of the bed. I flipped my gaze to her, pulling at the thick cotton covers out of modesty.

Annie entered with a smile and a glass of water. She helped me sit up and propped another pillow behind me. I asked her to hand me my satchel. She did, and I pulled out more pain killers and another antibiotic shot. At this rate, I'd run out soon.

"How bad is the injury?" I asked, peering at the bandage on my shoulder.

"The bayonet went all the way through," she said. "I had to clean and stitch each side. I was afraid it would become full of pus, but so far, no signs of that. The bayonet, I suspect, was quite painful but as thin as it was, it didn't seem to cause much damage."

"How long have I been out?" I asked.

"Two days," she answered. "I think it was more from the head wound than the shoulder."

"Two days," I repeated in a panic, trying to keep my eyes open. "We need to get out of here. Captain Bonifield will be on his way back with more men. He can't let this insult and challenge to his authority go unanswered. We're in danger."

She put a hand on my chest, and with no effort at all pushed me back down onto the bed.

"Easy, Thomas," she told me, her voice tight. "We're at a friend's house. After I got us back home, Ben said the same thing you did, and we loaded up the wagon and cart and came straight here. We're at the Cornel farm, about three miles west of Ben's farm. We even hid the horses and wagon in the barn. They'll not find us here. We're safe."

"Did you tell him?" a male voice asked from the doorway.

I turned my head slowly. Ben stood there with a smile on his face.

"Tell me what?" I asked returning my gaze to Annie.

"No," she said. "Not yet."

"Tell me what?" I asked again.

"What they're calling you," Ben answered, with an ever-growing smile.

"What? Who is calling me what?" I asked Annie. My head pounded at the conversation.

"The British and the Colonists," Ben answered.

"What are they calling me?" I asked Annie, confused. "How do they even know about me?"

"That's enough Ben," Annie commanded, the pitch of her voice rising. "I'll tell him later. After he's rested."

"Annie?" I said, the question hanging in the air.

"Father rode into the city yesterday to see how things were going and get whatever information he could. He took the cart and sold some apples so that no one would get suspicious."

"And?"

"Everyone seems to know about you. Different people are calling you by different names," she said, with a hint of sadness in her voice.

"Such as?" I asked.

"The British don't know your name, so they are calling you Pale Rider," she told me. "Some people say that death follows you. Others say that you bring death with you, like a hungry dog on a leash. The whole British army seems to know what you did to General Howe's encampment, single handedly at that. Some of the British soldiers are saying that you killed hundreds in Howe's camp. There were witnesses that saw you ride away alone, but no one saw you ride to or walk into the camp in the first place. Then you killed all but three of Captain Bonifield's men."

She glanced at Ben before she continued. "They say that Captain Bonifield had never lost a battle before the night at the farmhouse. General Howe couldn't believe him or his men when they reported that only one man had attacked them in the middle of the night. The General doesn't understand how they had four sentries on guard and not one of them gave out an alarm."

I raised my eyebrows at her. Ben had learned a lot in town. So much for trying to stay under the radar.

"There was a Sergeant Major that they say you killed," Annie added. "Ben heard a few of the soldiers say that he was a real son of a bitch. They sent men back to the farmhouse. His body was burned, but they found your knife in his charred body. The fact that you killed him seems to be enough to scare most of the soldiers. The fact that you killed him with a knife scares them even more. The British seem to think you're something between a monster and a shadow. They say you can see in the dark, and you kill without mercy."

"And the Colonists?" I asked. "What are they calling me?"

"The Colonist are calling you, Washington's Assassin," she said. "They think that you were raised by Indians and serve the General. Ben heard someone say that General Washington met you back in the Indian War. They seem to think that you are using Indian magic to walk among men without being seen."

"There was also talk about Washington being captured," Ben interrupted, "and that he was rescued by a single man in a white shirt, black leather vest, with two pistols. They say that after Washington was captured, you rode into town that same night and found the General, killing those who had assaulted him. Some say that Washington sent you to distract the British so he could walk out of the city with his men.

Other say that he sent you to avenge the assault on his person."

"The part about me distracting the British is true," I told them dryly.

"You can bet your horse that you're so fond of that the loyalists have told General Howe about that," she said poking a finger lightly in my chest.

"Did it work?" I asked. "Did Washington get out of Philadelphia with his men?"

"Yes," Annie said, a slight smile dimpling her cheek. "But you're not listening to me. The British are after you. They're searching everywhere for you. They have a basic description of you and are looking for anyone with two pistols or a black vest."

"I *am* listening to you," I told her. "What happened in Philadelphia?"

She blew out a lung full of air. "The British attacked and found Philadelphia empty. A few British loyalists but no soldiers. General Howe wasn't happy about that. He put a price on your head."

"How much?"

"Too much."

"Annie, how much?" I asked again.

She dropped her gaze to her hands. "General Howe is seizing and giving away Ben's farm, plus two thousand English gold coins," she answered, refusing to meet my eyes.

My jaw clenched. I was afraid this would happen.

"Help me up, Ben," I directed, turning to him again.

"Don't you dare!" Annie spun and admonished Ben.

Ben raised both hands as if surrendering and backed out of the room.

"Thomas, you have been shot in the leg, arm, *and* head, and let us not forget the bayonet through the shoulder," she said. "You can't keep this up. You need to rest and recover."

"The leg wound is nothing more than a scratch and the head wound is a graze, they look worse than they are," I explained. "The bayonet wound only stings a little. It went through me and caused a lot of blood loss, but you said it yourself, that it didn't cause much damage. The bullet wound to my arm is the worst injury, but it's my left arm, and the bone wasn't hit, so it still works, only some torn muscles. Besides, apparently, I've done nothing but rest and recover for the last two days."

The truth was that my head injury was what worried me the most. Another pounding headache blossomed in my skull. Headache or no headache, I was going to have to get going soon, if I wanted to help General Washington. But she was right about me needing rest. Back in my old world, I would have been in bed for weeks, but this wasn't my old world, and time wasn't on my side.

Now that General Washington had made it out of Philadelphia alive and with most his men, the timeline had been changed. I just didn't know in what way. The next part of the plan was for me to travel to Saratoga and help fight the British. The French would be watching the outcome of that battle, and the Colonists needed a notable showing to prove to the French they wouldn't be backing a losing horse.

I had nine days to travel the ninety miles to Saratoga, seven if I wanted to give myself two days to come up with a plan to help win the battle. I had already wasted at least four of them here. A wave of shame churned with that thought. Saving those two girls was anything but a waste of time.

I asked Annie, "How far can you travel per day on horseback?"

She squinted at me with questioning eyes, trying to figure out how I didn't know the answer to such a simple question.

"If you stay on the road and not travel over hills and through the woods," she said thinking about the answer, "I would say you could make thirty miles a day. Depending on the horse, that is. You can't keep that pace up for more than a day or two without killing the animal, and you'd have to rest at night."

"Ben!" I yelled, causing a spike of pain to bust in my head. Ben's head poked around the corner as I swung my leg over the side of the bed to stand. "Saddle Little Joe and three other horses for me, I need to ride to New York."

"You're not going anywhere," Annie dictated, standing with her hands on her hips.

"I'm sorry, but I have to," I told her. "I'll come back when I'm done with what I have to do, but I do have to leave."

Silence filled the room as we stared at each other. She blinked rapidly, and a single tear ran down her cheek. She wiped it with her dress sleeve.

"I know," she finally said. "I will be waiting for you. We will be waiting. All I ask is that you do not throw your life away. Come back to me."

"You know I'll do my best," I said with a weak smile. "That much I can promise. You've given me a reason to live. That'll make my job harder, but I'll do my best to get the job done and come back. For now, I need to ride to Saratoga, then to Valley Forge."

She nodded her head and threw herself in my arms. I stumbled a bit as I caught her in arm. We stood there for a while, holding each other. She buried her face in my neck, and I didn't want to let go of her.

Ben stood there awkwardly, not knowing what to do, until Annie turned to him and with tears openly running down her face, yelled at him. "You heard him! Saddle the horses."

Standing in my underwear, I asked Annie to help me dress. Without another word she retrieved my clothes and helped dress me.

"It's getting cold," she said, and she handed over my jacket.

Looking around the room, I didn't see my backpack, and she seemed to read my mind. She reached under the bed and pulled it out, placing it on top of the mattress. Reaching into the backpack, I pulled out one of my extra knives and placed it in the sheath behind my back. I tugged out my night vision goggles from my cargo pocket and placed them in their case that laid in the backpack. Then I withdrew a few more pistol magazines, dropping them in my cargo pocket, and made sure that my 30-30 ammo band around my arm was still filled. I also grabbed one of the two grenades from the backpack and put it in the satchel with the one I still had in there.

The last thing I did was pull out my money pouch and pour half of the coins into Annie's hands. It was a small fortune in coins. She could buy a new farm with all that money. She pushed it back at me until I grabbed her hands, forcing her fingers to close around the coins.

"I'll be back." I gave her a hollow promise. "We can start a life together, if that's what you want."

She threw herself into me again and we again held each other for several more minutes before she pushed herself away. "I'll make some food for you to eat on the road."

With that, she exited the room. I pulled my jacket on over my vest and, grabbing my backpack, I headed outside. The sun was up, trying its best to brighten the day, but the air was even colder than it had been several days ago. It had to be about thirty degrees out and my breath puffed in the air.

The barn was to my left and the large barn doors were open. Little Joe and two other horses were saddled and tied to the picket post. I hung my backpack on Little Joe's saddle horn and ducked into the barn as Ben was finishing up with a third horse.

"We need to talk," I told him.

"I suspect so, lad," he said.

"I'm sorry about your farm Ben. We both know you can't return there until the British are gone."

"Aye, lad, I know," he responded.

"You can't go back into Philadelphia either," I said. "Too many people know you, and it only takes one to turn you into the British."

"Aye, lad," he said. "I know that as well."

"I plan on coming back when this is all over," I said, staring him directly in the eyes.

"Good lad. You should."

"You're fine with me and Annie. . ." I trailed off, letting the rest go unspoken.

"Lad," he said, taking a deep breath. "My only son is dead. I love Annie as if she were my own daughter. Should I deny her whatever happiness she's able to find in this wretched world? What about my granddaughters? Should I say they don't deserve a father just because my son can't be there to raise them?"

His words were powerful and heartfelt. "Thank you, Ben," was all I could think to say.

"If you get yourself killed and break her heart," he continued, "I'll track you down, dig up your rotting corpse, and piss on whatever flesh is left on your body."

His voice lacked any humor, as did his face. This old man would do his best to do what he promised. Then he stuck out a hand and we shook. Annie approached them with several cloth wrappings in her hand. Ben went back to saddling the last horse, and I left the barn to meet Annie. She placed two wrappings in Little Joe's saddle bags and two more in the saddle bags of one of the other horses.

"Some cold, fried squirrel and rabbit," she explained. "Also, some cheese and bread."

I thanked her, and as she turned away, I grabbed her arm and pulled her back to me. She leaned into me, and we kissed. It was a long, soft kiss, delicate and meant to last a person a lifetime.

"Come back to me," she whispered in my ear.

"I will," I told her, searching her face. "For the first time in years, I have a reason to live. Thank you for that."

In the back of my head, I thought about how much harder my job was going to be if I wanted to live through this. Until this moment I wasn't worried about getting killed. I needed to cause enough damage to the British to change the timeline. Now, with Annie and her family, things were getting complicated.

Annie turned her head so I wouldn't see more tears roll down her cheek as she walked off towards the house. I turned around as Ben led the last horse out of the barn.

"I put two bags of grain on this one and a feeder bag," he said. "You'll have to feed them one at a time."

"Thanks, Ben," I said.

Ben helped me tie the horses in a line with Little Joe last. I lifted my leg to mount the first horse when Regan and Molly came running from the house. I scanned the yard for any signs of danger.

"What's wrong?" I hollered, ready to draw my pistol.

138

I was surprised when they threw their arms around me in hugs. I didn't have any children of my own, and I was out of my element. I cast a helpless glance over at Ben, who smiled at my awkwardness. Unsure of what to do, I bent to one knee and returned their hugs. Molly told me to be careful, and Regan made me promise to come back. Then she made me promise to take care of Butterfly. Ben saved me as he pulled the girls away and told them that I needed to go.

I started off on the road heading north. Once I was far enough from the farm, I used my phone and pulled up a map of the east coast circa 1777. The battle took place on September nineteenth, at Freeman's farm, located about nine miles south of Saratoga.

I rode the horses hard on the first day, making sure to switch out the horses every hour, and never riding Little Joe. I was going to need him strong and fresh when we got there. After riding each horse once, alternating galloping and trotting, I got off and walked with them for an hour. I munched on beef jerky from my backpack and drank from my canteens.

By the time the sun was starting to set, I had ridden each of the horses several times, only stopping once to cool them off and let then drink from a stream. I'd spotted British soldiers on the road twice. The first time I turned the horses off the roadway and bolted away as fast as I could. For the most part, the British were foot soldiers, so it was easy enough to stay away from them. The second time, a few of the soldiers shot at me, but I was too far from them to be in any real danger. I made it to the Hudson River and followed it north.

As night began to creep across the sky and the sun sunk over the horizon, I came across an abandoned farm. The house had been burned down, and the smell of scorched wood still lingered in the cold air.

Ropes hung in a nearby tree that somehow managed to not catch fire. While the ends of the ropes had been cut, I knew what had happened and it made my stomach roll. The British had hung the farmers who had lived here, for an act they claimed was treason. Maybe the farmers wanted to be paid for food that the British took from them, or maybe the farmers were suspected of giving aid to the Colonists. Either way, the four ropes that swayed in the wind, like snakes that had bitten into the branch and refused to let go, told me enough of the story. At least, the important part of this story – how this particular family's story ended in tragedy and death.

Four mounds of dirt were set off to the side of the tree. Two of the mounds were shorter than the other two. *Children*, I thought, a final resting place for the family that lived their lives on this farm. Each mound had a small wooden cross pushed into the dirt, two pieces of wood tied together with some string, but the act itself was a kind one. A final gift from some neighbor who risked their own freedom, maybe even their lives, to bury friends.

The barn was a little run down but still in one piece, untouched by fire. It was a large barn meant to hold horses and cows, though it was now empty. The two large doors, screamed in protest, as I pushed them open. The pens were built against the walls and left enough room in the middle for a wagon. I put each of the four horses in their own stall. Plenty of hay was piled on the floor, but I gave each horse some grain and fetched some water from the well. Little Joe got a granola bar, because I was afraid, he was getting jealous of me riding the horses and not him. Then again, maybe it was my imagination. He was just a horse after all.

By my estimation, I had covered over forty-five miles today and was ahead of schedule. Riding three horses meant fewer breaks and faster travel time. Each of the horses had to run long distances without stopping, but each only had to carry me one hour every four hours. I didn't know if the horses could keep up this pace, but I was going to push them even harder tomorrow. I sat down in one of the stalls and pulled out my phone to review the battle records while I ate cold rabbit and bread.

According to the records, British General John Burgoyne led his men south from Canada. A few miles outside of Saratoga, he met up with British forces marching north from New York City, led by a Major Davenport. After the battle started, the British received reinforcements the next day, from forces marching east from Lake Ontario, led by Major Campbell. All three of the British officers later published their personal journals and wrote about the battle, detailing the routes they took and the part they played. The two British companies attacked the Colonists at the same time from two different sides and were later aided by the third. The Colonists were prepared for General Burgoyne and had placed sharp shooters north of the farm in hopes of causing mass casualties on the British. They were horribly unprepared for, nor did they know about, the other two companies until it was too late. The Colonists were outnumbered four to one and were slaughtered down to the last man.

The battle went down in the British annals as one of the bloodiest in the war.

I had the British's plans in my hands, and they could be defeated if I came up with a plan before I got to Saratoga. My biggest problem was I lacked a way to convince the Continental Army that I was one of them, and they had no reason to believe me. They'd most likely believe me a spy and shoot me on sight. General Washington might vouch for me, but it would take too long for a messenger to ride to him at Valley Forge and back. I was going to have to find a different way to help defeat the British. Putting my phone away, I fell asleep in the hay, thinking about this problem.

NINE: Fear My Name

I WOKE TO THE BEEPING of my watch alarm, which I had set for five o'clock in the morning. After I ate some powder eggs and smoked salmon, I fed the horses what I figured was a half portion. While I didn't know much about horses, I didn't think I should feed them a full amount and then run them hard.

I was ready to get on the road before the sun had started to grace the horizon. The morning was cold, and a thick fog lingered in the air. We walked first to loosen up. After an hour of walking, I mounted the first horse again and sped into a slow gallop. By the time, the sun breached the horizon and the fog started to burn off, I was on the second horse and had made up my mind on my next course of action. If studying history and the art of war had taught me anything, it was that the soundest idea in this case was to divide and conquer. If the Continental Army wouldn't accept my help, I'd have to do this on my own.

Turning east and using my small watchband compass, I set a path to intercept Major Davenport and his soldiers. British General Sir Henry Clinton was busy on the coast, and instead of taking his battalion east, he elected to send Major Davenport with only a company of men. From what I read, a British company consisted of anywhere between eighty and one hundred and fifty soldiers. I was really hoping for the former and not the latter.

I rode the whole day without stopping, but the horses were starting to slow their pace. I knew I was pushing them too hard, but my only chance of surviving was to find an ambush spot and wait for them. Following the path that Major Davenport indicated in his book, that he traveled from New York, I thought I had found a great spot on the map – a wide clearing that made for a killing field. I just didn't know if I could get there in time.

I raced against the clock as I traded one horse for another several times. The first horse that I had started with, fell behind and started to slow us down. Exhaling a long breath, I had to cut him loose and let him go. I hoped he'd be Ok, but then again, I was sure he was going to be safer than I would be.

An hour later, I neared the open field and slowed the horses to a walk so that they could cool down.

We made it to the clearing with no soldiers in sight. I was starting to worry that I was in the wrong place. I studied the terrain, convincing myself this was the correct open field. It had to be about five hundred yards long and just as wide. I didn't think I had time to set up traps, and there was no way I could win in a straight-up fight with eighty to a hundred and fifty soldiers, no matter what the rumors about me claimed. Not even if I never missed.

Swallowing hard, I focused on my one and only idea. My lone chance was that Annie was right about the whole British army knowing about me. General Howe wanted me dead so badly that he might have sent word to the other British forces. From the talk in the town, I was almost certain of it.

I tied the horses about fifty feet into the tree line so no one could see them. I withdrew my range finder and marked a spot in the field that ranged at three hundred yards.

When I was practicing with the Thompson Contender, I made a few decent shots all the way out to four hundred yards, but not consistent enough to try that today. Three hundred and fifty yards was my max range for consistent hits.

I searched around and found a six-foot branch on the ground. Taking one of the horses, I rode to the spot I had marked in my mind. I slid off the horse, and using my range finder again, I looked back to the tree line, confirming the distance. Then I stuck the branch into the ground sticking up so I would know right when they were three hundred yards away. I rode back to the tree line, and tied the horse with the others.

I found a thick four-foot log about twenty feet away that would serve as cover and concealment for me. After rolling, flipping, and dragging the log, I finally got it into position between two smaller trees at the tree line.

With my position set up, next I took off my jacket, placed it in my backpack, and extracted an extra box of 30-30 ammo. I hooked the backpack onto Little Joe's saddle horn along with my satchel and fed and watered the horses. I retied the horses in reverse order this time, with Little Joe at the front. He was the one I wanted to be on if I had to ride out of there fast.

I was feeding Little Joe another granola bar when two British soldiers broke through the tree line on horseback and rode toward me. *Scouts!*

I stood behind one of the trees and waited patiently as they rode across the field, getting closer with every step. With my Thompson in my left hand and my Tec-9 in my right hand, I stepped out from behind the tree, when they were only ten yards away. They stopped and raised their muskets until I lifted my pistols. From the way their eyes widened, I knew that the black vest and two pistols announced who I was and had the effect that I was hoping for. Without me saying a word, the soldiers dropped their muskets onto the ground, their pale faces whitening more.

"Off the horses," I ordered. "You British call me Pale Rider. Do as I say, and you might live to tell others what you see here today. If you don't, neither of you sons of bitches will ever leave this field."

They nodded in unison and slid off their horses. I made them sit down in front of two small trees facing the open field but with trees blocking their view of where I would be. They were far too compliant as I tied their hands behind their backs and then their feet together. I stuck a piece of duct tape over each of their mouths so they couldn't yell out a warning before tying their horses to my little caravan, bringing my total up to five horses. Then I settled back down behind the log and waited.

After another ten minutes, the steady staccato of drums filled the air. Definitely no focus on stealth. I pulled out my Thompson and range finder and waited the few minutes until the British rode into sight.

They broke through the tree line on the other side of the field right where the scouts had. Using my range finder scope,

I eyed them as they enter the field as if they had nothing to fear. What audacity these Brits had.

With the powerful magnification of the scope, I could make out their faces clearly. Major Davenport rode at the front of his company, like he was leading a parade in front of the Kings palace, on the royal birthday. I recognized him from a drawing in his book. He sat atop a large white horse and stared straight ahead like a true British officer. The next four officers, Junior Lieutenants, rode about ten feet behind him and were talking to each other with easy smiles on their faces. Behind them, the rest of the company marched on foot in two columns. There were about six drummers, then soldiers, and lastly a wagon pulled by two horses. I estimated about one hundred men in total.

They continued through the open field. In my century, soldiers avoided open fields. They were too easy to die in. In this century, the British thought that only savages would fight in the woods. Open fields are where they felt more comfortable, civilized.

That was going to change today.

I set down my scope, picked up my Thompson, and aimed in on Major Davenport. He felt safe because he was an officer, and soldiers didn't try to kill officers; they killed the men that the officers led. Rules of civilized battle in the eighteenth century.

Too bad I didn't follow those rules.

Like a bully with a mob behind him, the Major continued through the field as if he didn't have a care in the world. As he drew even with the branch that I'd placed in the middle of the field, I fired my first of many shots. Blood exploded out of the Major's back in a red shower, and his body slowly rolled over backwards, off his horse, as the spirited mount leaped forward in a panicked run. The other four officers froze, scanning the field as they juggled their muskets, trying to identify where that shot had come from.

As the British panicked, I kept my hand calm and focused, and my eyes on the remaining officers. I thumbed the release button on my Thompson. Without looking I removed the spent cartridge and reached over and under my right arm, removing a new cartridge from its leather loop that held my bullets. Placing the cartridge into the barrel of my Thompson and snapping the barrel up into the locked position, I was now reloaded again. Having never moved my head or taken my eyes off the officers, I brought my pistol back up, so that my sights were in front of my eyes again. One of the Junior Lieutenants had dismounted to check on his fallen Major. The other three officers started yelling orders to their men on the ground behind them.

The foot soldiers ran forward through the snow and set up two lines in front of the Major's dead body. I fired again, and one of the three officers still on horseback flew backwards off his horse like his Major had just done.

As I reloaded my Thompson again, the other two officers had finally realized that being up high was detrimental to their health and crouched on the ground.

One of the more experienced common foot soldiers was paying attention and figured out where I was. Thirty or more soldiers fired their muskets in my direction. At this range, their bullets didn't reach me. When I finally saw one of the other officers rise up a little bit, I fired my third shot, killing my third officer. Again, with steady patience, I reloaded again and aimed in on one of the two remaining officers standing up. He drew his sword to order a charge. I fired, and instead of giving that order, he grabbed his throat and dropped to his knees.

I reloaded again and searched the field for the last officer. He was laying down in the grass behind his men, so I couldn't get a decent shot at him. Not wanting to waste time, I turned my aim and shot the soldier on the wagon. He didn't fall off, rather he slumped over onto his side.

I found my rhythm again. Fire, reload, fire, reload, fire, reload. I concentrated on the soldiers in front of the last officer. All the other soldiers were firing and reloading as fast as they could. Small thick clouds of smoke billowed in front of them as they fired their muskets. None of them seemed to notice that their rounds never quite made it to me. The dirt was being churned up about thirty feet in front of me. I finally had a shot at the last officer and killed him as he hid behind a bush.

With their officers dead, I aimed for the soldiers with the most stripes on their uniforms. My figuring was killing the senior and most experienced soldiers first would cause confusion and a distinct lack of leadership. Five shots later, I didn't see any more soldiers with stripes on their arms.

Now was the time for my *real* plan. I stood up for all to see me and calmly moseyed over to the two soldiers that I had tied up. With all the casual calm I could muster, I pulled out my knife and cut the ropes at their feet and then the ropes behind their backs.

The soldiers in the field were still firing at me and their rate of fire only increased when they saw me stand. The ground seemed to move as if it was alive. The impacts of their rounds seemed to be getting closer and like a stray dog who was afraid to get too close to me, the whipped-up dirt did follow me as I walked. I was three times farther than their maximum effective range, so I didn't think they had much chance of hitting me.

Looming over these two soldiers, I spoke in a tight, commanding voice. "Run. Tell them that the Pale Rider stands before them. Tell your friends to throw down their muskets and run back to New York harbor now, or I will kill every one of you goat licking bastards. I will leave their bodies in the field for scavengers to feed upon, and with my magic, I will tie their souls to this field where they will be trapped forever."

The stricken men whitened impossibly more and nodded their heads as fast and as hard as they could. One of them had wet himself, a dark patch coloring the front of his pants and staining the snow yellow. They climbed nervously to their feet and took off running for their British compatriots, waving their arms, and hoping not to get shot.

When they made it to their comrades, the shooting halted for a moment. The two soldiers were yelling and pointing towards me, then towards the way they'd come earlier. Without hesitation, a dozen men threw down their muskets and ran for the tree line behind them, led by the two I had released.

Unfazed by my threat, the rest resumed their shooting. I stepped back into the tree line and waited. Each time one of the soldiers gathered enough courage to stand up and move forward, I fired my Thompson and they fell over dead. Each time I killed a soldier, three more dropped their muskets and ran. When only thirty-five or forty men remained, they seemed to decide as a group and ran in full retreat as one. The mostly white, snow-covered field was now covered with deep red spots, where blood had soaked into the snow.

Taking my time, moving slow and with caution, I circled around the open field to make sure they were not setting up an ambush. It took unnecessary time, but better safe than sorry. I didn't see a single living soldier. The tracks in the snow were hard to miss. They had all run straight back the way they had come. The tracks leading into the field were clear and straight after a hundred men had walked in a line behind each other. The tracks leading out of the field were all over the place, as if no one were leading or following. Just a mass retreat. I wondered if the British Empire was going to hang those men for cowardness or cover this up to save face.

The wagon they had abandoned was filled with gun powder, shot, blankets, barrels of salted beef, and some sort of pickled meat. Taking a page out of Annie's playbook, I quickly collected as many muskets and powder tins as I could and placed them in the wagon as well.

As I worked, I needed to decide what to do next. General Burgoyne was still marching south from Canada and Major Campbell east from Lake Ontario. General Burgoyne was closer but would have at least twice as many men as Major Campbell. Major Campbell was the easier target, but I ran the risk of running into General Burgoyne on accident. After weighing all my options, I decided that I would intercept Major Campbell, and the Colonists would have to fight General Burgoyne without me.

Once the wagon was full of its precious cargo, I couldn't leave it sitting in the field, so I tied the horses to the back of the wagon and headed back the way I had come. I rode at a faster pace than the wagon horses were used to but slower than the other horses had been ridden. It took all day of non-stop riding, but I made it back to the burned-down farmhouse and barn as the sun made its final descent into the western horizon.

I hid the wagon and the horses inside the barn with plenty of hay and a freshly filled water trough. Then I tied the barn doors together from the inside so that no one could sneak in on me. Laying down in the same stall that I slept in last night, I made a dinner of the rest of the cold rabbit, bread, and cheese. Every bone in my body ached, but nothing more than my head and arm. Pushing those aches out of my mind as best I could, I pulled out my cell phone and powered it back on. More work beckoned, and I wanted to read about Major Campbell again, to commit as much as I could to memory.

Major Campbell had written in his journal that his company had followed what was now called the Mohawk River all the way down from Lake Ontario to Saratoga, on the north side of the river. Unlike Major Davenport, Major Campbell didn't go into details about his travel route, just his personal life and his skirmishes. I was lucky enough that he mentioned that he had one hundred and sixty-three men. He even went into details about their specific numbers. My eyes skimmed short passage that talked about his company's movement to Saratoga and the details about his men. Rubbing my eyes, I read it again, hoping to catch something new this time.

I took command of one hundred and sixty-three of his Majesty's finest fighting men. They are disciplined and well trained. I have under my command: one captain, four junior lieutenants, eight drummers, two wagon drivers, one hundred and forty-four infantry men and four of his majesty's finest riflemen. My four sharpshooters have been given the new, long rifles that shoot much more accurately than our common rifles. One of my men, a John Brooks, has promised me that he can kill a rebel from three hundred yards, yet I shall not give him credit for this until I see him do it myself.

The Major went on and talked about following the river to Saratoga. Then he went into more details about the battle itself. I didn't care about the battle because it was my goal to prevent him from making it to Saratoga. If I accomplished that, then his participation at Saratoga would never happen.

The only other interesting fact that I read was that he mentioned that it had begun snowing right before they reached Saratoga. The four sharpshooters could shoot from almost the same distance I could, so I lost my advantage to stand far away and waste ammunition like I had with Major Davenport's men.

A wave of shivers covered my skin in goose pimples. Unlike my horses, I didn't have a coat of fur to wear against the oncoming cold. The time had come to put on my thermal underwear. I had never worn long johns before, and their warmth immediately comforted me. Cozy in my warmer clothes and on a bed of hay, I fell asleep contemplating my resources and trying to come up with a strategy to stop this Major Campbell.

I pried my eyes open the next morning while the barn was still shrouded in darkness. I choked down the last of my powdered eggs and smoked fish. When I rubbed my hand over my jaw, my fingers caught on the scruffy beard, and I realized that I had not shaven in several days. Rising on stiff legs, I pissed in the corner of the barn, then packed up my blanket and other items. I nudged Little Joe awake and saddled him. I fed grain to him and the other horses and hung my backpack on Little Joe's saddle horn again. Then I secured two barrels of black powder to one of the spare horses and headed out with Little Joe.

The morning was still early, gray, and even colder. White puffs of breath formed as I exhaled, and dismal, angry clouds were coming my way. According to Major Campbell, snow would begin to fly tomorrow or the next day. I thought about General Washington and how cold his men had to be. When

I was finished with Major Campbell and his men, I was going to need to do whatever I could to help at Valley Forge.

I stayed on the south side of the river until I found a bridge. The bridge and the fast-running water below gave me an idea. I rode across and stopped to set one of the barrels of gun powder down, standing it up in the middle of the bridge. I then placed the other barrel against a tree on the other side, also standing it up on its end so that it could be seen from the south side of the river. I rode back across the bridge to the south side of the river and tied the horses off about fifty yards into the tree line.

The tree line on my side of the river to the tree line on the other side of the river was one hundred and fifteen yards, according to my range finder. That meant that one hundred and sixty-three rifles would be able to reach me from the farthest points. The truth was, it was impossible for me to kill one hundred and sixty-three men on my own, rumors or no. The way Major Campbell bragged about his men, I didn't think I could scare them off as I had with Major Davenport's soldiers. This was a battle I couldn't win. My only hope was to get them to chase me south, causing them to miss the battle all together.

Whoever came up with the saying *better late than never* wasn't talking about war.

TEN: Brown Coats

THE SUN HAD RISEN into the sky but was blocked by the darkening clouds. At midday it was still cold, but at least I could no longer see my own breath. I settled between a tree and a large rock with bushes surrounding me for coverage. I had set up a secondary position, twenty yards behind me. If I ran from there, I was just going to make a break for the horses.

It had warmed up to about fifty degrees, and even laying on my jacket and with my thick pants, the ground was damn cold and damp. How long could I lay here without the cold affecting me? And shivering would ruin my aim.

After about two hours, two scouts rode slowly into view. One was riding right next to the river and the other was at the tree line. They rode on, passing by the bridge. Thanks to the bushes I placed in front of the barrel, they didn't see it. I was waiting for the Major to appear when a horse snorted behind me and to my left.

I slowly turned my head in the direction of the noise. Two additional scouts on horseback were on this side of the river and riding straight towards me. *Fuck.*

Major Campbell was smarter than I'd given him credit for. He had scouts on both sides of the river. Cursing at myself under my breath, I shook my head. Why hadn't I considered this? It's what I would have done if I were in his shoes. Major Campbell wasn't as foolish or as arrogant as some of the other British officers.

This new development left me no choice. I was going to have to kill them. Even if they rode by without spotting me, they might find my horses. If for no other reason, I didn't want them on *this* side of the river when the shooting started.

I slowly rolled onto my back, praying the dying grass and leaves didn't crunch and announce my location. I pulled out my Tec-9 and stayed low. Move to better cover was a sound idea, but if I sat up, they would see me. Once they were about twenty feet away, I closed my eyes and pretended to be dead. A horrible plan, but what other options did I have?

One of them yelled, "Over there!"

Even with my eyes closed, I sensed they had seen me and would be on me in a few seconds. From the sounds of the horses halting and the creaking of leather, I knew they were getting off their horses. Before the echoes of those sounds ended, I raised my head and pistol and fired two quick shots into each of them. They collapsed backwards onto the cold grass. Neither moved, and I thought I was safe until a yell came from across the river.

I rolled back over. The two scouts had stopped and were looking my way. I didn't know if they saw me or not, but they sure as hell watched the other two scouts fall over dead. I holstered my Tec-9 and grabbed my Thompson again. The two scouts fired their muskets. Their shots missed me by four or five feet, but it was obvious that they found me. Breathing lightly through my nose, I aimed and fired, hitting one of the two men, knocking him off his horse. The other galloped towards the bridge, and I scrambled to reload. I wasn't ready for this to kick off yet.

With a steady gaze, I waited for him to get closer as I holstered my Thompson and pulling out my Tec-9. When he was halfway across the bridge, I fired my last two rounds. He flew off his horse and landed face first on the bridge. The horse kept running and galloped across the bridge at full sprint. I reloaded my Tec-9 and holstered it. Pulling my Thompson back out, I laid back down to watch what would happen next. My jaw tensed as I waited. I had a feeling this wasn't going to go down the way I had planned it.

Major Campbell, resplendent in his formal red coat, and two officers broke through the tree line, searching for danger. Foot soldiers ran alongside the horses, trying to keep up. Major Campbell held up a hand, and the officers halted as the Major yelled orders that I couldn't make out.

The soldiers formed two ranks, one going across from the river to the tree line on their side and one along the river. Major Campbell wasn't sure where the threat was, but he was covering both his front and side. *Smart man.*

I estimated about seventy or eighty men, so I figured the other half of his men, and the rest of his officers were covering his rear and the other flank. The foot soldiers marched in step, moving forward, with the right flank that faced the river marching forward with them. They stayed in step and appeared confident. Major Campbell had not embellished the fact that his men were well trained.

I wasn't going to be able to hold out against this force. Once I fired my first shot, I wasn't going to survive the return fire. I had hoped to let these men go by and come up with another plan. When the soldiers stopped at the bridge, the Major pointed to the dead scout in the clearing and then to the dead scout on the bridge. He was searching for the other two scouts on my side of the river. I hoped that the bushes and trees hid their bodies, but my hopes were crushed into a sour ball in my stomach when he pointed my way. I glanced over my shoulder to find the two horses that the scouts had been riding were still standing behind me. He looked for his now missing scouts.

This wasn't my best plan, and it was going to shit fast.

The Major was still yelling orders at his men, his commanding tone carrying over the river. Two soldiers were dressed differently than the rest of his men. They wore brown coats and not red coats and carried muskets longer than the regular muskets. These two soldiers must be two of the four sharpshooters I'd read about. A detail of about thirty men formed up and were crossing the bridge. My original plan was simple. I was going to wait for the Major to get close to the first barrel of gunpowder and shoot it, hoping to kill him. Then, as the soldiers came across the bridge, I'd shoot the second barrel, killing more soldiers and blowing up the bridge at the same time.

Now that the soldiers were coming across without Campbell, I was going to have to shoot the barrel on the bridge first. If I were lucky, the explosion from the barrel would hide the sound of my pistol. As the soldiers closed in on the barrel, they stopped to check on the dead scout laying face down. With another light breath, I fired my Thompson and the barrel detonated in a brilliant flash of light and a deafening ear-piercing thunderclap that moments later became a high pitch ringing in my ears. I ducked down against the explosion but peeked my eyes open to see the result.

The blast killed the men on the bridge and a few on the other side of it. The explosion also did a wonderful job demolishing the middle of the bridge. Wood and debris rained down on both sides of the river. Soldiers covered their heads or dived to the ground, trying to protect themselves from the onslaught. Other soldiers ran for the trees for cover. One of the sharpshooters, recognizing the Major was an easy target high on the mount, reached up and yanked the Major unceremoniously off his horse.

The ringing in my ears was followed by the agonizing screams of those soldiers lucky enough not to have been killed by the blast, but unlucky enough to have been hit by the concussion of the shock wave or wood shrapnel.

I reloaded my Thompson slowly, moving as little as possible while still hiding. The two sharpshooters had their muskets up and were looking for me. The sound of my last shot had been hidden by the explosion of the gunpowder. If I shot the Major or one of the sharpshooters, I'd be giving my hiding spot away. The rest of the soldiers scattered blindly in all directions, and a few fired randomly into the trees.

One of the officers yelled at the men to not shoot unless they had a target as he tried to regain control and return order to his ranks. Once the debris stopped falling from the sky, soldiers began to climb to their feet or run out of the tree line and back into formation, as if they had never run off in the first place. The Major was searching for a way to send his troops across the river. The water was running too swiftly and was too deep for the soldiers to cross. Realizing his conundrum, the Major waved his arms to order his men to fall back into the tree line. They were abandoning those dead and wounded men where they laid. I didn't think I could have done that to my men.

The sharpshooters leaned into the Major, and he nodded, heeding to whatever they were telling him. I hated it when enemy officers listened to sound advice. Either they were going to seek cover and wait for me to pop up, or they were going to abandon this distraction and continue to Saratoga. I still wanted to kill the Major or get him to chase me, and I laid hidden for nearly ten minutes, trying to figure out what they were planning. I had killed twenty-five or thirty of their soldiers but was still losing this chess match and was unsure what to do next. *Does the Major know that?*

It was time to try a different type of ambush. If I were going to run for the horses, a distraction was necessary. Time to shoot the other barrel, even though it was such a waste of gunpowder. I most likely would freak them out a little, but I doubted that I would kill more than the few that happened to be close to it.

When I shot the barrel, I wasn't surprised by the explosion that was a magnificent twin to the one on the bridge, accompanied by yelling and screaming in pain. With the soldiers' attention on the explosion, I ran for the tree line with my pistol in one hand and my jacket in the other. The tree I had set the barrel up against was falling over and landed on several more men that had run over to help the soldiers killed by the initial explosion. *Not bad.* I might have taken out eight or ten in total.

Shots rang out, splintering the tree trunks around me. A few soldiers yelled, "Pale Rider!" They must have recognized my white shirt and black vest, or maybe they thought that every bump in the night was the Pale Rider. Either way, the chase was on.

I made it to the horses and rode down river trying to get ahead of them, pushing the horses as fast as they could go. At a spot where the water was shallow, I slowed. From here, I could cross over to ambush them on the north side, but this was a significant risk. This Major was smart, and worse than that, he was shrewd, listening to advice from his sharpshooters. By the way they dressed, they were either Colonists or men from the countryside back in England. Either way they knew their way around the woods. They also knew to pull the Major off his horse before I decided to shoot him, so they understood guerrilla warfare. In many ways, these sharpshooters were a bigger threat to me then the Major. *I'll have to kill them first.* Not in my plan, but necessary.

Staying to the south side of the river, I hoped that the Major or one of the sharpshooters would have the same idea that I had. I had raced on horseback to get here, so I figured I had about twenty or thirty minutes before the Major and his men arrived in their measured march. Setting up traps would have been helpful, but I didn't have enough time for that.

There was only one thing to do. I took the bridle off the spare horse and left him between two trees where he could be seen easily enough by anyone walking into the tree line. I back tracked with Little Joe to a safe place where he wouldn't be seen. I then picked a large, thick maple tree between the horse and riverbank where I guessed they would come from. I also stuck a few rocks in my front pockets, just in case I need to get someone's attention. Silly maybe, but I was thinking of what my father always told me: *better to have it and not need it, than need it and not have it.*

Wrapping the horse bridle around the tree, I used it as I shimmied up the first ten feet of the tree trunk like a lumber jack. From there, I climbed higher from branch to branch. I was about thirty feet up and standing on a thick bough, with the bridle tied to my belt to prevent me from falling. I screwed my suppressor onto my Tec-9, settled down onto the branch like a deer hunter, and waited.

161

I only had to wait about twenty minutes before four scouts came into view. All were on foot and not horseback this time. I guess none of the officers wanted to give up their horses to the scouts.

A scout noticed the shallow spot in the river where I could have crossed over, if I had chosen to. They paused and began talking. One of them rushed back the way they had come while the other three hid in the tree line. A few minutes later, the rest of the company came into view.

Major Campbell dismounted from his steed and spoke with two of the sharpshooters. One of the men was the same who had pulled the Major off his horse. I didn't know if I was right, but I thought this man was the John Brooks that the Major had written about. The man I thought of as John Brooks pointed to the tree line on their side of the river. He was sure I was over there, on that side already, setting up another ambush. It had been my first thought, so he wasn't entirely wrong. Was this man trying to get into my head, and anticipate my next move?

The other brown coat pointed across to my side of the river. Then his arm waved upriver. I presume he wanted to cross over and try to come up behind me, just in case I was still on this side.

The Major must have decided to listen to his men. The man I was calling John Brooks, ran off with about forty soldiers into the tree line. They spread out searching for me, like dogs trying to flush out a fox.

The other sharpshooter waded across the river with about ten soldiers.

The Major climbed back into his saddle and rode off again, heading down river with the rest of his company and two wagons.

The brown coat and his ten men crossed over and headed to the tree line for cover. The sharpshooter was out front, and he must have instructed the others to stay behind him. I was betting he was afraid that they would make too much noise and alert me to their presence.

He spotted the horse right away and froze. He now knew I was here, close, but didn't know where. His eyes flashed — he didn't yell out, not wanting to give away his location, but he needed to flush me out. He moved closer to the horse, stopping about two trees in front of me, with his back to me. I had him in my sights when he waved to the others to move up to him. They poked around the woods, but none of them bothered to look up. I spared a glance across the river. The Major and his company were rounding the next bend and almost out of sight.

The sharpshooter whispered something to three of the soldiers, and they moved off to the right. He leaned in and spoke to three more soldiers, and they moved off to the left. He tapped two of the soldiers on their arms and pointed back the way they had come.

The edges of my lips curled up. *Impressive.* He was being careful about this. The two stopped at my tree, directly under me, and watched behind them. The sharpshooter took the last two men and moved slowly towards the horse. Waited until they were almost to the horse, I then leaned around the thick branch I was standing on.

The two soldiers were right there, straight down. I could have dropped on them but instead I fired one round into the top of each of their heads. They gave off a low grunt and made more noise falling over into the now blood-soaked dirt, than my pistol made firing the two rounds.

The sharpshooter made it to the horse and scanned the area. The soldiers from the left and right moved in and they met up. The sharpshooter crouched a bit, studying the ground. He must have found my tracks. The trees were thick and close together. The ground in that area was free of snow. My boots did leave deep enough boot prints in the dirt that any half-trained scout could follow. *Why didn't I cover my tracks better?*

He followed my tracks straight back to the tree I was in.

I couldn't remember – had I come straight to the tree, or if I had walked around? At first, I thought I'd come straight to the tree. If I was right, he was going to find me right away.

The sharpshooter turned left and crept silently away from me. He wasn't following *my* tracks; he was following Little Joe's horse tracks. The brown coat left two soldiers with the spare horse and took the other six with him. I waited until they were far enough away then focused in on the two minding the spare horse.

They were about forty yards from me, and that was too far to shoot with the Tec-9. The weight in my pockets as I moved gave me an idea.

I waited until neither was looking my way, then I threw a rock halfway between them and my tree. They each heard it plunk into the damp grass and moved in that direction. They did their best to move quietly, but they stepped on every twig they came across. I rolled my eyes. I was starting to think they were trying to make as much noise as possible.

When they were about twenty yards away, I threw another rock passed them, and they turned, presenting their backs to me. I took the shot and fired one round into each of their backs. They dropped hard to the ground, breaking more twigs, and I cringed. I changed my magazine out, putting the almost empty one in my other cargo pocket. With the one round left in the chamber and the fresh magazine of six rounds, I now had seven shots.

The sharpshooter came back into view, still studying the ground, inspecting my boot tracks this time. He only had four men with him, so I assumed he left two men with Little Joe. He froze in place when his face turned to the two dead soldiers. His eyes scanned around my tree and squinted back at the two dead soldiers beneath me. I held my breath, hoping he didn't glance up. His head twisted slowly to the left and then to the right. He didn't want to move. The expression on his face shifted as he finally realized that he wasn't hunting me – he was being hunted.

I tried not to smile at the nervous sensations that must have crawled over his skin. Four dead men, and he didn't hear any gunshots. He had to assume that I'd killed them with a knife or something up close. He stiffened and his eyes went wide as he searched the bushes right next to him, thinking I was a ghost or something worse. Pale Rider indeed.

One of his men started to say something, and he held a hand up to quiet him. These soldiers didn't have the training or patience to hunt a man in the woods, and the sharpshooter knew it. He would have been better off by himself.

He sent his four men forward, hoping to flush me out. They didn't know it, but they were prey. He knew I was near, and if I didn't miss my mark, he was hoping to shoot me as soon as I killed another of his men. His musket was set in his shoulder, his face tight against the stock, aiming his musket in the direction of his men – waiting for me to pop up so he could take me out. It really wasn't a bad idea. He was heartless about it, but I had to give him credit. His men were just assets to him, and he was using his assets to find me.

I waited until his men passed me so even if they did hear me, they wouldn't see me on this side of the tree. Once they were far enough away, I aimed my Tec-9 and fired three quick rounds at the sharpshooter. The first round hit his musket with a loud ping, like a hammer striking a piece of metal. The second shot hit him in the upper chest or shoulder. The third shot hit home – striking him low in his face. He plummeted backwards and dropped his musket, but he wasn't dead. His legs kicked out and he was trying to yell, but all that came out was a sick, wet gagging sound.

His four men were out of view behind me, and the sudden lack of twigs snapping, and crackling leaves told me that they had stopped. They listened to their leader kicking his legs in a panic as he spurts out his final few breaths. Hoping to shoot his killer, they fired their muskets into the bushes where their leader laid dying. Then they were running away from me, toward the river. They knew death lurked behind them, and they were trying to outrun it.

Bracing myself, I leaned around the tree trunk and fired my final four rounds at the last man in line. I didn't know where or how many times I hit him, but he splashed face first into the water. The other three paused to glance back at their friend who was being swept away by the shallow but swift current, but they didn't attempt a rescue. The three men turned and doubled their efforts, lifting their knees high to run faster through the water to get away from this killing field. I grinned at their retreat and had to wonder what they would tell their Major and how the ever-growing story of the Pale Rider would spread.

I shimmied down the tree and reloaded my Tec-9 again. Slowly and quietly, I made my way back to Little Joe. The two soldiers that remained had no idea what had happened to the rest of what used to be eleven-man detail. They must have heard the four muskets fire, but they didn't appear worried, figuring their friends had killed me. They were standing upright, and one was trying to calm down Little Joe who kept trying to draw away from them. The other soldier was digging through my saddle bags. Little Joe made so much noise that they never noticed me walk up behind them until it was too late. They each died with two quick shots.

My father once told me that if you're fighting fair, then you're not trying to win. I thought about those words as I unscrewed my suppressor from my Tec-9.

Little Joe didn't like standing next to two dead men at his feet, so I led him away from the soldiers. I fed him a granola bar to help distract him and calm him down. His large teeth and eager tongue devoured the bar, and he head-butted me for more.

Digging into my backpack, I pulled out a box of ammunition and reloaded my magazines. It wouldn't take long for the three survivors to catch up to their Major. I didn't think they would return and try crossing here, but what would they do? So far, the Major had lost over forty men, but the question was, what he'd do next. I thought that he'd have to come after me now.

My mind replayed the events today, and I realized it was the sharpshooter John Brooks that I was worried about. He seemed to understand the concept of a sniper and guerrilla fighter. I'd bet my last granola bar that he could predict what I was trying to do. If I were right, he would advise the Major to move faster and get to Saratoga without delay. His men were on foot, and I had two horses. I could stay ahead of them, so chasing me was a no-win situation. Letting me pick them off one by one was also not an ideal situation for the Major.

Time to review my options and conceive a new plan.

Second Chance

ELEVEN: The White Flag

THE DISTANCE BETWEEN Lake Ontario and Saratoga was about two hundred miles. The Major had already marched his men about a hundred and fifty miles, through dirt, then mud and now snow. They still had about fifty miles to go. His men had to be getting tired. I was sure John Brooks, and the Major were plotting a third option. Maybe moving away from the river? Maybe leaving an ambush behind them? If I were right about this John Brooks, I was sure he would want to hunt me down in the woods. The question was what course of action the Major would decide was best.

I needed to get ahead of them, but it wasn't safe to follow the river any longer. Too many places for them to set up an ambush. I'd have to move slowly, and I didn't have time for that. I was going to have to move away from the river, then cut back over to it, ahead of them.

I tied the spare horse to Little Joe and led them away from the river. When I was about a mile away, I stopped and fed the horses, then gave them some of my water. I sat down on a large rock and ate the last of my squirrel and weighed all my options.

What if they didn't follow the river? Then I might lose them. The Major had written in his journal that they had followed the river all the way to Saratoga, but I had changed the timeline when I attacked them, so I couldn't count on that. I didn't want to follow them on this side of the river for fear of ambushes. I couldn't try and get ahead of them for fear of losing them. As I picked squirrel from my teeth, I realized I had only two options. Either I was going to have to give up, or cross over and harass them until they gave chase.

Looking on my map, I found the next bridge, five miles upriver. I rode the horses hard, kicking up cold mud, trying to get there before the British so I could cross the river. When I neared the bridge, I dismounted and trekked to the tree line to make sure it was clear. There was truly little snow here. It was getting colder, and I knew it would start snowing here in a few days, but right now the snow was only less than an inch deep.

I froze where I stood before whipping behind a tree.

The sharpshooter that I had been calling John Brooks was standing on the bridge. He was alone with a horse tethered to the bridge railing. He also had a branch in his right hand with a white handkerchief tied to the end of it – a makeshift white flag.

What is this guy playing at?

I stood behind my tree, just watching him for a few minutes. He leaned the branch against the bridge, making sure it could still be seen and pulled out a small pouch. He packed a tobacco pipe and lit it. Then he picked up the branch again and stood there patiently, smoking his pipe.

I could have shot him right where he stood, but then he was standing in the open with a white flag, and if I shot him, I would never have known why he was there. I shrugged off my jacket, so my vest was visible, and I'd have freer movement of my arms. I stepped out into the open with my right-hand hovering over my Tec-9. His eyes flicked my way, and I barely made out a smile widening on his face. He turned his pipe upside down and tapped it against the bridge railing a few times. He methodically inspected the bowl and then blew in it, freeing any ashes that had not fallen out. He tucked the pipe away in the same pocket that he had pulled it from. We walked towards each other, meeting at the end of the bridge on my side.

"So, what's all this?" I asked him.

"I told the Major, this is where you would cross to get a head of us," he stated in a bored tone, his lips stained with tobacco. "I told him you'd harass us the whole way to Saratoga. Picking us off, one by one."

"John Brooks, I presume?" I asked.

I knew I was right by the shocked expression that crossed his face. To his credit, he covered it quickly, spat to the side, and smiled.

"At your service, sir," he countered with a dip of his head. "And you are . . . the Pale Rider?"

I nodded my head. "Personally, I think it's a little melodramatic. Then again, you British gave me that name."

"I like Washington's Assassin best," he said, laughing. "Then again, you didn't pick that one either. The Colonists seem to think it's true. You are a bit of a mascot."

He stated it as a fact, but the statement sounded like a question. I think he was hoping for confirmation on whether I was Washington's personal assassin or not.

"You said you knew I was coming across this bridge," I told him, pointing to the bridge itself. "How'd you know I wasn't going to shoot you?"

"You learn lot about a man when you hunt him," he said somewhat smugly. "You killed my friend and seven other soldiers, and no one seems to know how, but you let the last three live because they had their backs turned to you and were running away. No, I have reason to believe that you're an honorable gentleman."

"Whoever told you that was mistaken." I told him. "Four were running away from me, and I shot the last one in the back."

His hazel eyes went wide as he realized that he had made a huge miscalculation and was lucky to not be dead right now.

"I guess the three that got away didn't tell you that?" I asked. "Why are you here and not just setting up an ambush for me?"

"I thought we could settle this like gentlemen and in a way that didn't involve you killing any more soldiers," he said.

He didn't seem like the kind of guy that would give two shits if I killed more of the common foot soldiers. He definitely wasn't going to risk his life for them.

"Sure," I replied. "Tell Major Campbell to turn around and go back to Lake Ontario, and I won't kill any more of his men."

His eyebrows rose at my mention of the Major's name and where they had come from. It was, after all, a hundred and fifty miles from here. George Washington had spies everywhere, and even he might not have known that Major Campbell was heading to Saratoga.

"I'm afraid the Major will never agree to that," he said. "He is under orders after all. I'd like to make you a counteroffer. The Major is a practical man and understands that, without a cavalry unit to chase you down, it would be difficult to neutralize one man on horseback. He has agreed to allow me to handle this my way. I have advised him to move several miles away from the river and wait for me to return."

"What'd you have in mind?" I asked.

"A fight between just you and me," he said flatly.

"Rifles?" I looked around but didn't see his musket.

"Two professionals hunting each other in the woods would be the best way to prove who's best, but no. That would take too long. I was more thinking knives."

"What's in it for me?" I asked. "Why don't I shoot you right here and right now?"

"The Major is camped with his men," he explained. "He will wait for me to return in the morning with your head. If I win, I get to take your head to him, and maybe even receive some small notice by his Majesty King George. I'll tell you right where they are camped, before we fight, so if you win... Well, we both know what kind of damage you are capable of doing tonight, since you'll know right where they will be. Don't we, Assassin?"

That final word held a note of derision. "Not good enough," I said. "Too much risk and not enough reward. You need to put more in the pot to make it worth the risk."

He scowled and thought about it for a few seconds. "I cannot give you any secrets. That'd be treason."

"Not if I'm dead," I retorted.

"True," he said, more to himself then to me. "We know that your General Washington is regrouping his men at Valley Forge. Major Campbell has orders on his person for General

173

Burgoyne to take Major Davenport and Major Campbell's companies and attack Saratoga. After that, they are to report to General Sir Henry Clinton and inform him of General Washington's location. The information came from one of our spies. If you stop Major Campbell, then General Burgoyne will never get those orders, and General sir Henry Clinton won't learn of Washington or of this, Valley Forge place, where Washington and his men are hiding. Your precious General Washington would be safe, for a little longer at least."

He said the name Valley Forge as if it was a cursed graveyard or something. Then again, he didn't say the name Washington with any love in his voice, either.

"Ok," I said. "But we go deeper into the woods." I jerked my thumb behind me pointing to the trees on this side of the bridge.

I didn't want to take the chance that he might have men hidden in the tree line, on the other side, waiting for me to be distracted. He nodded as I gazed over the trees on the north side and understood my concern.

"Agreed," he said cheerily.

We headed back to where I'd secured Little Joe and the spare horse, about twenty feet into the tree line. He pulled out a large but thin boot knife with his left hand. It appeared more like a dagger then a real knife, like something his mother might have given him. He then extracted a larger hunting knife from his belt with his right hand – one with wide blade with a smooth redwood handle. His mother didn't give him *that* one. I held up my left hand to stop him from moving forward and kept my right hand on my holstered Tec-9, ready to draw and fire.

"First the location," I said.

"Two miles due north of the bridge, on a hillside," he said. "They'll have extra sentries out tonight."

Of course they will.

I took my hand off my Tec-9 and pulled out my two twelve-inch knives.

"Why knives?" I asked again, while we side-stepped to our left, circling each other. "Why not pistols? A duel of sorts."

"Did you really kill Sergeant Major Brown in a fair knife fight?" he asked, his face stony and his eyes hooded.

"Yes," I answered plainly. "He was a tough bastard."

"That bastard was my uncle," he said. "My favorite uncle. On my mother's side."

I found myself hoping that his favorite uncle had not bothered to teach him knife fighting. His uncle had been a truly tough son of a bitch. The thing I remembered most about that fight, even more then the bayonet in the shoulder, was the relief of fighting him in the dark. I was happy that I hadn't fought him in the light. He'd been a really scary motherfucker.

John held his knives easily with his fingertips, with blades pointing at me. I held mine a little tighter with the blades facing down. His knives were in front of his body, ready to stab forward with either hand. I held my hands up in a boxer stance, with both blades in front of my face. He was going to go for stabs, while I was going to go for slashes. We were well met.

In a sudden move, he lunged forward and faked a jab, testing me. I shifted back and blocked, so he hit nothing but air and blade. We circled each other again. Neither of us was walking away unbloodied. I spun the knife in my right hand, so it was facing up, leaving the other facing down. He pushed forward with another fake, still testing me. This time I surged

175

forward, blocking with my left hand, and stabbing with my right. My block hit only his blade again, but the knife in my right hand sliced the air close to his flesh. He jumped back at the last second and barely avoided a cut to the face.

Something didn't feel right here. My brain worked overtime, trying to assess his motives, his behavior. This guy was trying to kill me in a way that avoided being cut himself. If he knew anything about knife fighting, he should know everyone gets cut in a knife fight. If he weren't adept enough at knife fighting to know this, then why would he choose knives instead of guns? He had faked an attack twice, keeping me at a distance. Sergeant Major Brown attacked with no regard for his own safety. His only concern was killing me, even if that meant sacrificing his own life. This guy was holding back, waiting for something, but what? Looking for an opening? Hoping I made a mistake? I was still missing something.

And I didn't like it, not one bit.

Then it happened – time simultaneously slowed down and sped up and I knew in an instant what was going on. The distinct sound of a dead twig snapping under the weight of a heavy foot broke our silence. Out of reflex and survival skills, I dove to my right without thought. As I combat rolled, a gunshot rang out. I came up ready to face John Brooks and whatever unknown threat had stepped into our arena of death.

I wasn't surprised to find a British soldier in a brown coat, holding a flintlock pistol, standing about ten feet behind where I had been, moments ago. Gun smoke drifting from the barrel. A mask of shock and horror marked his face as he stared ahead. I followed his gaze and shock clamped down on my chest. John Brooks was sprawled on his back, a dark red stain seeping through his coat. He held his stomach with both hands, as blood was oozing between his fingers. Again, without a second thought, I threw the knife that was in my right hand at the distracted newcomer, and then the knife in my left. He smacked the first knife out of the air with the discharged flintlock pistol. The second knife, however, hit home and buried itself deep into the right side of the man's chest.

Diving through the air again, I rolled to my feet with my Tec-9 in my hand. I scanned the woods and listened for any other threats. The only sounds were the moans from the two British soldiers. I trudged over to the man who clutched at my knife sticking out of his chest. His eyes went wide as I stepped into his view. He knew who I was, and fear painted his face in a grotesque mask. This man had the look of a child laying eyes on a boogieman. I raised my pistol, and he held up a hand in a futile attempt to block my shot and closed his eyes as he turned his head away. As if any of that was going to save him.

Instead of shooting him, I bent over and rested a boot on his chest. I grabbed my knife handle and yanked with a hard jerk, tearing the knife out of him. He screamed as his chest skin and muscle ripped, and his back arched as if he thought it would hurt less to go with the knife instead of resisting its exit. I caused more damage pulling the knife free, than it caused going in. I'm sure the knife hurt like hell when it was stuck in his chest, but like a cork in a wine bottle, it was also holding his blood in and keeping him alive.

With the cork now removed, his blood spurted free in fountain. In a real asshole move, I crouched and wiped my knife clean on his jacket, adding insult to injury. I picked up his pistol, tossing it into the bushes. Then I retrieved my other knife that laid a few feet away and forgot about the man. He was going to shoot me in the back, so, fuck him.

I went over to John Brooks, who laid in the wet grass under a tree, on his back, holding his stomach with his hands. His two knives laid on the ground and I kicked them away from him.

"It was a respectable plan," I told him in a casual voice.

Who was I to judge? I had shot plenty of men in the back these past few days. He was only doing exactly what I'd done.

"Not good enough," he gasped between heavy breaths.

"Was he hiding on this side of the river, the whole time?" I asked.

"Yes," he answered breathlessly. "I figured you'd expect a hidden surprise on the other side."

"Is Sergeant Major Brown even your uncle?" I asked. I had to know. It had been a good tale.

He barked out a wet laugh, red droplets spraying from his mouth. "Never even met the man. I heard what you did and thought it made my story more believable."

I couldn't help myself and laughed a bit with him.

"What about the camp and the orders that you mentioned?" I asked. I pointed my pistol at him as I stopped laughing. "Speak true."

"I spoke the truth about both," he told me. "I thought you'd be dead by now and didn't see any reason to lie about that."

I lowered my pistol as he started coughing up blood in crimson bubbles. Turning my back on him, I strode away with purpose. Without any medical attention, both men were as good as dead anyways.

"Well done, Pale Rider," he wheezed out from behind me.

As I rode Little Joe toward the bridge, the hair on the back of my neck stood up. I stiffened and peered over to where John Brooks laid. Major Campbell wrote that he had

178

four sharpshooters under his command. I'd killed three so far. I had the sinking feeling that this John Brooks wasn't the gracious loser that he was pretending to be.

My gaze shifted from where he laid, to across the river at the tree line and the bridge that I was preparing to cross. Did he really guess that I was going to want to fight on this side of the river? Did he only put a man on this side of the bridge, or did he cover all his bases? The bridge appeared to stretch out before my eyes, and now looked to be a lot longer than it had a second ago. And I already knew the answer. I just needed to confirm it.

I reined Little Joe around and rode back into the tree line where John Brooks still held his stomach. His eyes widened when I returned.

"Who's on the other side?" I asked in a sharp voice, as I swung down from the saddle.

"What? No one. You won. The Major is camped and waiting right where I said."

My stare didn't waver, and I stepped up next to him. "You didn't plead or barter for your life," I said out loud, as I pieced it together myself. "You knew your man across the river would come find you after he killed me."

The sharpshooter didn't say a word. His eyes held mine steadily, and his smile contracted into a scowl. The lines around his eyes twisted and twitched, as the laughter he had a minute ago, turned to scorn, then contempt and lastly settling on hatred.

"I can see it in your eyes," I said. "Even after being shot, you thought you'd won. You knew I was as good as dead."

I pulled my pistol out with the full intention of ending his life.

"No, wait," he gasped, panic finally tinging his voice. "You're right. Don't shoot, please."

"Like I said, it was a fine plan, but you lost. This round at least. I can't take the chance of your man finding you and getting you to a doctor. I can't have you coming for me, looking for revenge."

"I won't," he pleaded. "I swear."

At that, I snorted. I couldn't believe a word this snake said. Why had I trusted him to begin with? No honor among snipers.

"I surrender!" he hollered. "You can't kill an enemy soldier who surrenders."

"Yell for your man," I commanded.

"What?" John asked confused.

"Yell for help," I clarified. "Call him over."

"You'll shoot him as he crosses the bridge," he argued in a weak voice. He was fading and would die if he didn't get help.

"Yes," I said coldly. "I will. That's what he was going to do to me. Call him over here, and you can have his horse. I'll let you ride for Fort Stanwix. It's controlled by your people and only twenty miles from here. You might make it there before you die."

Getting shot in the stomach was one of the most painful places to get shot, but it usually took a long time to die. And it was a painful, miserable death. As cold as it was this time of year, the temperature might slow his blood flow enough to keep him alive for a bit longer.

"Don't do it, John," the soldier who was bleeding from his chest cried out.

The soldier's voice was weak and his breathing ragged. He tried to stand but crashed down on his face. Most people don't realize how much more damage a knife laceration can cause than a bullet hole wound. People also bleed more from

180

a knife gash. A lot more – death from blood loss alone was common.

"Good advice from the man who shot you," I said to John Brooks. "He'll be dead in a minute. Is this how you want to die? Protecting your man, while you lay there, holding guts, bleeding to death? Or do you want to grab whatever chance you have? You can ride his horse to the fort and be treated by a doctor." I tipped my head to the side. "You might live."

He didn't say anything out loud but nodded his head in answer. Trading his friend's life for his was one thing, but saying you'd do so out loud somehow, made it different, worse even.

John Brooks yelled into the air. "Fredrick. Fredrick, get over here. I need you."

I led my horses away as he continued to yell. I tied the horses to a tree and found a spot where I could observe the bridge. My range finder was in my backpack, but I found a point on the bridge that I estimated was fifty yards from where I hid. I pulled out my Thompson and had to wait a mere minute before the other, and I hoped last man came into view. He trotted his horse across the bridge with his rifle in his left hand and a snide smile on his face. The beating of horseshoes against the wooded bridge was loud. It had a pleasant but rushed sound to it, making the sound of the horse seem faster than the horse was actually going. He believed I was dead, shot in the back by his two associates and fellow sharpshooters.

There was a weird respect regarding snipers. A sniper might shoot an unexpected enemy who had no idea they were in danger, but at the same time, the sniper was usually behind enemy lines, on their own, with little to no help. Being a sniper was more than just pulling a trigger. In fact, pulling the trigger was the easy part. Getting close enough to the enemy to take the shot without being seen, finding the right place to shoot, knowing elevation and windage, and most of all having the patience to lay in one spot without moving for hours, maybe days, waiting for the right moment, those were the real challenges to being an exceptional sniper. I had respect for snipers. I had been trained as one, in my anti-terrorism training.

What these men did wasn't sniping or even open warfare. They held up a white flag under the pretense of an honest parley only to shoot me in the back. This man coming over the bridge right now planned on shooting me as I came across the same bridge. I had no respect for him.

I paused to clear my mind. If I were going to kill this man, I wanted to do it coldly, without emotion not with any fiery anger in my heart. Killing was a fundamental part and a necessary evil in war and not an action that should be done with any joy or fury.

I cleared my mind and justified what I was doing as true sniping. I was killing the enemy as he foolishly came across the bridge in the open. That was my final thought as I pulled the trigger.

My job done; I ran out into the roadway to stop the riderless horse. Grabbing the horse's reins, I was able to calm him down. Once calmed, I searched through the horse's saddle bags, where I found some survival tools and personal gear. I commandeered the saddle bags and water bags and placed them on my spare horse. Then I led the horse over to John Brooks, who was still down, grasping his stomach.

"Take off your coat," I directed him.

"Why?" he asked in surprised grimace. "You promised to let me go."

"I never promised to let you keep your coat," I replied. "If you don't get to a doctor soon, you'll die. Bleed to death or freeze to death, but you'll die. You can try to warn Major Campbell that I'm coming, but you'll have to admit that you failed, and unless he has a doctor with him, you'll also die. You can find a doctor at Fort Stanwix, but you'll die of frostbite unless you ride nonstop."

Without saying a word, hatred burning in his eyes, he held his stomach as he struggled to his feet. He tugged off his brown coat, first one arm, then the other, keeping one hand on his gaping midsection at all times. With a low deep moan of pain, he climbed onto the horse's back and trotted down the road the way I had come. I had no doubt he'd go straight to Fort Stanwix. He cared too much about his own life to warn Major Campbell, and I knew from Major Campbell's own words that he didn't have a doctor with him anyway.

I also pulled the brown coat off the now dead soldier in the grass. Walking my two horses across the bridge, I stopped to collect the fourth and last sharpshooter's rifle and coat as well. I collected John Brooks' horse and located the soldier's horse hidden behind some trees. I examined all the rifles they'd had, and the weapons did seem nicer, longer, and better built than the more common muskets I'd seen so far. I searched the saddle bags and found some maps and food. After gnawing on some dried beef, I'd found in one of the saddle bags, I put the maps into my own saddle bags. Giving Little Joe a break, I decided to ride John Brooks' horse for a while.

Second Chance

TWELVE: Working at Night

I TRAVELED NORTH, hoping that John Brooks wasn't lying. After about a mile, I located Major Campbell's tracks and followed them. I wasn't a great tracker, but half a dozen horses, two heavy wagons, and over a hundred men, leave a lot of tracks in their wake. Major Campbell liked to march in the open fields. I didn't know if this was his mentality or if it was due to the wagons, but it made it easy for me to follow them. The worrisome part of following them was that this left me in the open. When I caught up to them, I'd be easy to spot.

As the sun tucked itself into the pinkish-gray horizon, and the wind blustered cold and sharp, I finally spotted their camp. I hesitated to call it a hill, but John Brooks was telling the truth – they had set up camp on a rise in the middle of an open field. The closest tree line was a good five hundred yards away from them. Sentries stood guard around the camp, and another had a post at the top of the rise where he could see in all directions.

The temperature was dropping fast and plenty of fires had been kindled in and around the camp. Snow had not fallen this far north yet, but the grass under my feet had frozen as night came on and crunched with every step. There was no way for me to get close and not be seen or heard. I couldn't fire from the tree line at that distance, so once again, my options were running low. I hitched the horses onto the trees and moved as close as I dared to the camp without being spotted. After wiping the horses down and feeding them, I picked at some food while sitting on a log and observing the camp, weighing my options. Towards the center of the camp, four soldiers were bound and guarded. They wore blue coats, marking them as General Washington's men. If I could save them, I would, but I had to remind myself that this wasn't a rescue mission.

By the time I had finished eating, I had only come up with two ideas. The first was to wait to see if an opportunity presented itself tomorrow. *Ahh, my good friend procrastination.* That plan involved riding ahead of them and picking off a few men at a time. This was the safer choice.

The second was to harass them all night tonight and deny them sleep, causing fear as the primary objective. This notion was more dangerous, but I decided it was the more effective option. A tired soldier was a weak soldier indeed.

Using the three brown coats I had liberated from the British, a bit of high grass and the black duct tape in my backpack, I made myself a poor excuse for a Ghillie suit.

Ghillie suits employed by snipers were designed to break up their form and blend into their surroundings. What I had made was more of a Ghillie blanket that I could hide under and crawl with. Not quite the design intended by its creators. I'd use it at night, so mine didn't need to be as good as a twenty-first century Ghillie suit. Mine was a far cry from that.

By the time I was ready to go, my watch said it was a little after eight o'clock. I removed my coat and satchel so that I wouldn't snag them on anything. I placed a few extra Tec-9 magazines and 30-30 rounds in my cargo pocket. Then I put one of my dirty pairs of socks in with the extra rounds to block any flash from the gun when the time came. Crawling from the tree line with the blanket over me, I crept fast at first, knowing no one would be able to see me at night, in tall grass, from five hundred yards away. Once I reached about three hundred yards, I slowed down and became more cautious. Right around nine o'clock, I was within two hundred feet of the camp.

For a ghillie suit, my blanket wasn't as useful as I would have liked it, but in a time when men stood out in the open to shoot at each other, it was the finest and first ghillie suit ever made to date. In fact, the next Ghillie suit wouldn't be made until one hundred and thirty-nine years from now. No one would think to look for a man hiding under a blanket, disguised as a bush. By Colonists' standards, I was invisible.

The British chose the high ground in the field and that made military sense. It also gave me a clear view of fire to any spot in their camp. Peeking my head out, I searched for the easiest targets first.

Most of the camp was bathed in darkness, and from this distance, it was hard to make out anything with detail. Three soldiers lingered around a fire, trying to stay warm. I decided to rely on the fires to make it easy for me to pick out and aim in on individual people.

I pulled out my pistols, setting the Tec-9 under the blanket next to me in case I needed it, and held onto my

Thompson. The three soldiers were passing a bottle back and forth as they tried to stay warm. They didn't seem to be on guard for any enemies. In their defense, the tree line was five hundred yards away, so in theory, no one should be able to get near them without being seen. These thoughts went through my head as I pulled out one of my socks and slipped it over the barrel of my Thompson. I pulled a strip of duct tape and wrapped it around the sock, halfway up the barrel of the pistol. I ripped the top of the sock, pushing the front sight through so that I could still use it.

There were only two ways they would find me if I fired my pistol. The first was if they could pinpoint where I was by sound. For that, I hoped that the gun shot would echo off the trees and make it hard for them to determine my location.

The other way they might find me was if someone happened to be looking my way and caught the flash that my gun would put out when I fired. I had never tried this before, but my hope was the sock would cut the flash down. The bullet would go through the sock, leaving a hole, but the sock would still catch and hide much of the flame that the barrel would produce. The flame itself was tiny and not noticeable in the daylight but could be particularly noticeable at night.

No one appeared to be facing my way, so I aimed at one of the three standing by the fire. I picked the one whose face I could see. The other two had their backs to me, which would help cut down on the chances of being seen. I carefully and slowly squeezed the trigger of my Thompson, and the sound waves from the shot bounced off the trees in a vibrating echo. The soldier hit the ground while the echo was still reverberated, sounding like four shots as the sound wave bounced back and forth.

I ducked back down under the blanket as men in the camp yelled and scrambled for safety. Officers screamed orders, and the whole camp was now awake and moving. Muskets were aimed in every direction as men hollered about being under attack.

With one finger, I set the alarm on my watch for an hour and rested my head on my arms, my entire body hidden under the blanket. Time to nap while they panicked.

When my watch vibrated on my wrist at ten, I blinked awake and pushed the button that turned off the vibration of the alarm. I poked my head out of the blanket to investigate. The soldiers were on alert, with some of them awake but most sleeping at their post. Their lazy behavior might have shocked me if I hadn't already encountered it.

I aimed my Thompson and fired again, watching one of the soldiers who a minute ago had been awake, collapse backwards. Again, my gunshot reverberated off the trees and echoed back and forth. I ducked back down and reloaded my Thompson, listening to the whole camp come back alive. This time men yelled, "Pale Rider!"

Why, yes, it is, I laughed to myself.

I laid there for about ten minutes and finally peeked out. Soldiers with torches stalked the tall grass between the camp and my position. They only covered about fifty feet from the camp, not even coming close to me. The thought that someone could aim and shoot one of them from any distance beyond that, in the dark, was implausible to them. Even for Pale Rider.

I returned to the cover of my blanket and set my watch to wake me at midnight. I fell back to sleep only to be awakened by my watch in what felt like no more than a few minutes. I rubbed my eyes to wake myself up.

This time I crawled to my right about two hundred yards. I was afraid the Major may have ordered the men to watch for the discharge of my pistol the next time I fired. It's what I might have done if I was in his shoes, and he had to be catching on. It took me an hour to crawl the two hundred yards and find a spot that I was sure I blended into. This time, when I peered out of my blanket, I found that the whole camp was still alert. The campfires had doubled, and a few fires burned outside the camp on the side I had last shot from.

I adjusted my sock so that it would still prevent most of the flash and propped up the front of my blanket with two twigs that I found as I had crawled through the field. This time, I'd fire from inside the blanket and hoped no one could see the flash. I used a pair of earplugs this time, since the blanket might hold in most of the sound.

With a steady finger on the trigger, I fired on one of two men who were closest to me. I was still two hundred feet away, and he was sitting on a log, and I wasn't sure if he was awake or asleep. I dropped the twigs and laid there, not moving. This time I didn't hear my gunshot bouncing off the trees. The soldiers fired their muskets in all directions, shooting at a ghost.

One of the officers yelled at the men not to fire unless they saw movement, but discipline had gone right out the window and they kept shooting. Two impacts sounded close to me, and I ducked my head. Two more officers joined in on the yelling, and they finally got their men under control and the shooting stopped. The night went deadly quiet. I could picture every man in camp staring into the field and beyond to the tree line. I pictured their conundrum of hoping to find me while at the same time fearing to see the devil himself.

Ten minutes went by before I registered any movement. I risked a peek. About sixty men arrived, broken up into three groups. Each group had an officer screaming at them as they marched through the grass. A few men held torches high while others stabbed bushes with bayoneted muskets. The men kept glancing back at the camp, as if every step they took away from it was a step closer to death.

When they made it a hundred feet from the camp, the men talked about going back. The officers kept herding the men like cattle, shouting for them to keep going farther and farther from the camp. One officer threatened to make a soldier go all the way to the tree line if he didn't stop acting, "like a stupid under paid superstitious whore."

With every step they came closer to me, but the soldiers also pushed back harder on the officers, arguing that I wasn't out here, even though they knew I was. Some of the soldiers were whining that they needed to get back to the camp. The soldiers shot into the bushes and at any rabbit or field mouse that moved. When they made it within thirty feet of me, I broke into a worrying sweat and forced myself to remain still, even as my sweat dripped into my eyes.

One particular officer pushed a group of men harder than the other two officers were. Propping my blanket up again with my twigs, I knew something had to be done or they'd either randomly step on me or shoot me by as they fired into bushes. I pulled out and aimed my Tec-9 with suppressor in the officer's direction and waited, letting the barrel follow him as I studied his men. As one of the men raised his musket to fire into what he must have thought was a menacing bush, I squeezed back on the trigger. He fired his musket at the same time I fired my pistol. Dropping the twigs and holding still, I listened to what happened next.

The soldiers panicked, and without the officer to keep them in line, they raced back for the camp and the safety of the campfires. Panic can be like a disease, spreading quickly from one person to another. The other two groups, seeing the panicked men run for the camp, joined them in an all-out sprint. I knew Major Campbell wouldn't stand for this and would have the men back out here one way or another.

Once the soldiers had retreated, I resumed my crawling to the left. I made it about twenty yards before soldiers started shouting again, followed by a shot ringing out in the night. I froze and stuck my head out of the blanket to take note of the camp. Major Campbell stood like a monument over a slain soldier. Maybe he refused to go back out into the field, or maybe Major Campbell was making an example out of one of his men. He needed to regain command, and there were only two ways to do that. Respect or fear, and respect was no longer working.

I decided I had done enough damage for the night and turned back towards the tree line. While I had only killed two soldiers and an officer, I had also caused sufficient havoc within the camp to the point where Major Campbell had killed one of his own men.

By the time I had made it back to Little Joe, Major Campbell had men out in the field, setting fire to the grass and bushes. It was far too cold for this to have the effect he hoped for. I led the horses away farther from the camp. After finding a thick copse of trees, I settled the horses and laid down amongst the tree roots to get another three hours of sleep, confident that Major Campbell's men wouldn't be getting any sleep themselves tonight.

When I woke, I left the horses dozing where they were and headed back to the tree line. The camp was packed up and the men were moving out. They moved around noticeably slower than they had earlier in the night. The officer sent out scouts, then led the weary company themselves. It was a smart move, because to do anything else would show fear to the men. The soldiers marched behind them with the wagons last. The four prisoners were at the end of the column, tied to the rear wagon and forced to walk or be dragged.

I crept back to the horses to feed and water them. I wasn't in any rush; it wasn't like I couldn't follow their tracks or even that I didn't already know where they were going. It was only a matter of how I would harass them today. I took care of the horses, then took care of my own needs – going to the bathroom, eating breakfast. I even took the time to clean and oil my pistols, which had seen more than enough use over the past few days. Not for the first time, I wished I had thought to pack some instant coffee before I left my timeline. My eyes struggled to open, and I really craved a cup right now.

An hour later I was settled into in the saddle and rode through the field, following the deep tracks. The officer's body and that of the three dead soldiers remained where they had fallen. The British didn't even bother to bury them. I was slow to realize that Major Campbell was a cold-hearted motherfucker. I still didn't know what I was going to do next if and when I did catch up to them, but several options started to form in my mind. I stopped at the soldier whom Major Campbell had shot and regarded him with a hard stare for several seconds. Stepping off Little Joe, I went down on one knee, pulled his large red coat off this young man, and picked up his hat that still laid next to him.

Apologies, man, I thought. But he didn't have a use for them anymore, and I did.

The trail that the Major followed narrowed from the wide-open field to a thirty-foot-wide trail with trees clustered on both sides. I stayed off the trail but moved at a much faster pace than the soldiers could walk. At the pace they were going, I estimated they'd reach Saratoga tomorrow after noon. I understood the Major, and I believed he might not

193

stop to camp at all tonight. He'd march his already fatigued men all night until they reached Saratoga and sleep there. His men had marched all day yesterday, stayed up last night, and began their march at first light this morning. They were exhausted, with sallow skin, purple half-moons under their eyes, and were starting to resemble zombies.

Perfect.

When I caught up to them, I tracked them from a distance, staying far enough back not to be seen. They were so focused on ambushes up ahead that they weren't overly concerned about a rear guard. That was a mistake that I was going to take advantage of. I followed for about two hours, letting them tire out even more and relax, hoping they'd fall into a false sense of safety.

I pulled off the road and sped up to catch up to the column of soldiers. When I was somewhere in the middle of the column, I tied the horses to a tree, and jogged towards to the road. By the time I made it, the last wagon had passed my position. With the dead soldier's red coat and hat on, and John Brooks' rifle in my hand, I came out of the bushes like a man who had pissed on a tree and was trying to catch up to the rest of the company. Increasing my stride, I came up alongside the rear wagon. The four prisoners cast their sad gazes over my way, and I held a finger to my lips, stopping any of them from saying anything. They were dirty and underfed and just as weary as the soldiers marching in front of them. Two of them had black eyes but they all had bruises on their faces. One of the men's arms hung in a makeshift a sling constructed from his own jacket. Two of them had no shoes but what might have been shirts wrapped around their bloody feet.

As I came along the right side of the wagon driver, the driver laughed at me. He was a stern, gray-haired man in his sixties. He appeared no longer able to march with the company, and I assumed was rewarded with an easy job of driving the wagons.

"Better get your ass back up there, boy, or the Major will have you whipped."

Instead of answering, I grabbed the side of the wagon and climbed up onto it in a fluid move and flopped down on the seat next to him.

"What's this?" he yelled. "Get your ass off my wagon, boy! You can walk with the rest of them."

Before the man could say another word, I brought the butt stock of John Brooks' rifle up and jammed it into his face, hard. His head snapped back with a crack. He went limp and slumped over to his side as I grabbed the reins from him. The other wagon driver ahead of me never looked back. His head drooped, and I wondered if he was asleep. His horses followed the soldiers a head of them like they have done day after day, with little guidance from him.

I glimpsed back at the four prisoners, and they stared at me with open mouths. I tossed the first man my knife underhanded, and he caught it in a steady hand. He cut himself loose, then the others. I pointed to one of the other men, and then pointed to the wagon driver. They didn't hesitate. Two of the men ran up next to the wagon, and one pulled the unconscious wagon driver off the seat and into the mud as the other climbed up the wagon next to me. One of the two men without shoes was pulling the wagon driver's shoes off his feet before joining us.

"Who the fuck are you?" the man on the bench whispered, handing me my knife back. I palmed the knife.

"The man saving your asses," I said.

The same colonist who had pulled the driver off the wagon ran back up and tossed the wagon driver's coat up to the man sitting next to me. They were taking my idea and going with it. These men were smart.

"Keep the wagon going," I told him. "I think the other wagon driver might be asleep. Slowly fall back. When they are far enough ahead, turn the wagon around. I have horses hidden back the way we came. We'll meet you on the road."

"The hell with the wagon," he said. "Let's run for the horses."

"No," I said in a harsh voice. "General Washington will need these supplies."

He pursed his lips but nodded his head in slow understanding, and the wagon slowed a bit. I jumped down and moved to the rear of the over loaded wagon. I handed John Brooks' musket to one of the other three men, told them about the horses I had hidden, and explained what my plan was.

"You three come with me to retrieve the horses," I said. "The road curves up ahead. He'll turn the wagon around after he falls back far enough that the British won't notice."

I didn't add the phrase *I hope*, even though I was thinking it.

I had expected more questions and was surprised when they followed me back down the road in a run without question. The horses weren't that far away, and it only took a few minutes to get back to them. One of the Colonists tried to mount Little Joe, but Little Joe wasn't having any of that and strained away from him.

"He's mine," I said. "Pick another horse. Those two horses have muskets on them. Make sure you're loaded before we reach the roadway. Just in case we find ourselves in a fight."

"Are you really the Pale Rider?" one of the Colonists asked. He was the tallest of the men.

"Yes, that's what the British call me," I answered. "But you can call me Thomas."

They gave me their names, and I nodded my head to each of them one by one. We made it to the road, and the wagon was already coming our way. I directed them to the burned-out farmhouse and told them about the wagon of supplies and extra horses hidden there.

"General Washington needs both, this wagon and the other wagon of supplies, if he is to survive the winter."

Marcus, the taller one, was raised in the area, and said he knew of the farm and where Valley Forge was. One of the other men, Peter, asked if I'd be going with them and was surprised when I said no.

"Why the fuck not?" Marcus asked, spitting on the ground.

"There are two possibilities," I said. "The British come after us and that wagon. With the tracks the wagon leaves in the mud, they'll be able to track us down easily enough. In which case, I will be here to stop them. The other option is that they don't come after us, and I will still need to stop them from reaching Saratoga."

As the wagon rode up to us, a shorter man named Jonas volunteered to stay with me. He was the one I had handed John Brooks' rifle to. I investigated the wagon and found that it was filled with salted meat, bags of potatoes, medical supplies, and a couple hundred blankets.

"No," I said to Jonas. "This wagon is too important. You need to make sure this one and the one I left in the barn, get to General Washington."

With that said, shots rang out from two hundred yards down the road. We ducked under the wagon and peered around the sides to find two officers on horseback, flanked by about fifty soldiers, racing around the bend.

"Go!" I yelled to the men as I pulled out my Thompson. "I'll be right behind you!"

I fired and one of the running soldiers crumpled to the ground. The other soldiers ran around him as if he were nothing more than a hole in the road. I turned Little Joe around and galloped down the road behind the wagon, passing Jonas who was off his horse and had his musket laid over the horse's saddle. He fired with assurance, and another soldier fell face first into the mud. He remounted back on his horse and kicked his horse to follow me.

We raced back the way the company had just come from. As I searched the soldiers, I realized that Major Campbell wasn't in front. Other than the wagon, the officers were the only ones left with horses, and they had no desire to race ahead of the foot soldiers, so it was easy enough to stay ahead of them. I didn't want to get bogged down in a battle with the soldiers here. We wouldn't have a chance, but I also didn't want the soldiers to give up and stop following us.

The soldiers finally began to chase me, and I didn't want them to give up too soon. I didn't have to stop them from actually reaching Saratoga, only delay them long enough that they couldn't join in with General Burgoyne. If I delayed them just one full day, maybe two, the battle might be over long before they made it there. Then the Colonists would have to deal with Major Campbell's lone company of men.

I was sure they could do that by themselves, yet I hoped that they wouldn't even have to. If Major Campbell learned that General Burgoyne had already been defeated, then he'd likely turn around and leave without engaging the Colonists in battle. I still needed to stop him from reaching General Clinton, the top British dog. If he gave up General Washington's location to General Clinton, the war was nearly over and not the way I wanted it to be.

By the time we made it back to the open field that the soldiers had camped at the night before, they'd given up the chase and turned back around, marching towards Saratoga again. Our ploy had delayed them a few hours but not near long enough.

The taller man raised his sharp eyebrows at me. "We thought you were here to rescue that French officer."

I parted my lips to answer no but stopped myself. "What French officer?"

"The British came across a French officer on the way here," Jonas explained. "I think he was French. He wasn't British, and not from around here. Two of the soldiers were talking and said that the French officer was looking for General Washington."

What did this mean? Was this French officer important? I couldn't recall any important details about any significant French officers from my history downloads, but then, history had been written by the winner. Maybe he was the one who could tell the French government about Saratoga. I had to figure out if I needed to rescue him now or stick with the plan of delaying Major Campbell.

"Ok," I said. "I'll figure out what to do about the French officer. You men follow through with the plan and get the two wagons to General Washington."

"You can't do this on your own sir," Jonas said, protesting. "At least let me help."

The rest nodded their heads in serious agreement. Well, two of them were. The third man busied himself pulling the boots and coat off one of the dead soldiers I'd killed.

"Ok, Jonas," I relented. "You're with me. Look in the back of the wagon and take whatever you need. It's getting colder, make sure you grab two blankets for you and two for the horses."

Second Chance

THIRTEEN: Sweet Revenge

THE YOUNG MAN was only in his early twenties, but he seemed abundantly capable. Jonas grabbed a few blankets and extra gunpowder with a small leather bag of shot. He had picked the horse with extra food in the saddle bags, so I wasn't worried about rations.

Now that I had some time, I drew a map in the dirt, showing them the bridge I'd crossed and where to go from there to get to the barn with the other wagon. I didn't know how much two wagons loads of food and blankets were going to help thousands of men, but it was better than nothing. General Washington probably had hunting parties out killing deer and whatever else moved in the woods to add to his rations. The potatoes, bandages and blankets would be needed even more than the salted beef and gunpowder.

The wagon and Colonists rode in the direction of the bridge as Jonas and I rode back towards the British soldiers. I reined Little Joe to a stop and squinted at Jonas who'd had pulled up next to me.

"I don't like the idea of chasing them down the same road," I said, tilting my head in that direction.

"You think they may have left men behind?" he asked. "You think they left a trap for us?"

"I don't know," I answered. "It's a coin flip. If the Major thinks I was after the wagon and you men, then he'll head to Saratoga with his men. If he guesses I'm trying to prevent him from reaching Saratoga, then he might have left men behind to kill us on the road."

"So, what do we do?" he asked, peering into the trees for soldiers.

"We need to go around this road and get ahead of them," I said. "Do you know this area of the country?"

"Yes."

"Can you get us ahead of them?"

"That shouldn't be a problem," he said.

He quickly dismounted his horse and scratched in the dirt with a twig, drawing the road the British were taking from where we were to Saratoga. Then he marked the different farms on the way between us and Saratoga. One of the farms, the Foster's farm, was known for an incredibly special item that caught my attention. The farm was two or three miles before Saratoga, which might prove to be to our advantage. It was far enough ahead that, if we rode hard, we would get there eight or nine hours before Major Campbell. He'd be close to Saratoga and might think I'd given up. I liked this plan. I settled back onto Little Joe and told Jonas to lead the way. He led us off the road, and we kept up a gallop as we went around the trees through the woods.

We stopped a few times to walk the horses, and I gave Jonas some of the food. He must have been starving but forced himself to eat slowly. I hoped it wasn't because he didn't want to embarrass himself in front of the Pale Rider by wolfing down his meager meal. I was starting to fear that his expectations of me were too high. He seemed to believe the myth that I wanted the British to believe about me. The difference here was that Jonas, unlike the British, was walking, riding, and talking with me. He watched me eat and drink. Hell, I had to take a bowel movement break, and if that didn't make me human in his eyes, I didn't know what would. Legends didn't take bathroom breaks.

We chatted during our walk breaks, and he told me that his father worked in Philadelphia as a candle maker. Jonas worked alongside his father until the war started. He had plans of taking over the business when the war was over and when his father decided he was ready. He talked about his mother and what a wonderful cook she was. His older brother had been killed by the British, but he still had two younger brothers at home. Jonas hoped that the war would be over before they were old enough to fight. From his tone, he came from a loving family. He seemed like a pleasant kid, and I found myself enjoying his company.

I asked Jonas about this Foster family, whose farm we were going to. He assured me that they had no love for the British, and even though Mr. Foster, at the age of sixty something, was too old to pick up a musket and fight with the Colonists, he and Mrs. Foster didn't stand for the British marching across their property or taking their belongings *in the name of the king*. Jonas loved my plan and promised that Mr. Foster would love it too.

It took us about six hours of riding and walking to reach the Foster's family farm. An hour before we made it there, clouds clustered in the sky and a light drift of snow began to fall. Not a heavy snow, yet giving us warning of what was to come. From our location, we heard sporadic musket and cannon fire from the battle. The main battle would have begun yesterday but was still miles away from us. Other small skirmishes had sprung up between the Freeman's farm and the Foster's farm.

I glanced at the thick clouds above us. We had only three hours before sunset. If the Major marched his men all night without stopping, then they'd be here between eight and ten in the morning. If they made camp, and after what happened last night, I didn't think they would, then they'd be here between two and four in the afternoon. Either way, I wanted to get everything set up and ready to go tonight, and then try for a little sleep while we waited for the Major to arrive.

When we arrived, we spoke to Mr. Foster, who it turns out, loved my plan, and laughed so hard I thought he was going to give himself a heart attack. He and his wife agreed to help us set up and put my plan into action. In fact, Mr. Foster did most of the work with his wife's help, while Jonas and I stayed as far away as possible to stay out of their way.

When it was all done, Mr. Foster insisted that we sleep in the barn, and his wife cooked a chicken with roasted onions and potatoes for us. She took one look at Jonas and the mother in her took over. After we ate the chicken, Jonas and I settled in for some sleep. I couldn't see any way for Major Campbell to get here before morning, so we were safe enough to get a few hours of sleep. As much as I hated to admit that I was getting used to sleeping in hay, but as cold as it was outside, even the barn felt like a luxury. Jonas thanked me for telling him to grab two blankets and not just one.

As I laid down, I thought about how cold and hungry General Washington's men had to be. How bad it was going to get for them. My mind worked non-stop, formulating a plan to help with that when we were done here. As my eyes slipped shut, I thought about Annie and her girls. What was I doing? Those girls deserved better than me. I didn't have any kids and had no idea how to raise two daughters, even if they did have a way of making me feel like a better man. With visions of Annie in my eyes, sleep finally overtook me and I drifted off.

The vibrations on my watch woke me before sunrise. I could still hear canon fire in the distance, but no musket fire. The battle must be concentrated at the Freeman's farm now. We were too far for the sound of muskets to reach us, but cannons were significantly louder. I shook Jonas awake and we saddled the horses, rolled our blankets, ate the last of the food in the saddle bags, and prepared for the day. Digging into my backpack, I gave Jonas some beef jerky and smoked salmon to eat while we hid. I also made him fill the water bags on the horses. People sometimes forget to drink when they're cold, and I didn't know how long we'd end up hiding in the cold grass, but that we were going to be damn cold was a certainty.

I hid under my Ghillie blanket near the opening of the woods where the road met the Foster Farm. Jonas was about a hundred yards from me, deeper into the woods, yet near enough to the road. We each held sharpened knives in our hands and a rope tied to a stake in the ground near us. The ropes went up into the trees, then around the trunks and over to a thick branch that crossed over the road.

According to my watch, it was nine o'clock when the sound of drums came from the road. I had a higher opinion of Major Campbell than the other British officers and had expected him not to be announcing his arrival like this. I was a little disappointed to learn that, like all the other pompous British officers, he wanted to declare his coming to the world. Some people never learn.

I snuck a peek out of my blanket. Major Campbell sat tall on his horse, riding my way. A man rode at his side. Jonas had been right – the man in the pale blue uniform with unfamiliar insignia appeared to be a French officer. The French officer lost his hat somewhere on the road because he was the only person on horseback who didn't wear one. Two more British officers rode behind Major Campbell, then the drummers, followed by the foot soldiers. The foot soldiers seemed to be sleep walking. Some of them held onto the barrels of their muskets, the butt stocks dragging lines in the dirt behind them. They had marched two hundred miles without sleep for the last two nights.

It was time to wake them up a little.

The Major halted his horse in front of the large wooden sign at the entrance of the farm's property line that proudly proclaimed they were coming upon Foster's farm. The sign also informed the reader that the farm produced fresh chicken eggs, the largest pumpkins in the state, and last but not least, the cleanest and sweetest fresh honey ever produced by the farm's own beehives.

The night before, Mr. Foster and his wife dressed in their baggy, eighteen century beekeeper outfits, and picked up and loaded two of their four large, manmade, wooden beehives onto the back of a wagon. This turned out not to be as difficult as it sounded since it was so cold out the bees were highly dulled and inactive in the cold. The wagon was slowly and carefully walked to the road, and with ropes thrown over branches high up in the trees, the hives were hauled up high into the air, a hundred yards apart from each other.

My right hand reached out, and with a fluid movement, my knife sliced through the rope tied to the stake next to me. The beehive that hung in the air high above the

Major and about twenty feet back hurtled toward the ground, landed on the head of one of the foot soldiers directly, and killed him. The sound of the wooden contraption crashing into the soldier's head and then to the ground was loud enough for Jonas to hear. He immediately cut his own rope that held up the second beehive. A few moments after the first beehive hit the ground, a second crashing sound followed.

Here is an interesting fact. Bees get aggressive when they see dark colors, like dark red. It turns out that colors like black, dark blue, and dark red, are colors of their predators. The British wore dark red uniform coats, whereas I sported my brown coat. Jonas had removed his coat this morning, leaving it on his horse. Another interesting fact is that each beehive can hold about fifty thousand bees. With our two beehives, we had a total of about one hundred thousand bees.

So, there were about fifty thousand really pissed off bees in the front of the British column and another fifty thousand bees just as upset, at the rear of the column. There were over a hundred exhausted dark red coat wearing British soldiers between the two beehives.

The buzzing that ensued was extraordinary.

The poor bees in those beehives were really addled, having their hives destroyed like that. They must have thought that they were the ones under attack. It was in their nature to protect the hive and their queen, even at the cost of their own lives. I couldn't see Jonas's hive, but tens of thousands of bees emerged from my hive, and I could hear them buzzing from where I was. They sounded like an empty blender set on high speed.

Bees filled the air in a frightening grey cloud and attacked the soldiers in their bright red coats, and unfortunately the poor, innocent horses. The soldiers swatted their arms at first, trying to kill the bees. Then the swarm seem to attack as one against what they assumed was their enemy.

Some of the soldiers tried hiding in their coats. The smarter soldiers dropped everything and ran in all different directions. The dumb ones panicked and fired their muskets at the swarm, upsetting the bees even more. The unluckiest of the soldiers suffered the full brunt of the bees' anger and died of hundreds of stings.

The horses didn't fare any better than the soldiers. They bucked and reared up, thinking that the riders were somehow causing the pain, and wanting to be rid of their unpleasant masters. As each horse threw its rider into the air, it bolted for safety, which was probably the best thing for them – to get far away from the bee attack.

The French Officer wisely jumped off his mount, not waiting to be thrown as the other officers had been. Major Campbell didn't wait either but instead of fighting his horse or jumping out of the saddle, he kicked his horse into a run. As the Major raced by me, I jumped up and fired my Thompson, hitting the Major and knocking him off his horse.

The French officer and the two British officers ran from the bees right towards my spot. After I shot the Major, the British officers that were still alive, spotted me and drew their flintlock pistols. I shifted the Thompson into my left hand and drew my Tec-9 with my right. I fired first, and one of the officers dropped onto his face. I was going to fire and kill the other officer, but the French officer, thinking I was there to save him and that both my pistols were empty, decided to intervene in what he thought was my death. He grabbed the flintlock pistol from the officer and snatched it away from him, turning the pistol on its owner. The French officer fired the flintlock point blank, and the British officer died, his mouth and eyes wide in shock in a grotesque death mask.

I waved to the French officer, calling him over to me and under the blanket. He didn't hesitate for a second. He ran at me then dove under the blanket. Now that I saw him up close, I was surprised at how young he was. From how he held himself, I thought him to be an older man. Instead, he was only twenty to twenty-five years old. I yelled for him to stay under the blanket, then I chased after Major Campbell.

The Major, though still alive when I reached him, was not in the best condition. He was unconscious, but I didn't know if it was from my bullet or from the fall off his horse. A fall headfirst off a running horse could easily kill a person. He was lucky to still be alive. The horse had been at a full sprint when I'd fired, and I hit the back of his right shoulder. The exit wound in the front of the shoulder was larger than the entry wound, and he suffered for it. Bone shards stuck out of the gaping hole in the front of his shoulder. He'd never use that arm again and would be lucky to live long enough to have it amputated off. Despite the horrific nature of the wound, I had to force myself not to smile sadistically at that.

The road rash on his forehead from the fall off his horse bled profusely. Viscous blood stained his face and caked in the lines, but head wounds bleed a lot, so it didn't necessarily mean a severe injury. His flintlock pistol was tucked into his belt. It was a superbly made pistol with a deep red cherry wood stock. I grabbed the pistol and tossed it to the side.

Then I dragged him over to my blanket and the French officer. By the time I reached the blanket, I'd been stung by six or seven bees on my arms and twice on my face, which throbbed against the stings. I was sure bees hit my legs, but my deer skin pants provided me with plenty of protection.

None of the soldiers paid any attention to me. They were either running for their lives or dead in the roadway. The bees seemed never to run out of energy or anger and were either attacking the soldiers or looking for someone to attack. Those soldiers who'd been swatting at the bees lost that fight and now joined their comrades in running for their lives or were also dead in the road.

We hid under the blanket for about ten more minutes until the buzzing sound faded. Slow footsteps sounded around me, telling me that Mr. Foster was next to us. If it had been one of the British, they would be running, and no one was dumb enough to walk into a swarm of bees on purpose.

Except someone who knew how.

"Ok," Mr. Foster yelled. "You can come out now."

I peeked my head out of the blanket and found Mr. Foster standing in front of us smiling. He didn't have his bee suit on but did hold a torch. The torch must have been covered with pitch or something else because it made a lot of smelly dark smoke. Mrs. Foster worked in the road, setting fire to a bucket of something that poured out fountains of black smoke, upward into the sky.

My new French friend and I stood up hesitantly and stared ahead. Over thirty dead soldiers littered the roadway. Drums, muskets, and blanket rolls laid discarded in the road, where they had been dropped by panicking men. I didn't see any living British soldiers around.

"The soldiers?" I asked.

"They are still running," Mr. Foster said.

"The bees?"

"Most are dead," he answered. "They die after stinging a person. Almost all of them died stinging the British. It was a strong plan. Give it another ten minutes and the smoke will get rid of what is left of the two swarms."

Mrs. Foster waddled over to us, wringing her hands.

"You two come up to the house," she said in a matronly tone. "I'll put something on those stings that'll help with the pain and swelling."

I looked at the French officer who sported a few welts on his face and hands.

"Who are you, sir?" I asked him. Time to make introductions. The French officer brought his feet together in a snap and bowed at the waist.

"Marie-Joseph Paul Yves Roche Gilbert du Motier de La Fayette. You may call me Marquis de Lafayette. At your service sir. Are you the one, the British call the Pale Rider?"

"Yes," I told him. "But you may call me Thomas."

"Is not the Pale Rider the fourth horseman of the apocalypse?" he asked, his lips quivering in a slight, derisive grin. "In the Christian scripture, I mean."

"He is," I answered with emphasis. "Keep in mind, *I* didn't pick that name. The British *gave* it to me."

He made a show of gesturing at the dead soldiers and then down at his feet where Major Campbell laid, not moving.

"I cannot imagine why they would pick a name like that for you," he said with a dry note of sarcasm.

I laughed. "I didn't know you French had such a refined sense of humor."

"Oh, we don't," he said. "But the irony is overwhelming here."

"What are you doing in the colonies? Why are you here?" I asked.

"I was on my way to Philadelphia to speak to General Washington, when I was captured by these men," he answered.

Jonas rode up in the wagon that had been at the end of the soldiers' column.

"Look what I got!" he yelled with a cheery grin plastered on his face.

"How did you get that?" I asked.

"The driver jumped off and ran. I jumped up with the blanket wrapped around me and rode off with it. Nobody turned their head my way. The horses were stung a bunch, though. I think they may be sick."

"Jonas, this is Marquis de Lafayette," I said. "Marquis de Lafayette, may I introduce my companion, Jonas." I realized I didn't know Jonas's last name. I'd have to ask him later.

The two men nodded their heads to each other in greeting. Jonas's nod was friendly, deep, sincere and with a smile, but the French officer's nod was somehow quicker and dismissive, his lips tight. I didn't think the French officer was trying to be rude. In his mind, he was probably being formal and polite by making the effort to nod. He made me feel like I had introduced him to a servant, or someone not worth his time. I had to remember what year this was. The French guy probably thought of Jonas as the help. Someone to drive the wagon or shine his boots. He didn't know much about me except that I had just rescued him, but he thought he had Jonas all figured out – a lower social class and therefore not one to speak to. I hoped this wasn't going to be a problem.

"Jonas," I said, getting the young man's attention again. "Would you be so kind as to take the wagon to the barn and tend to the horses?" Feeling the two bee stings on my face, I added, "Were you stung by any of the bees?"

"No, sir," he answered with that same cheerful smile on his face.

Then Major Campbell moaned. I narrowed my gaze at him.

"Let's take the Major to the house and have Mrs. Foster look at all three of us."

I tied a quick torniquet to the Major's shoulder to slow down the bleeding. I wanted to take him back to General Washington if he lived that long. It might take us days, maybe several, to get there. Horses could go over hills that through streams, but a wagon had to stay on the road in this weather. General Washington needed the supplies, but even if he didn't, we'd have to transport the Major in the wagon anyways. I patted down the Major and found several sealed envelopes in his coat pocket. More good luck. I stuck them in my cargo pocket for now to read later.

Back at the house, Mrs. Foster used a red-hot knife to cauterize the bleeding in the Major's shoulder. If he wasn't unconscious before then, the searing pain of the cauterization surely knocked him out. She picked out the bone shards that she could see, and then sewed up the entry and exit wounds like a bad piece of quilting. Patting her fine workmanship, she said he'd live if we were able to keep any upcoming fever down, which confirmed my thoughts that he'd never use that arm again.

She put a smelly gray mud-like paste on my bee stings. I didn't want to know what it was made of – the stuff smelled like cow dung, but the itchiness faded away quickly. She promised that the welts would go down in a day and gave us some extra stinky paste to use on the horses.

I wanted to leave right away, before the British returned, but needed to make sure that Mr. and Mrs. Foster would be ok. They agreed to leave the farm for two days, just in case the British returned. While the Fosters loaded up a wagon of belongings that Mrs. Foster refused to leave behind, Jonas loaded our wagon with any muskets and gear he'd liberated from the British. From my count, sixty-three muskets, four drums, and thirty bed rolls littered the road. We left the drums and the dead soldiers where they laid. I didn't feel good about that, but burying the soldiers was too time consuming, and the drums would have taken up too much room in the wagon. Besides, what did I need drums for, anyway?

When the Fosters were ready to go, I shook Mr. Foster's hand and thanked him for everything he did. I really hoped nothing unfortunate happened to him after we left. Mrs. Foster gave us several dozen chicken eggs in a basket and eight jars of honey. Jonas put the smelly paste on the horse's bee stings and then volunteered to drive the wagon, giving Lafayette the use of his horse. Lafayette, delighted after he found his superbly crafted sword and flintlock pistol that the British had taken from him in the back of the wagon, mounted with a sense of refined glee.

Then we rode off south on the same rode from which we'd come, with Major Campbell asleep in the back.

FOURTEEN: Bedtime Stories

AFTER WE STOPPED to camp the first night, I pulled out the maps that marksman John Brooks had packed in his saddle bags and plotted a course for Valley Forge. The four of us had a ways to go, and the snow was only going to slow us down. Though it was still a light snow, that snow melts into water, and water turns dirt into mud, which was going to be the real problem for the wagon. To make things worse, I had no idea how we were going to make it the rest of the way without running into anymore British soldiers.

Changing my train of thought, I threw another small log onto our campfire and turned to Lafayette.

"Why are you looking for General Washington?" I asked.

"I came here to fight in this war," he said in his accented English. "I do not know for which side, as of yet. I am a member of King Louis the Sixteenth's court, and which side I choose will have consequences. France and England are not at war, but we have never been what you might call true friends either. As it stands now, war with England may be around the corner for my countrymen. If I choose to help England, then I help strengthen peace between our two countries. If I help General Washington, then I might be helping the enemy of my country's biggest threat. It's not an easy decision. Help strengthen peace and prevent war with the English or risk trying to weaken the English war machine, to ensure peace with strength."

A choice between the enemy, or the *enemy of my enemy is my friend* philosophy. The man was smart. He evaluated the dangers of either choice, and instead of staying home where he'd be safe, he chose to jump into the lion's den and make a decision that would affect his whole country.

"What do you think will happen if the British win this war?" I asked in a terse tone.

He thought about that for a second but before he could open his mouth, I answered for him.

"The British will have all the resources the land has to offer," I said with the knowledge that my words would likely influence him. "This land is a lot bigger than your government realizes. As people come here to live, they will live under British rule. The Empire will take young men into their army, then with all the timber, and ore this land has to offer, they will increase the size of their army and navy tenfold or more. There is a lot of gold in this land, a thousand times more than France and England put together. That, plus the money the Empire will receive through taxes, will make King George the richest king in the world. With that additional manpower, plus natural resources this land has, combined with the wealth the King will acquire, how long until he can afford to go to war against France again? How long before the French are forced to call him King?"

Deep in thought, the young Frenchman stood up and left me to gaze pensively into the horizon. The answer was simple for me, but for him it meant he might be dragging his people into a war they didn't desire.

He stood away from us for about ten minutes then he returned, climbed under his blanket, and rolled over to sleep.

"I will decide what to do after I talk to General Washington," he said at last, before closing his eyes.

I didn't think the Frenchman was really going to fall asleep but decided to let him rest just the same. I wasn't the only one with much at stake in this war. Sitting on a log next to the fire, I pulled out the three waxed sealed envelopes that I had taken off Major Campbell.

The first envelope I opened were the orders that John Brook had told me about —orders to attack General Washington. The second envelope was a letter to the quarter master in Philadelphia with a schedule consisting of ship names and approximate dates of their arrivals. The schedule only covered the next two months and included the ship's basic manifest. Several ships coming from Canada had food and medical supplies for the troops. Other ships were coming from England, laden with weapons, black powder, and reinforcement troops.

The third letter was addressed to General Howe and was the most interesting. At first it read like a letter between two friends. The sender, who wasn't named, asked about the General's family, and even mentioned his dog. The letter was written in a way that I thought was personal, but it jumped around a lot, touched on random ideas. Strange. After I read it a second time, I realized it was coded. I had no way of reading the real message without the secret code to decipher it. I stashed the three letters in my satchel to give to General Washington later.

The snow was still falling at a light pace, catching on my eyelashes. I rose and made sure the horses were covered, as was the Major. The last thing I needed was for him to die of exposure. Jonas was asleep, and I decided not to set up a guard. We needed our sleep, and I doubted anyone would be marching at night in the snow. Laying down under my thermal blanket. I let sleep overtake me, as I wondered if I would be dreaming about saving Jenny, and the life she would have without me, or would I dream about Annie and the life we might have together.

The next day, we agreed to the only plan I could think of. Jonas knew the area the best, so he would scout ahead on the horse while Lafayette drove the wagon, following Jonas's trail as best he could. I'd bring up the rear, watching for anyone coming up behind us.

Lafayette didn't like this plan and insisted that he should scout ahead and Jonas drive the wagon. He didn't seem like a dreadful man, but growing up in a world based on stations, he lived in a society that determined what jobs were appropriate for which person based on their station. Driving a wagon wasn't fitting for someone of the King's court. I had to pull the young man aside and explain what I thought was the obvious. Jonas had been born and raised in this part of the country and was the best choice to scout ahead. The plan had nothing to do with one's station in life.

Lafayette shook his head but complied. He still hadn't figured me out and wasn't sure where I stood on the hierarchy in the world. I think he agreed to drive the wagon more out of fear of being rude to me than because the plan made sense to him.

Jonas fell back to the wagon every couple of hours, and we would eat, confirm our location on the map, and make any necessary changes in our direction. This system seemed to work nicely, and we were moving faster than I had expected. We had plenty of food in the back of the wagon, and water wasn't in short supply with the streams around us. The first few days were uneventful, and we didn't see another person on the road.

At night we talked and told each other about our lives and families. Lafayette and Jonas were of a similar age but that was the extent of their similarities. The two young men were from completely different worlds. Whereas Lafayette was from France, rich, highly educated, already married, and came to the colonies at his own expense, hoping for experience and adventure, Jonas was from Philadelphia, poor, home schooled, had most likely never even kissed a girl, and was thrown into this war for the most part against his will.

As for me, well, keeping track of lies and separating the whole truth wasn't my strong suit, so I kept it simple. I told them that my wife had been murdered, and I was here for revenge. This way, if either of them ever repeated what I said, it wouldn't give anything away to who I really was and might even add to the whole Pale Rider legend.

Young men being young men, every night they'd ask me to tell them why the British called me Pale Rider. I'd recite a watered-down version of how I saved General Washington, how I blew up a wagon and killed hundreds of General Howe's men, but the story they wanted to hear over and over was the one about me saving Annie's daughters. They seemed to enjoy best the part about the knife fight. Neither of them was willing to believe me when I told them how scared I was of Sergeant Major Brown. They believed, and straight out told me, that I was being modest or making light of it.

Despite myself and my desire not to form bonds, I found myself liking these two men more and more each night. We formed an improbable camaraderie. Lafayette let his guard down and the two younger men seemed to have formed an unlikely friendship with each other as well, although I didn't think they'd acknowledge each other in public. They were from two different classes, and each of them knew that they'd only be friends in private.

Lafayette told us about being born in the Auvergne region of central France, and of his stunningly beautiful wife, Adrienne de Noailles.

Jonas talked more about his mother and father. We learned that he had plans on marrying a young lady whose father owned a local Inn not far from his father's candle shop.

Lafayette was well trained with the sword and flintlock pistol. He was surprisingly patient as he gave Jonas lessons on both, and for his part, Jonas was a quick learner. In return, Jonas gave Lafayette lessons on shooting the musket and how to lead a target, shooting where the target would be, not where he was. Jonas then gave Lafayette John Brooks' fine musket as a gift and took up one of the British muskets from the back of the wagon for himself. Lafayette gave Jonas Major Campbell's fine flintlock pistol. I hadn't seen Lafayette pick up the pistol the day I had shot the Major, but at some point, he had.

The men asked me for lessons on knife fighting, and I even taught them how to throw knives. You never knew when that skill would save your life.

As for Major Campbell, he slept the first two days and we had to force water down his throat to keep him alive. I secretly gave him an antibiotic shot to keep any infection or fever away. He woke on the third day in a great deal of pain.

Although I really didn't care about his pain, I did want to keep him quiet, so I also gave him one of my few shots of morphine when he first woke up and then two pain killers every few hours after that.

Mrs. Foster adhered her word and our bee stings had healed up good as new.

On the fourth day, I trailed behind the wagon, but kept it in sight. Jonas rode back to the wagon at a full gallop, waving one arm wildly over his head. I kicked Little Joe into a run and made it to the wagon seconds before Jonas. He pulled his horse up short and yelled excitedly about British soldiers. Before I could say a word, Lafayette held up a hand and told Jonas to slow down and catch his breath.

"British soldiers," Jonas said excitedly, pointing behind him.

"How many?" Lafayette asked in a calm voice.

He was trying to get information and quiet Jonas down at the same time. I was impressed with the Frenchman again. Lafayette was a natural leader.

"About thirty," Jonas said. "All on horseback."

Now, I understood why he was so excited. These weren't foot soldiers he was talking about, and we wouldn't be able to go around them or outrun them. If they were coming our way, they'd find the wagon tracks. They would have to be blind to miss them in the mud. If they followed our tracks, they'd catch up to us in minutes.

"How far away?" Lafayette asked, pinching his nose.

"Two, maybe two and a half miles," Jonas said. "They're walking their horses, but they'll be here in twenty minutes. Sooner if they stop walking and start riding."

Lafayette took a deep breath, composing himself, and observed his surroundings to take inventory of what we had and weigh our options.

"We have two choices," Lafayette stated. "We turn off the road and cut through the woods, hoping not to get stuck and that they don't follow our tracks. I do not like that choice because we'll most likely get stuck at some point, and they'll certainly follow the tracks, wanting to know who we are and why we left the road to avoid them. The other choice is we kill the Major and abandon the wagon, riding off on the two horses. They will certainly follow us, but at least we'll be on horseback and can stay ahead of them."

Jonas was nodding his head in agreement, and Lafayette pulled out his flintlock, glancing back at the Major. He'd already made up his mind and was going to decide for us. He might be a natural leader, but I had enough and was going to have to remind him of who had saved who and who was in charge.

"No!" I commanded in my best no-nonsense voice.

Both men froze.

"What?" Lafayette asked.

"I said no," I told him. "We're not killing our prisoner. General Washington will want to talk to him. We're not leaving the wagon behind, either. The General will need everything in it."

"Look here, *monsieur*," Lafayette said, in an attempt to take charge.

This wasn't the time to let him try his hand at usurping leadership. We had a cavalry patrol coming our way. If that patrol happened to be commanded by a certain Captain Bonifield, then this young man was going to have his ass handed to him, and that meant mine and Jonas's as well. You didn't break your teeth learning to command men against someone like Bonifield. He was too smart, too ruthless, and too capable. I needed to take command back and fast.

"Lafayette," I interrupted him, raising my voice. "I like you. Please do *not* make me slap the shit out of you. I am in charge here, not you."

This took him by surprise, and his jaw dropped. He had most likely never been talked to this way in his entire life. Jonas didn't know what to do, so he to sat on his horse with his mouth parted, an eager onlooker.

Lafayette's eyebrows furled in anger, and he moved his mouth to speak. I knew he was going to say something that would end up causing me to knock him off the wagon. Then he'd demand satisfaction, and I'd be forced to kill him. That was not the outcome I wanted.

"Think!" I yelled. "Before you say your next words."

The young man inhaled a deep breath through his nose and blew it out through his mouth. Someone had taught him how to keep his temper under control. Again, I was impressed.

"Do you have a suggestion for me?" he asked, his voice level.

He was still trying to keep control and thought of himself as being in command. I needed to push a little harder to ensure he followed my instructions.

"Suggestion?" I asked. "No, I don't have a suggestion. I do however have orders for you to follow."

I waited to see how that would set with him. After about three seconds of staring each other in the eyes, the younger pup finally dropped his chin and nodded his head.

"Good," I said. "You'll pull off the road and stay with the wagon and the Major. You can unharness one of the horses and be ready to kill the Major and ride away as fast as you can if Jonas and I fail. But only if we fail."

I turned my attention to Jonas. "You grab as many of those muskets that you can carry and ride with. We are going to find an acceptable ambush sight and surprise them."

"No," Lafayette said. "Have Jonas stay with the wagon and let me go with you."

He tried to say it as a command, but with pleading in his eyes. The man still thought war was a game and wanted to be baptized in British blood. If I wanted to keep him with me and keep him under control, I was going to have to give in a little.

"Fine," I responded. "Take Jonas's horse and grab some rifles. Jonas, take the wagon and look for a decent spot to hide. If you see the British and not us, kill the Major, leave the wagon, and ride to Valley Forge to tell General Washington."

The men nodded their heads and traded places. Lafayette harnessed two rifles on his back and held one in each hand. I grabbed two rifles and brought the slings over my head, so they hung on my back. As we rode off back down the road, I was surprised that Lafayette stayed at my side and didn't try to ride ahead of me.

We crested a small hill and saw the British coming our way, about a half mile from us, on their horse but walking, not riding hard. The road we were on was more of an open field. The ground was bare grass for about sixty feet with trees on both sides, a clear shot from them to us. Lafayette followed me as I turned off the road and into the trees. Looking through my range finder, I counted the horses.

"I count twenty-two riders," I said. "I don't see Bonifield. The lead rider might be a Lieutenant."

"Do you have a plan?" Lafayette asked. There it was, that deference I was looking for.

I withdrew the two muskets from my back and handed them to Lafayette. "Yes. Load all six muskets and stay ready. I'm going to ride across the field to the other side. They'll see me and give chase. At three hundred yards, we open fire." I pointed to John Brook's musket. "You can shoot that far with that musket. At a hundred yards, forget about reloading and keep switching muskets."

He nodded his head. "I understand."

"Here is the hard part," I said, grabbing his arm. "If you shoot the men in the front, the rest might break and go into the trees. We do not want that. We can't win a fair fight against their numbers. Shoot the men riding in the back of the column and work your way up to the front. If the Lieutenant doesn't see his men falling off their horses, he might think we are missing and keep coming. As long as he keeps coming, his men should follow. They won't break away from their leadership."

He nodded his head again as he loaded the muskets. I patted his back and told him that he'd do great.

I mounted Little Joe. "Take your time Lafayette. Remember to lead them like Jonas taught you, to breathe between shots, shoot the riders at the rear of the column first, and if they get close, don't forget you have your flintlock and sword."

With those final words, I knickered Little Joe and we took off across the open field for all to see us.

Lafayette yelled after me. "You forgot to take a musket."

I crossed the field, knowing the British would see me and head my way, thus putting themselves at a better angle for Lafayette. They were about a quarter mile away when I broke through the trees on the other side. I scrambled to tie Little Joe to a tree twenty feet into the woods and ran back to the field. The riders were about four hundred yards away when a musket fired.

"Too soon," I yelled across the field to Lafayette.

Crap. He was scared and rushed it. I yanked out my Thompson, and when the last horseman on the far left was three hundred yards out, I fired. He tumbled backwards off his horse. Lafayette fired again as I reloaded. The last rider on their far right, was flung to the ground. At two hundred and fifty yards, I fired again, and another rider fell. Lafayette was still loading John Brook's rifle, so I fired my third round as they were two hundred yards out.

By this time, all the riders had drawn their swords and kept coming harder. I fired my next round at about a hundred and fifty yards, as Lafayette fired his next shot. I knew Lafayette would now start switching muskets and not bother reloading. We are on borrowed ammunition and time.

Six of the horsemen broke off and turned towards Lafayette. I fired again and then switched to my Tec-9. My Tec-9 didn't have the suppressor on it, so they would hear the blast every round fired. Maybe they'd think there was one of us for every gunshot they heard. It was the natural assumption. Lafayette was firing his five standard muskets at what I thought was too fast a rate. He couldn't have been aiming very well for as fast as he was shooting, but I didn't have time to see if he were hitting his targets or not.

With nine horsemen still bearing down on me, I started firing, aiming at the Lieutenant first. I struck the Lieutenant on my third shot, and he plummeted off the side of his horse, hitting the ground in a solid mass. I missed my fourth shot, but the remaining soldiers noticed their numbers had dwindled down from twenty-two to eight, plus the few still on horseback over by Lafayette.

They must have thought that dozens of Colonists hid in the woods, because as soon as their Lieutenant's dead body hit the ground, his soldiers lost their enthusiasm for battle. They pulled their mounts up short of the tree line, their horses sliding to a stop in the mud. Jerking the poor mounds heads around to turn them, the soldiers then kicked the horses into a full run back the way they came. Pulling the trigger twice more, I fired another two rounds. I managed to shoot one more of the retreating soldiers in the back, as they rode away, kicking up semi-frozen mud. He stiffened then slumped over the horse's neck, but I didn't know if I'd killed him or not.

Reloading my pistol, I returned my attention to Lafayette. Four of the soldiers laid on the ground, unmoving. Horses galloped in all directions in the field between us. Lafayette gripped his sword with his right hand and faced down two of the soldiers who were still on horseback, trying to hack at him with their own swords and run him down with their horses. The young man was fast. He dodged around the horses and blocked their swords with his.

"Get to the trees," I yelled to Lafayette, waving my arm.

If he could get into the trees, the soldiers would have to dismount and fight him on foot. Lafayette tried to edge closer to the tree line while dodging the two horses. I broke into a run across the field, hoping to get there in time. One of the horses clipped Lafayette, and he was thrown to the ground, landing on his face and splattering mud everywhere. The rider who'd knocked Lafayette down reined his horse around and was now going to run over him, letting the horse stomp him to death.

I was only halfway across the field, and the Tec-9 wasn't made for a shot at this distance, especially not when the shooter was breathing as hard as I was. On whim and a prayer, I fired with my shaking hand and was lucky enough to clip the rider on his left arm. He screeched and grabbed his wounded arm with his sword hand, but I didn't knock him off his horse. His attention was now on me and not the man lying face first in the mud.

Thinking I had fired my one and only shot from my flintlock pistol, he turned his horse and charged me. The other soldier had enough of this dancing around with Lafayette and dismounted from his horse. He must have believed Lafayette was an easy kill lying face down on his stomach the way he was and wanted to finish him off with his blade that he lifted over Lafayette.

The injured soldier bearing down on me as I fired all five of my remaining rounds at him. At least one of the five hit him because he flew off his horse, and I dove to the left, barely avoiding being trampled over by the riderless, runaway horse.

I scrambled and rolled in my dive – I needed to get up and save Lafayette before he became a pin cushion.

Lafayette had rolled to his back, and out of reflex brought his sword up, just in time to stop the blade that was chopping down towards his neck. Not deterred by his first failed attempt and with ever growing anger, the soldier chopped down again and again, trying to remove Lafayette's head. Lafayette rolled in the mud back and forth to avoid the slashing blade.

I reloaded my pistol while still on my back and clambered to my feet to get a better shooting platform. My pistol was jammed with mud and wouldn't fire.

Fuck!

In between chopping motions, Lafayette swung out wildly with his sword, causing the soldier to jump back. Lafayette came up smoothly in a fighting stance with his sword pointed at the soldier. The two men crossed blades, and the clamoring of clashing steel filled the roadside. Lafayette was calm and seemed to know he was the better swordsman. He blocked and attacked with grace.

In a final blow, Lafayette delivered a deadly back swing and his blade bit into the soldier's throat. The soldier spurted blood, dropped his sword, and crumpled to his knees as he attempted to hold his throat with his hands. A spring a red fluid poured out between his fingers, and he collapsed forward onto his face.

Lafayette and I were now coated in a thick layer of freezing mud. He was attempting to wipe the thick mud off his face with an equally mud-covered sleeve as I strode over to him. Looking around at the death and carnage around us, I patted Lafayette on the back.

"What was your first mistake?" I asked him.

"Mistake?" he asked with eyebrows squeezing together. "*Non*, I made no mistake. I won. I am alive and they are dead."

"Learn from your mistakes now, Lafayette, or you'll die later when you repeat them," I said. "Now think. What was your first mistake?"

Anger left his face and his features softened. His gaze moved from the first horseman he shot to the soldiers he had just killed.

Taking a deep breath, he said, "I fired my first shot too soon. I wasn't sure how far three hundred yards was, and instead of firing after you did, I guessed and wasted my first shot."

"Yes, very good," I responded. "And your next mistake?"

"When the six riders broke off, and came at me, I didn't take enough time to aim each shot. I only hit three soldiers out of the five shots."

"Three?" I asked. "You mean four."

"No, three, *trois*," he corrected, holding up his fingers. "The fourth I killed with my flintlock pistol."

"So, you forgot to aim," I instructed. "But you didn't panic, and you remembered to use your flintlock. It's hard not to panic when men on horses are charging down on you. What was your next mistake?"

He thought about that question for a few seconds and then shook his head, not knowing the answer.

"You stepped out onto the field to meet them with your sword," I informed him.

"You said to not forget my sword. Only after I shot the six muskets, and my flintlock, did I draw my sword, just like you said."

"I didn't say to step out from behind the trees," I answered. "If you had stayed where you were, they would have dismounted and fought you on foot. As it was, you were not only fighting them, but you were trying not to get stepped on by their horses."

He glanced back towards the trees where he had been hiding earlier. Seeing his mistake, he nodded his head in agreement again. His pretension notwithstanding, Lafayette was a strong student.

"And you?" he asked accusingly. "What was your first mistake?"

"Me?" I asked, taken aback. But we are always a student, so I, too, considered my actions. I thought about it for a second. "Always make sure your men not only know what your orders are, but that they understand what it's you want. I should have ensured you knew where three hundred yards was. Your first mistake, shooting too soon, was really my failure, not yours."

"And your second mistake?" he asked. Oh, he was really getting me. I like to think he learned from the best.

"A few of the soldiers rode off," I told him. "They'll report our location and return with greater numbers. I should have trusted you to fight your own fight and rode after them. It's too late now. We'd never catch them."

"Anything else?" he asked me with wide eyes.

He seemed taken back that I was willing to admit my mistakes and worse than that, I was willing to say them out loud. He didn't seem used to this from a leader or commander. In his world, leaders didn't make mistakes, even when they did. They blamed their men for their failures.

"Weapons failure," I said showing him the mud packed into my Tec-9. "I should have protected my weapon better."

Lafayette squared off with me and gave me a simple and short bow.

"Thank you, *monsieur*," he said. "I will remember each of these lessons."

"Go get Jonas," I said. "I'll start collecting what I can."

By the time Lafayette and Jonas rode up with the wagon, I had collected three muskets, twelve flintlock pistols, ten swords, but only four of the horses. The rest either ran off or were in the woods but wouldn't let me get close to them. We need to get going and didn't have time to chase them down.

Major Campbell was awake and not in the best of moods. He may have been smarter than most British officers, but he wasn't one for enduring pain. He sat up in the back of the wagon, his face whitening at the sight of the dead calvary soldiers.

"Two of you killed all these men?" he asked, horrified. "Who are you, sir?"

That question was directed to me, but I turned my back on him, and meandered away. No one bothered to answer his question. Jonas watched him with his flintlock in his hand, while Lafayette and I tried to clean up as best we could. The stream water was freezing cold – it would have a sheet of ice covering it in the morning – and neither of us was willing to take a bath in it. We did manage to wash off our hands and faces. We'd have to brush our clothes after the mud dried. Having learned my lesson, I did insist that we clean our weapons before moving out. We had time for that, but since we didn't know how far the closest company of British soldiers were, we didn't know how long it would take the survivors to report us.

With the extra weapons in the wagon, I had Jonas tie the Major's hands together. The last thing I needed was the Major getting ahold of a gun. We still had a long way to go before we reached Valley Forge and keeping our location a secret was getting harder and harder.

Between the heavy, overloaded wagon and six other horses, we left a wake of tracks in the mud behind us. Lafayette led two of the horses, and I pulled two behind me. If anyone were counting tracks, it might appear like a wagon and six riders, not just the two of us. Part of me wanted to leave the wagon, kill the Major, and ride off on the horses. It would be so much easier to avoid any more British contact that way. I had to remind myself that I was here to ensure General Washington's survival and his victory in this war, not to play it safe and avoid contact. He'd need this wagon, and that meant we couldn't leave it behind. George Washington had twelve thousand men to feed at Valley Forge. The wagon was teeming with salted beef and potatoes, but I knew it wasn't enough to feed all those men even one meal each. He was going to need more food than this.

FIFTEEN: Introductions

I LINGERED BEHIND the wagon to watch for danger at our rear. This also gave me time to power on my phone and study maps of the area. Lafayette was up ahead scouting this time. Not as far out as Jonas had been when he scouted, but then Lafayette was new to this and less familiar with the landscape.

If I was right about our location, then we would be coming up to a fork in the road. We could continue south to Valley Forge or turn east. Going south was the quickest route to George Washington, but also the best chance of running into more British soldiers. Those British survivors from our last fight were riding as fast as they could to report what had happened.

How much time we had before they came after us depended on how far reinforcements were. If they were a day or more away, then they might not bother with us. It would be too far to march foot soldiers in the snow in hopes of finding a couple of men and one wagon. If they were closer, or if they had any more cavalry soldiers, then they could be on us in hours. And if they were coming, then making it to the fork in the road and heading east was our only hope of survival. But turning east when they weren't coming after us would delay our arrival at Valley Forge by days, maybe a week.

I stopped the wagon and fired one round from my Thompson, signaling for Lafayette to rejoin Jonas and me. I explained my concerns and asked for their opinions. Lafayette and Jonas agreed that the risk of going straight wasn't worth the reward of possibly getting to Valley Forge a few days sooner.

Major Campbell spoke up and thought we should take the chance and go straight. Jonas wasn't sure how to react to this, but Lafayette and I laughed. The Major's comment pretty much decided the matter for us.

We decided to go against Major Campbell's advice and play it safe. Turning east at the fork, we knew we were adding days to our journey to Valley Forge. This road was less traveled, so we were able to travel faster on the harder packed dirt that was more stone and less mud. Plus, the road or open field at least, was only twenty feet from the tree lines.

Our nights were filled with Lafayette telling stories about France and his life there. Jonas never stopped asking questions, and Lafayette loved to answer them, or any excuse to talk about his home and family. Then when they grew bored my two young friends asked me questions about my life. I never volunteered anything but promised to say yes or no as they let their imagination run wild and tried guessing about my life.

Lafayette had been groomed to be a leader since childhood, so he already had strong beliefs on this subject. He asked me about what I thought made an exceptional leader. We had plenty of arguments about different leadership styles and roles leaders played in their men's lives. Jonas never became involved with that argument, but he hung onto every word. It was interesting watching these two men learn, grow, and change.

Jonas not only carried his recently gifted flintlock pistol but took to carrying one of the British cavalry swords. Lafayette tried to copy me and now carried two flintlock pistols. He was a notable shot with the pistol, so it seemed like a sound idea. Better to have it if he needed it.

Lafayette and Jonas seemed to enjoy each other's company. Lafayette had first taught Jonas how to use a sword and they often practiced against each other. Lafayette even talked me into taking up the sword. He was surprised to learn that I had never used one, which made sense. Men of this time were more familiar with swords than guns. I was a knife fighter, thanks to my dad, not a swordsman. Yet, I'd learned the value of the longer blade, and Lafayette seemed to take joy in being the one to teach the Pale Rider how to use a sword.

Lafayette's sword had a curve to it, whereas the British Cavalry sword that I used was thinner and straight. I practiced with the two younger men and won almost every time against Jonas but lost my matches against Lafayette.

Major Campbell remained tied to a tree or one of the wagon's wheels every night. He seemed to be getting better, with no sign of fever or infection. His arm was useless and hung against his side like the dead weight it was. We untied him several times a day so that he could use the bathroom, usually a nearby tree. Once he was strong enough, I had him walk alongside the wagon and not ride in it. I didn't want him attacking Jonas when the young man wasn't paying attention.

On the second day, we came to the south bound turn we had been watching for. This road would take us to Valley Forge, but at the rate we had been going, it would take us another seven or eight days.

The weather was still getting colder a few degrees each day, pinking the tips of our noses and ears. The snow still wafted down slowly and softly, but it never seemed to stop. In a few weeks, the snow would come down harder, thicker, and the wind would gust harder, increasing with the cold. I hoped to reach General Washington long before that happened.

On the seventh day of our south bound slog through the snow that was about six inches deep, I noticed at least ten British riders appeared in the distance behind us. They were in their saddles but keeping to a walk, trying to stay far enough back so as not to be seen. They were waiting for something, but what? More reinforcements I guessed. I kicked Little Joe to a gallop and headed for the wagon while pulling the other two horses behind me.

I couldn't believe they had tracked us down. I cringed on the inside – I'd been so certain we were in the clear. If they didn't come after us on the first day, that meant these soldiers had come from far off. It made no sense to me. Why did they spend days trying to find three men and a wagon? Maybe one of the survivors recognized my black vest and correctly assumed that I was the Pale Rider. Did killing me mean that much to the British? Or were they following me right to General Washington?

Lafayette saw me riding hard and turned round, meeting me at the wagon.

"Riders," I yelled. "Ten or twelve of them."

I order the Major into the Wagon and we boosted him in.

Jonas yelled to the horses pulling the wagon and slapped the reins against their backsides. The wagon took off, with Lafayette and me on each side of it. Snow kicked up as the horses galloped off at full speed. The British were done watching and were coming on fast. They were about six or seven hundred yards behind us, but even with the wagon going as fast as the horses could run, they'd overtake us in no time at all.

Jonas kept slapping the reins and yelling at the mounts. "Ya! Ya!"

The wagon flew up into the air every time the front wheels hit a bump. Jonas jounced on the bench and had the wagon going at an unsafe speed, but what other choice did we have? Major Campbell held onto the side of the wagon with his one good hand, yelling for Jonas to slow down. That wasn't going to happen.

Musket fire exploded from behind us. The British were too far back to hit us and too disciplined to think they could shoot well at that range. They had no hope of hitting us and wasted their shots.

We managed to run at a full sprint for about a mile, Jonas slapping the reins against the poor horses the entire time. We might not outrun them, but we needed to stay ahead of them long enough to come up with a plan.

I finally figured out what they were doing as we rounded a bend in the road. The wagon was going too fast for the curve and approaching an out-of-control speed when we realized the trap that we had already fallen into.

A large tree laid across the road, twenty yards ahead of us. Four British red coats stood behind the tree, aiming their muskets our way. Even as I cursed to myself, I had to admire the genius behind the plan. They used the cavalry to chase us and get us to run the wagon horses too fast to stop in time to avoid the tree after turning the bend. There was no way for the wagon to go over or around the fallen tree. A perfect trap. The wagon was toast, and we couldn't do anything about that. I kicked Little Joe and raced him up next to the wagon. I yelled for Jonas to jump onto one of the sweat-coated horses I was leading at full speed.

Four muskets fired, and the wagon's poor horses screamed as musket balls tore into their flesh. Their feet went out from under them and down they stumbled to the ground, necks snapping against the freezing, packed dirt under the snow.

The wagon's front end, with Jonas still on it, followed the horses, crashing down and digging into the earth. The wagon's back end went into the air as the wagon flipped end over end, over the already dead horses, flinging the Major into the air. The wagon came to rest only after crashing into the fallen tree. Lafayette and I released the spare horses, bent low on our mounts, and jumped the fallen tree. I pulled up Little Joe and spun around as I withdrew my Tec-9.

The destroyed wagon had run into and killed one of the soldiers standing behind the tree. I fired three shots in quick succession, killing the still standing soldiers who scrambled to reload their muskets. The horse riders still came on hard, having dropped their muskets and were now holding flintlock pistols. Major Campbell was sprawled on his stomach in the middle of the road. His neck was twisted at an impossible angle, with his head upward, and his eyes ghastly and wide open. Jonas laid in a heap in the road on the other side of the tree, and he wasn't moving either. A sour lump formed in the pit of my stomach. I prayed he'd jumped before the horses went down.

Lafayette was off his horse and crouching behind the tree for cover. He leveled his rifle and fired, killing one of the riders. I leapt off Little Joe and switched guns. I fired my Thompson at one of the riders, knocking him off his horse. Muskets scattered across the ground from the broken wagon – some were loaded, and some were not. Lafayette had the same idea and snatched up one of the muskets off the ground next to him. He had gotten lucky, as he seemed to do, and picked up a loaded one. He fired as the riders were right on us now. The riders fired their flintlocks right before they jumped the fallen tree, landing on our side. Tree bark hit me in the face as musket impacts ripped into the tree. They were firing at me and not at Lafayette. Their actions became clear to me as I juggled my guns. I was the larger threat, Pale Rider, after all.

I holstered my Thompson and drew my Tec-9 as they passed me. I fired my last three shots, missing my first two and hitting one of the soldiers with my third and last shot. The seven remaining soldiers dismounted, drawing their swords. I started with surprise when the soldier closest to me turned out to be Captain Bonifield himself.

They ran toward us, swords raised high. Lafayette calmly drew his two flintlock pistols, as though death wasn't running right for us, and killed the first two coming at him. With my pistols empty, I drew my sword for the first time in a real life or death fight, suddenly very thankful for Lafayette's training with the weapon.

Bonifield came in on me hard and fast. He had a reputation of being a swordsman, and I was as good as dead. As he moved within eight feet of me, Lafayette stepped in front of me.

"You're no match for him, Thomas," Lafayette yelled over his shoulder.

Thanks for the vote of confidence.

The other four came around Bonifield, and ignoring Lafayette, they shifted their focus to come at me. Transferring my sword in my left hand, I drew and threw one of my knives. The first of the four grabbed his chest, as my knife sunk deep into his flesh, buried to the hilt as a ruddy stain darkened the front of his coat.

Bonifield and Lafayette's swords clashed like two bulls locking horns. Bonifield wasn't holding back. He attacked and attacked. His swings were far from out of control, his form was perfect, and Lafayette was too busy blocking, deflecting, parrying, and counterattacking. The two combatants danced around each other in a circle, while trying to slip under the other's guard.

Shifting my sword back in my right hand, I refocused my attention and took up the fighting stance that Lafayette had taught me. A soldier rushed at me too fast and slid in the mud, falling onto his backside at my feet. I ran him through where he was sprawled and faced off with the remaining two. They weren't going to make the same mistake the first soldier made. They slowed to a walk but crept closer.

Lafayette's coat was sliced across his chest. Bonifield had a gash on his left arm and blood soaked his coat sleeve.

Reaching behind my back with my left hand, I grabbed my second knife. The two soldiers were separating, dividing my attention. I lunged at the one to my right, and he blocked my swing. Instead of following up with another swing, I spun and thrusted behind me without even looking. The other soldier had been moving in on me, stomping through the snow and mud. He was eager to stab me in the back and didn't realize how noisy he was. He was surprised when my sword pierced his chest. He twisted his body as he collapsed to the ground, pulling my sword out of my hand with him.

Now it was my knife against a sword.

I turned to face the soldier still standing, who was in the middle of a thrust. I blocked his sword with my knife, but I only deflected it a few inches and the tip went into my right upper arm. Rather than pulling back, which the soldier probably expected me to do, I stepped forward, driving his sword deeper into my arm, ignoring the searing pain, and brought my knife up into his gut. We sank to the ground together, holding our wounds. I grabbed my arm as his sword slid out of my wound as he fell, and he grasped my knife, still deep into his stomach. He now had his sword and my knife but lacked the strength to use either on me.

Lafayette and Bonifield were both out of breath and tiring. Lafayette was on his back, holding his sword high, trying to fend off Bonifield's attack. Lafayette's pants were ripped, and a laceration scored across his bloody upper thigh. Bonifield, for his part, managed to keep his feet and approached Lafayette. From my angle, Bonifield appeared to be missing half of his right ear.

With no weapon left on me, I did the only thing I could. Pushing myself up off the ground and onto my knees with my good arm, I shot forward like a linebacker and hurtled into Bonifield at the waist. We crashed down into the mud, rolling over each other. We stopped with me on my back and Bonifield on top of me. Bonifield was right on top of me but too close to use his sword the way it was meant to be used. He did a fair job improvising and punched me in the face with his sword hand. Getting punched by the sword guard around his hand reminded me of getting punched by brass knuckles. My jaw vibrated deep in the bone and stars exploded in my eyes. I bucked my hips up and forward, and he flew over me, landing on his face. He rolled onto his back and climbed to his feet. I had to give the man credit – he could fight with the best of them.

I grabbed my boot knife and threw it. I was tired and my throw was weak, but it was all I had left. With a smug grimace of contempt, Bonifield swung his sword and knocked my throwing knife out of the air.

Lafayette rolled onto his knees and tried to stand. He tumbled back, splattering into the mud. That cut to the leg must have been deeper than it appeared. No more time for fighting like this.

"Ok, you fuck," I said, standing to my feet. "Let's do this the hard way."

Bonifield laughed and stepped forward. I quickly yanked off my coat and wrapped it around my left hand. Bonifield stepped in with a back swing, aiming for my throat as I shifted backward to avoid the deadly cut. He stepped forward again but this time with a lunge for my chest. I deflected his lunge with my coat. He shifted at me a third time with a forward swing to my face. This time I brought my upper body back, dodging the swing but didn't step back.

After the swing missed me, I stepped toward him, bringing myself well inside his guard. As his right arm tried to come back around to the front of his body, I grabbed his sword hand with my right hand, holding on for all I was worth. I wasn't as fast as he was, but I was stronger, and I locked a vise-like grip around his sword wrist. Dropping my coat, I came up with a left-handed upper cut to his jaw. I heard more than felt his teeth break under the impact as his head snapped back, his eyes rolling up into his eyelids. His hand opened loosely, and he dropped his sword.

I spun him and locked my left arm around his neck, gripping his shoulder while grabbing his chin with my right hand. One hard quick jerk of his head to the right and his body to the left at the same time snapped his neck, a loud bone cracking sound that I would never forget. His body dropped to the mud, then I bent down and picked up his sword. Admiring his sword in my hands, I decided to keep it as a souvenir. I slid the sword into the scabbard at my side.

Walking over to Lafayette, I reached out a hand. I helped him regain his feet, and using one leg and leaning on me, he hopped over to the tree and broken-up wagon. I collected his two flintlock pistols that he'd dropped and told him to load them just in case any other soldiers were on their way. I reloaded my pistols and then collected my knives. The soldier that I had stabbed in the stomach was now dead, his blood mixing with the snow and mud.

With my weapons reloaded, I ran to Jonas. I had to stop a few feet from him.

He hadn't moved from the position I'd first seen him in, and my arm ached, as my head pounded against the inside of my skull.

The young man was dead, and there wasn't a thing I could have done for him. He was a first-rate kid, and if not for his help I wouldn't have made it this far. I crumpled to my knees, and with a shaking hand, I closed his eyes. Then I sat there with a hand on the top of his head, blinking back hot tears that burned in my eyes. I had begun to think of him as a little brother, and now he was just gone. All that energy and eagerness resigned to the heavens.

After a few moments, I managed to muster enough strength to pick up Jonas's limp body and carry him over to Lafayette. I laid him down and instructed Lafayette to watch over him while I gathered a few horses. Lafayette had tears in his eyes, and he wiped them with a muddy sleeve.

Lafayette's lips thinned as he studied the lifeless young man. "I am not ashamed to say he was my friend. *Va avec dieu, mon ami.*"

The wagon was utterly destroyed, and the supplies would now have to be left behind. All our work, all our efforts to save the wagon and in the end, we lost it and the supplies. What a waste.

I was surprised to find Little Joe standing off to the side. He had not run off amid all the chaos this time. I started to lose respect for him. Doing things like that would get a horse killed. Since my backpack and satchel were on his saddle, I wasn't going to complain about his sudden bravery or loyalty. At least, not this time.

I needed the first aid kit from my satchel for Lafayette's leg, but didn't have the energy to walk over and get it. Bone weary, that was the only way I could describe it. My muscles didn't want to move, no matter how much I commanded them to. I called Little Joe's name to see if he'd come to me, when musket fire erupted behind me.

Not again!

I spun around, and another twenty or more British soldiers plowed through the trees. Lafayette twisted around and, without pause, fired his flintlock pistols around the wagon. He didn't hit anyone, but the shots slowed them down. Drawing my pistols, I ducked down behind the wagon, next to Lafayette.

We were so screwed, and I had nothing left to give. My arms didn't want to lift, my legs where shaking, and my brain was still reeling from Jonas's death. I slid down the side of the wagon and was ready to tell Lafayette to hold his fire and give up. I'd be hung in the nearest tree, but as a French officer, they'd most likely not kill Lafayette. He'd be taken as a prisoner and tortured to give up information. Not a great ending for either of us.

Just as I opened my mouth, more musket fire rang out from the road in the opposite direction. Twenty men on horses trotted towards us, followed by over a hundred more running on foot. The only difference was that this group of soldiers wore tattered blue coats, not red coats. The men on horses rode straight at us while the men on foot ran into the trees, firing their muskets. The British decided this wasn't a fight they wanted to be a part of anymore now that they couldn't win easily and retreated at a full run. The Continental army gave chase, and I raised my hands, hoping not to get shot by mistake.

I recognized the first horse that rode up to us and halted five feet away. I didn't need to look up to know who the rider was, but I did anyways. He sat tall and regal, General George Washington, the Commander of the Continental Army.

I'd never been so happy to see a single man in my life.

Smiling, I pulled Lafayette to his feet and made a show of dusting him off.

"Mr. Nelson," the General said smiling.

"General," I answered back. "You have good timing, sir."

Lafayette straightened to his full height. "Sir," I continued, "may I introduce a member of King Louis the Sixteenth's court, Marquis De Lafayette, of France. Lafayette, may I introduce the Commander of the Continental Army, General George Washington."

General Washington bowed his head. "An honor to meet you, sir."

Lafayette didn't slap his heels together this time but did bend at the waist. "The honor is mine, *Monsieur.*"

"I met Lafayette on the road, sir," I said. "He came here from France to meet you. I didn't think you would mind me bringing him here to you."

I don't know if Lafayette meant it or if he was trying to paint me in a strong light, but he motioned his hand towards me. "Any General who can inspire such loyalty in his men, such as that I've seen in this man, deserves my respect, if for no other reason."

General Washington eyed the scar on my head and blood on my face and arm, his eyes full of questions. He stepped down from his horse and the body of Jonas caught his attention.

My gaze followed his. "His name was Jonas, sir. He was one of your men from Philadelphia. We never would have made it here if not for him."

General Washington nodded his head slowly. "I'm sorry."

He then called some of his men forward, and they tried to rush Lafayette off to one of the General's doctors. To his credit, Lafayette refused to go until two of the General's men had picked up Jonas and carried him away. The Frenchman gained more respect from me with the way he insured that Jonas' body was taken care of before he left the battlefield. Another officer led Little Joe over to me, and the General and I mounted on our horses. It took me a few tries, tired as I was.

The General spoke in a somber voice. "You're bleeding again, Mr. Nelson. Seems to be a habit of yours. A habit you might consider breaking."

Well, he wasn't wrong. I wiggled my arm and agreed with him. The General scanned the destruction and carnage and shook his head.

"I'll send for another wagon to collect this food and those blankets," the General said. "God knows, we need both."

"That reminds me, sir," I interjected, only to be interrupted by a wave of the General's hand.

"Yes, Mr. Nelson," the General answered before I could finish asking the question. "Your other two wagons arrived a week ago. Just in time, too. Thank you for those. We needed them."

As we sat on our horses, the General pointed to one of the dead bodies. "Is that Captain Bonifield?"

"Yes, sir," I said. "A real bastard, too."

The General nodded his head in agreement, as if he had known the man. We started down the road to Valley Forge, and the General pulled up his horse and looked at me.

"I have another important job for you, Mr. Nelson. After you have rested and if you are so inclined to help," the General said. "But first, I have one question for you."

"Yes, sir," I responded with a short bow of my head.

"Do you prefer to be called Pale Rider or Washington's Assassin?" he asked with a tight smile on his face.

"Thomas, sir. Just Thomas," I said, then added, "if you please."

"Your reputation has spread like wildfire," he said. "You have done a great deal, in bringing up the morale of the men. You have become somewhat of a legend."

A legend. All I had wanted was to escape the world that had stolen everything from me and try to change it for Jenny, that she might live in the future. And now, for Annie and her daughters, that they might live a life of freedom, too. Now I was a legend.

I nudged Little Joe and we trotted back down the road together towards this place called Valley Forge, a place that until I met Dr. Rock, I had never heard of.

THE END

If you liked this book, please leave a review!
Then continue the adventure with book 2, Another Chance!

Excerpt of Book 2 *Another Chance*

November 2ⁿᵈ, 1777
Windsor Castle

Lord Frederick North, the second Earl of Guilford, the Prime Minister of England, and the servant, advisor, confidant of King George the Third of England, stood in front of the full-length mirror, evaluating his appearance. He wasn't alone in this self-serving exercise. Two servants stood behind him, dressing Lord North in his formal robes. One was his valet, the other a woman.

Lord North's wig wasn't on straight, and he uttered a *tsk* sound, sucking air through his teeth and into his mouth. The female servant noted what he was in distress about and moved to straighten his wig, without a single word spoken between them. She added a touch of white powder to cover the bare skin of North's head that had become exposed when the wig had been adjusted.

This servant seemed adequately efficient at reading his needs, all of them. A skill that seemed ironically uncommon among the common people. His stomach jiggled as he chuckled at his own joke, even if it was only spoken in his own thoughts. He made a mental note to repeat the joke to the king.

Although he'd called this particular servant to his silk sheet-covered bed last night, he still didn't know the woman's name, nor did he care to learn it. He would, however, make a note to have her see to his requirements every time he stayed at the king's palace. She was a little bulky, with thick shoulders, muscular arms, and a big ass, but he liked his women durable. The thinner servants bruised too easily, and he couldn't afford to have rumors of him being an abuser jumping from ear to ear in the palace. His eyes dropped to her ample cleavage. Unlike his wife, this woman had huge, soft breasts. His wife, Anne, hadn't been blessed in that area. He wished his wife had a chest like this woman.

Today, courtesy of a tight corset, her boobs pushed up and out of her yellow dress. It wasn't an expensive dress by any means, but like most of the serving ladies' dresses, it was designed to draw the eye to certain areas of the female body. She must have realized last night he liked the size of her breasts, as she was showing a little more today than she had yesterday. His valet sagely kept his own gaze averted.

Also, and most importantly, unlike his wife, this woman knew not to engage him in conversation whilst they were otherwise occupied. Oh, if only his wife were more like her. He thought back to the previous night and could remember her speaking to him twice. When she did speak, it was to inquire if she could do anything else for him.

His own wife seemed to be acquiring her own opinions of late. She seemed to have an opinion about everything these days. He'd noticed the older she became, the freer her tongue wagged in sharing those opinions.

He thought about pilfering this servant from the king's service and bringing her into his own household. She hadn't put up a fight last night, and he found her to be quite accommodating. She was eager to please him. Lord North had no illusions about himself. He wasn't a young man, nor did he have a body that women found desirable. If she was eager to please him, it was because she had hoped for some coin afterwards, and she wanted to finish the act as quickly as possible.

In truth, he cared not for her motivation, but for her service. He appreciated a servant who knew their place in the world, and maybe some secrets about the palace. Most fools thought servants weren't real people and said things in front of them that they'd not say in front of their own family members or confidants. As if the servants didn't speak the same language. Lord North knew servants were people, he just didn't respect them as such. Their eyes and ears worked as well as everyone else's, though they weren't smart enough to know they had such important information in their underdeveloped brains.

He'd learned long ago most servants possessed a treasure of information. Like a buried pirate's chest, that information had to be dug up. His valet was a superb example. He hadn't protested at the irregular servant helping Lord North dress this morning. He kept his head down, ears open, and was fiercely loyal to his lord.

Lord North had found himself staying at the Windsor Castle quite often of late. When he first became Prime Minister of England, he'd visited the castle once a month to discuss the royal financial books with the king. The royal debt was ten million pounds when he first started, before Lord North had devised a brilliant plan of how to discharge the king of that large debt four years ago. Up until then, the treacherous colonists in America had not paid their share of taxes, and Lord North had swayed the king to implement the Tea Act.

This additional tax should have been enough to pay off the Empire's debts and more. The plan was flawless, if in theory, but not in execution. He didn't live in the colonies and was forced to rely on others to implement his lucrative schemes. If only the colonists had complied and paid their lawfully ordered taxes. Who were they to question his wisdom or the king's commands?

Since the blasted Tea Party incident in Boston, the colonists had forgotten who their king was and had revolted. The king sought to bring the traitors back into the fold, but it was Lord North who had convinced the king to force them to kneel to their betters. Not out of spite, but to ensure they never again tried to shake off the yoke of the British Empire's rightful rule. It was the best course of action for the Empire and, in the long run, for the colonists. The colonists were no better than willful children who had to be told how to live.

The Empire's debt was now over forty million pounds and rising by the day. Instead of the Tax Act solving the king's problems, it had made them four times worse. This was of no fault of Lord North's, of course, and surely the king knew that. The king, however, demanded answers for some hard questions, and it was Lord North's duty to provide those answers. Lord North would never allow someone else in the palace to provide information to the king that might falsely blame his actions and ideas for the revolt.

For a very specific reason.

Excerpt of Book 1 of *Chain and Mace*
Prologue

Descended

Most people seem to believe that angels do not have free will. The truth is that they do. Angels in heaven chose to follow god, just as those in hell chose to follow Satan. When an angel chooses to follow the Lord but breaks one of his commands, he is cast out from heaven, but not all are cast to hell. These angels are known as Fallen Angels. But where do fallen angels go?

August 18

David fled down the grassy hill as fast as his legs could carry him, looking over his shoulder every few seconds. He was breathing hard; his heart pounded in his ears, and he was so tired. *Where were they? What were they?* They were behind him a minute ago, and now they were gone.

He remembered how they silently came out of the darkness, these strange men, *no not men, they were too big.* Animals, or a kind of creatures, *but they walked on two legs, or some of them did.* Monsters? He tried to think of an argument against using that word but could not. They grabbed Jake, his cameraman, by the throat. Jake hung in the air by that giant hairy hand or paw that shook Jake like a rag doll. There were three of them, that much he was sure of. The first one stood about six and a half, maybe seven feet tall, the biggest bear David had ever seen, but it wasn't a bear. Bears didn't grab people by the throats. He thought perhaps they were wolves. They did look like wolves, but wolves don't walk on two feet.

They must be men in costumes, David thought. After all, that was the reason he was out here in the first place.

His editor had sent him and Jake out to investigate reports of a type of new religious cult. Well, they sure as hell found the cult, or the cult found them. Poor Jake was overweight at least by forty pounds. How could any person just pick up a two-hundred-and-thirty-pound man by one hand? Maybe they were on drugs, PCP, or something. David had done a report earlier in the year about how strong people can get when they are whacked out on drugs. They had heard rumors about a motorcycle gang in the area, maybe they had something to do with this. David's thoughts were interrupted by the rock he tripped on. He fell to the ground and fought to stay conscious as he rolled forward on the grass, the metallic taste of blood filling his mouth.

Kathy! His mind suddenly went to her. *What would Kathy do if he died here?* Crouched in the dirt, he decided he would live. He had to find a phone and call the police, and it was his most unfortunate luck that he dropped his cell phone when he ran. *Maybe a pay phone at a gas station?*

David forced himself to his feet and looked behind him, up the hill that he had fallen down, but it was too dark to see if anyone was still there. He must have run a mile by now. David had played high school football years ago, and he always kept himself in good shape. He thought he could move with decent speed, but these guys were faster. By God, they were fast. It was almost as if they were playing with him.

David thought about his cat and how she would pounce on the bugs she would find in the house, only to let them go, then pounce again.

"Stop thinking and just run," David said to himself out loud. He turned to run but was stopped by the very large hand that grabbed him by the back of the neck

About the Author

Michael Roberts is a Police Officer in Southern California. He also served in the United States Marine Corps for seven years. He wrote this story for himself twenty years prior to publishing it. It was not until he met the love of his life, and his motivation, Michelle Deerwester-Dalrymple, a published author herself, that he updated this story and published it. This is his second of book.

Also the Author:

Alpha Team Paranormal Military Series:

Chain and Mace – Book 1
Chain and Cross – book 2

American History Military Time Travel Series:

Second Chance – Book 1
Another Chance – Book 2
Final Chance – Book 3
Aden's Chance – Book 4

Made in the USA
Las Vegas, NV
12 October 2024

96521098R00152